Was it any wonder, Cat thought, that she'd reached the ripe old age of twenty-six without getting married?

What man in his right mind would give her a second thought with her four brothers glaring at him?

She hated bucking her family, but she had to take a stand. Her rebellious urges surfaced when Hank opened the truck door and she saw her family lined up on the porch—watching.

She stepped up on the running board and wrapped her arms around Hank's neck. "I'm declaring World War III," she murmured. "Care to be my ally?"

She felt him tense from shoulder to thigh, but he wrapped his arms around her. "This is one hell of a way to retaliate," he said.

Cat had never known a man could take such care with a kiss. Hank's tongue lightly traced her bottom lip. She moaned. Her tongue met his. She tasted the sweetness of strawberries blended with his own special flavor. And the sweet taste of revenge was bland compared to the rush of raw, consuming passion his kiss evoked.

Dear Reader,

In a world of constant dizzying change, some things, fortunately, remain the same. One of those things is the Silhouette **Special Edition** commitment to our readers—a commitment, renewed each month, to bring you six stimulating, sensitive, substantial novels of living and loving in today's world, novels blending deep, vivid emotions with high romance.

This month, six fabulous authors step up to fulfill that commitment: Terese Ramin brings you the uproarious, unforgettable and decidedly adult *Accompanying Alice;* Jo Ann Algermissen lends her unique voice—and heart—to fond family feuding in *Would You Marry Me Anyway?;* Judi Edwards stirs our deepest hunger for love and healing in *Step from a Dream;* Christine Flynn enchants the senses with a tale of legendary love in *Out of the Mist;* Pat Warren deftly balances both the fears and the courage intimacy generates in *Till I Loved You;* and Dee Holmes delivers a mature, perceptive novel of the true nature of loving and heroism in *The Return of Slade Garner.* All six novels are sterling examples of the Silhouette **Special Edition** experience: romance you can believe in.

Next month also features a sensational array of talent, including two tantalizing volumes many of you have been clamoring for, by bestselling authors Ginna Gray and Debbie Macomber.

So don't miss a moment of the Silhouette **Special Edition** experience!

From all the authors and editors
of Silhouette **Special Edition**—warmest wishes.

JO ANN ALGERMISSEN
Would You Marry Me Anyway?

Silhouette Special Edition
Published by Silhouette Books New York
America's Publisher of Contemporary Romance

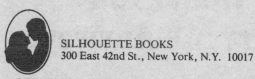

SILHOUETTE BOOKS
300 East 42nd St., New York, N.Y. 10017

WOULD YOU MARRY ME ANYWAY?

ISBN: 0-373-09655-0

First Silhouette Books printing March 1991

Printed in the U.S.A.

Books by Jo Ann Algermissen

Silhouette Desire

Naughty, but Nice #246
Challenge the Fates #276
Serendipity Samantha #300
Hank's Woman #318
Made in America #361
Lucky Lady #409
Butterfly #486
Bedside Manner #539
Sunshine #559

Silhouette Special Edition

Purple Diamonds #374
Blue Emeralds #455
Paper Stars #512
Best Man #607
Would You Marry Me Anyway? #655

JO ANN ALGERMISSEN

lives near the Atlantic Ocean, where she spends hours daydreaming to her heart's content. She remembers that as a youngster, she always had "daydreams in class" written on every report card. But she also follows the writer's creed: write what you know about. In twenty-five years of marriage, she has experienced love—how it is, how it can be and how it ought to be. Mrs. Algermissen has also written under a romanticized version of her maiden name, Anna Hudson.

Chapter One

"Cat's on the prowl," Bubba Clark grumbled. He thumped his knuckles on his hard hat. "I just bet this brain boiler she makes us wear that Cat's snoopin' around, lookin' for a reason not to pay me come Friday! She's gonna bankrupt Clark Electric, surer 'n hell!"

Hank Collins stopped hammering as he watched Bubba suck in his beer belly and attempt to squeeze his torso between the upright studs. He chuckled softly. Every Tuesday, the day the subcontractors on the Lemontree apartments project submitted their bills to get paid for the work they'd completed, Cat McGillis, who was the project's construction manager, tracked Bubba down.

"Why don't you quit billing ahead of the work you've completed?" Hank asked.

"If my electricians could wire a building as fast as your carpenters frame them, I wouldn't have to fudge a little bit on the bill." Wedged between two wall studs, Bubba squirmed and huffed until he could squeeze through. He looked over at the next apartment building where his men were lackadaisically stringing color-coded wire. "What are things comin' to when general contractors start hirin' a woman to fill a man's shoes?"

"Boots," Hank corrected, grinning. He drove an eightpenny nail into the doorframe with one well-aimed stroke and stood up. His wide carpenter's belt rode low on his slim hips as his hard-muscled legs jackknifed him upright.

Tipping his own hard hat off his brow, he wiped his sweat on the sleeve of his blue plaid shirt. None of the men liked wearing hard hats, but they didn't have a choice on this job site. No hat and boots, no job. Cat McGillis adhered to the safety rules with the same strictness she had for approving only the work that had been completed, tested and inspected.

"Is she still comin' this way?" Bubba whispered.

"Yeah." Hank watched Cat weave through the stacks of lumber, heading straight toward the entrance of the apartment building as though she knew Bubba had chosen it as his hiding place. "There isn't much point in avoiding her, Bubba. Goldcoast Construction isn't going to issue a paycheck without her signature of approval."

"It's called delayin' tactics. It ain't gonna take you long to learn about 'em if you keep subcontractin' carpenter work. I'm countin' on Cat's bein' inexperienced as a project manager workin' to my advantage for a change. If I can keep out of her sight for twenty-four hours, maybe she won't turn in the paperwork to the office. With a little luck, my men might get Building 6 finished."

Hank raised one dark eyebrow skeptically. Both he and Cat were new on the job, but neither of them had been born yesterday. He glanced toward Building 6, where his men had begun hammering floor joists in position. No studs yet. Bubba's men would have to be miracle workers to string wire where there wasn't any wood!

Bubba hunkered down behind a cardboard box filled with plastic plumber's fittings. "You ever notice how she signs her name? H. C. McGillis. It don't take a genius to know what that *H* stands for."

"Heavenly?" Hank joked, noticing how Cat's khaki-colored jumpsuit hugged her in all the right places. Big, blue-green eyes, high cheekbones and a pointed chin gave her a face that could haunt a man's dreams and fill his fantasies. And she was a more than competent manager, something few men on the job site were willing to admit aloud.

Attractive, bright and career-oriented, he mused, feeling the muscle along his jaw tense. Bubba Clark wasn't the only man who avoided Cat McGillis, but Hank did so for completely different reasons. He'd been married to a woman with the same qualities.

Married and divorced, Hank reminded himself. It hadn't taken Sharon long to discover he wasn't good enough for a career woman climbing up the corporate ladder.

"Don't let her angelic looks fool you," Bubba said. "That woman's own momma took one look at her and knew she was gonna grow up to be a hellcat. That's what the *H* stands for—hellcat." Bubba surrendered his hiding place when he heard Cat call his name. "If she asks, tell her you haven't seen hide nor hair of me, y'hear?" He vanished before Hank could agree or disagree to cover for him.

Hank sighed. He played along with the good-ol'-boy attitude that prevailed among Bubba and the other subcontractors, but he wasn't going to risk a confrontation with Cat to cover someone else's butt. Neither was he going to lie to their boss lady. His men had completed the work Hank had billed.

He slid the handle of his hammer into his leather belt, grabbed hold of the top of the doorframe and swung himself up on the skeleton framework of an interior wall. An old hand at balancing on a beam ten feet off the ground, he agilely moved to a position in the center of the building, where he could watch his framing crew work.

"Hey! Hank! How's Building 6 coming along?" Cat called from the center entrance.

She tucked her clipboard under one arm and moved gracefully between the studs, keeping her eyes trained upward to where she'd first seen Hank. She'd been around construction sites since childhood, but Hank Collins's show of muscular strength was too impressive not to notice. Beneath the cotton fabric straining across his back, she could see the play of muscles. Her eyes dropped to the backside of his faded jeans, then to his long powerful legs. Compared to Hank, the insurance agent she occasionally dated looked positively puny.

The closer she came to standing beneath the rafter where Hank stood, the louder her heart thudded in her chest. An empty thirty-gallon metal drum being slammed on the rim with a ball-peen hammer would have been silent in comparison, she thought.

Hank Collins is a subcontractor, she silently reminded herself, mentally painting an invisible wide red line between them. Tall, tan and decidedly good-looking, but nevertheless, a subcontractor. She couldn't allow the urge to dawdle every time she came near him to affect her job performance.

"We're working on the second floor," Hank called down from above her. He cleared his throat to remove the huskiness he heard. "I'm expecting a shipment of roof trusses by Friday. Early next week we'll be out of Building 6—ahead of schedule."

"Great." Cat smiled. The words *ahead of schedule* were music to any project manager's ears. Too bad I can't say the same for all the subcontractors, she mused. She'd been hot on Bubba Clark's tracks for the past hour, but he'd obviously eluded her. Again. "Have you seen Bubba?"

From his vantage point on the second story Hank could see Bubba hightailing it for his pickup truck. For an instant he was tempted to grab a scrap piece of lumber to hurl at the back of Bubba's knees to slow him down. Bubba and his men were the sort of guys who gave subcontractors a bad name.

"Never mind," Cat said, realizing she'd broken one of the unwritten rules on a construction site: never, ever pit the subcontractors against one another. That only resulted in the men vandalizing one another's work. "I'll catch up with him sooner or later. By the way, I approved your bill for this week's check."

"Thanks, boss lady."

"Thank *you*," she replied easily, grinning up at Hank. "Your framing crews make my job easy."

She plucked the clipboard from under her arm, turned and started inspecting the work completed on the first floor. Her heartbeat slowed to its regular rate as she distanced herself from Hank. Her eyes narrowed as she spied plastic plumbing fittings strewn haphazardly in the end apartment. Wads of rags stained with purple glue had been tossed into one corner. She leafed through the pages of her clipboard until she found the plumbing section and began making notes.

Bubba Clark wasn't her only problem on this job. Flint Martin not only beefed up his bills, he had to be the most slipshod plumbing contractor in Texas. It was bad enough that his crews cluttered every building with fittings and glue rags, but even worse that none of Flint's men seemed to know the meaning of the words *level* and *plumb*.

Why would they? she thought. Flint believed that as long as the pipes held water and didn't rattle his men had done a fine job. Unfortunately for Flint, Cat believed that a job worth doing and being paid for was worth doing right.

She removed a torpedo level from a loop on her belt. She perused the surface of the wood, tallying the number of nails holding the structure in place, as she placed the level on the trunk line of the plumbing.

"Off half a bubble," she mumbled, shaking her head.

"Impossible. I checked those pipes myself."

Cat whirled around at the sound of Flint's voice. "It is."

"Your level must be out of whack."

"Then use yours," Cat challenged. She stepped back and eyeballed the pipe, then glared at Flint Martin, who wasn't much wider than the pipe. "Frankly, I don't need a level to show a tilted pipe when I can see it."

"My level is in the truck." Flint shrugged. "So it's off a little. Big deal. Nobody's going to see it but you, me and the drywaller. Gimme a break, would you?"

"I want it plumb... You know—" her hand vertically sliced the air between them "—as in straight up and down."

"Do you realize how many man-hours you're talking about?"

Cat nodded. Flint assumed that because she was new to the job and a woman, she was inexperienced and weak. He'd assumed wrong on both counts. She could pipe this building without a set of blueprints, and she could be tough as nails when necessary.

"You could save a bundle by picking up the fittings you've left strewn around and using them."

"Those fittings aren't your concern, little lady. They didn't cost Goldcoast Construction one red cent."

"And while you're collecting the fittings," she said, holding a tight grip on her temper, "get rid of the rags, too. They're a fire hazard."

Cat unfolded her yardstick and began measuring the copper pipe stubbed out from the wall. The solder had dripped down the copper pipe like silver tears. The only good comment she could make about the plumbing was that it didn't leak.

She knew why Flint Plumbing had been awarded the contract on the Lemontree project—they'd submitted the lowest bid—but she hated sloppy work. It was her job to upgrade the quality of the work beyond minimal standards.

"Here's another place you can save money. Make your men wipe the joints. They're wasting silver solder."

She watched Flint's thin face turn red as he heard the ring of authority in her voice. He hooked his thumbs beneath the width of his belt and spread his feet apart as though he wanted to physically lash into her.

Cat wasn't intimidated. She'd been raised in a family with four older brothers who were twice her size. To her way of thinking, Flint's anger was misdirected. If the man had a smidgen of pride in his work, he would have been charging out of the building, raising hell with his crews for shoddy work.

Slowly, she straightened to her full height. At five feet eight inches, she was eye to eye with the plumber. Cold as the Freon running through metal pipe to an air-conditioning unit, she added, "I'm lowering the amount you billed for. You don't have the first piece of pipe strung in Building 6."

Flint inched toward her. "I don't take kindly to being paid less."

"I don't take kindly to paying for work that hasn't been completed," Cat said. She had no intention of backing down. The subcontractors weren't the only ones who'd trimmed their bids to get this job. Goldcoast Construction was working on a narrow margin of profit, too. "Don't bill ahead."

"Why don't you quit acting like my check is coming out of your bank account? You and I both know Goldcoast whittled the price per fixture I'm being paid down to nothing. Goldcoast is going to have to keep my cash flow moving or I'll have to drag up, move on to another job."

"Is that a threat, Mr. Martin?" He was bluffing. The price of crude oil plummeting on the world market had affected the entire economy of Texas, including the building trades. Competition was stiff; ten contractors bid for every project. Flint wouldn't leave this job; he didn't have another one to go to. "Unless I rubber-stamp your bill you're going to pull your men off this job?"

Flint pointed his finger in her face. "You're damned right, girlie. You'd better start thinking about the hell of a mess you'll have trying to replace me at the price I bid."

Tempted beyond measure to grab his finger and twist his arm around his back until he yelled "uncle," Cat restrained herself to pecking the front of his shirt with her forefinger. "There are two ways to do things on this job site, mister, my way and the highway. It's your choice."

Just as Flint grabbed her wrist, a voice from overhead shouted, "Hey, Flint. How's it going?"

An instant later, Hank Collins swung down from the rafters and landed beside Flint. The menacing tone of Flint's voice had carried over their heads to where he'd been standing. Going along with the good ol' boys or not, Hank wasn't going to let Flint physically abuse a woman while he was within earshot.

He slapped Flint on the back in a friendly way and said, "I was just getting ready to go grab a bite of lunch at the roach wagon. Want to join me?"

Cat hadn't the vaguest notion of how long Hank had been eavesdropping, but she resented his intrusion. She could handle Flint Martin blindfolded, with one arm tied behind her back. Her arm dropped to her side as Flint released her wrist.

She shot Hank a hot glance that clearly read, *Butt out, this is my business.*

"You're going to get ptomaine poisoning eating the food from one of those drive-through trucks," Flint answered through tight lips. He backed farther away from Cat, giving her a dirty look. "It's expensive, too. I'm stuck with a daily ration of peanut butter and jelly sandwiches from home."

Poor man, Cat thought unsympathetically. Did he think he could tug on her heartstrings, or more accurately, Goldcoast's purse strings, by implying she was starving him to death? Not likely, she mused. Two minutes ago she'd have cheerfully cleaned his pipes with rat poison.

"How about you, Cat? Could I interest you in a submarine sandwich?" Hank's offer didn't change the stubborn thrust of her chin. "My treat."

"Watch it, Hank," Flint said with a snide snort. "She'll think you have ulterior motives."

Cat ignored Flint's gibe. She knew Hank didn't have to resort to sneaky tactics to get his bill approved. Rather than involve Hank in her dispute with Flint, she replied, "A submarine sandwich sounds good." She turned to Flint. She had to show both men that she was in control of the situation. "We'd finished our discussion, hadn't we?"

Cat could tell Flint was biting his tongue. He wanted to continue the quarrel, but the icy edge she'd injected into her voice cut through the heat of his anger.

"Yeah," Flint grumbled, simmering down. Determined to get the last word, he added, "While I'm eating my peanut butter and jelly, I'll be checking out the highway."

After they'd left the building and were headed toward the food wagon, she explained Flint's parting remark to Hank.

"Flint has a reputation for having a mean temper when he's riled," Hank cautioned. Frowning, he slammed his right fist against his left palm.

"Flint isn't the only one around here with a hair-trigger temper. I've been known to shoot from the lip, too." With a cheeky grin, she added, "Flint will thank you later for saving him from bodily harm."

A small grin tugged at the corners of Hank's mouth. So much for the idea of rescuing a damsel in distress, he mused dryly. "You're a feisty cat, huh?"

"I don't like confrontations, but with four brothers built like brick houses, I learned how to defend myself at an early age," Cat said. She wasn't bragging, merely stating a fact. What she lacked in size and strength, she made up for with dexterity and sheer determination. Not wanting to belabor the subject, she glanced up at the sun high overhead and said, "It's a real scorcher today. I have a pitcher of iced tea in the office trailer. Why don't we stop by and get a couple of glasses of it before we get the sandwiches?''

Hank's frown deepened. The air-conditioned trailer would be a welcome respite from the heat, and iced tea would quench his thirst, but he knew his men would razz him unmercifully about sipping iced tea with the boss lady. His eyes moved from the spot under a huge oak tree where he usually ate lunch with his men to the office trailer.

He also realized the other men on the job might get the wrong idea if they saw him entering Cat's office at lunchtime. Half of them would probably think he was in scoring brownie points with the boss, but the other half would think he was trying to score with a good-looking woman.

He wouldn't have given her suggestion a second thought if Cat were a man. But she wasn't. She could claim to be tough as nails, but in his eyes Cat McGillis was a woman. All woman. From the top of her blond head to the soles of her narrow boots.

Too much of a woman for him.

"I'm not sure that's a good idea," he declined softly. "It might cause talk."

His thoughtfulness pleased Cat, but his protectiveness irked her. "Your men know that you don't have to charm me to get their work approved. It's not exactly uncommon on any job site for a project manager and a subcontractor to be friends, is it?"

Hank delayed his response, thinking of the one woman he'd once thought of as his best friend, Sharon. He raked his tongue over the roof of his mouth to remove a bitter taste. "I don't have any friends who are women."

"No?" she repeated in disbelief. "Not even one?"

"Not even one."

"Why?"

Because friendship has to be based on mutual respect, Hank silently replied. He'd put Sharon up on a pedestal; she'd ground him beneath her spiked heel. He'd learned from Sharon that wise men hid their weak spots from a woman. If a man was foolish enough to expose his vulnerabilities, he shouldn't whine when a woman poked and prodded at them. Better, much better, he thought, to keep silent.

Hank shrugged. "I haven't given the subject of having women as friends much thought. My work is uppermost in my mind. I use my energies to build apartment projects rather than building a relationship with a woman."

"A monk disguised as a carpenter?" Cat teased, not believing him for one moment. With his good looks he probably had to carry a two-by-ten on his shoulder to keep the women away from him.

"Just a carpenter doing his job, earning a living." He sure as hell couldn't tell his boss lady that the few encounters he'd had with women since Sharon had divorced him were purely carnal in nature. Eyes on the ground, he nudged a clod of dirt loose on the unpaved road and gave it a swift kick. He'd prefer for Cat to consider him a celibate monk than a eunuch or a womanizer. "I'm a sports fan. The Astros are playing a doubleheader this weekend. I'm hoping it will be a sellout so I can watch it on television."

As they passed by the office trailer without stopping, Geraldine, Cat's secretary, stuck her head out the door and called, "You've got a phone call, Cat. It's your mother."

"Tell her I'll call her back in a few minutes." Cat wasn't a sports fan, but for the sake of establishing camaraderie with Hank, she would have listened to every hit, run and error the Astros had ever made just to keep him talking to her.

"I already did," Geraldine replied, "before I saw you walking by here. She said to tell you it's important."

"I'll be right there," Cat said. Pangs of guilt tightened the muscles in her stomach. She'd dodged her mother's calls at home during the past week. Cat had to take this call or her mother would pester her every hour on the hour until she did pick up the phone. If stubborn tenacity was hereditary, Cat knew exactly whom she'd inherited the trait from.

She started toward the wooden steps leading into the trailer, then turned and looked up at Hank. Certain he'd feel uncomfortable waiting for her in the trailer with the men on the job speculating about his reasons for being there, she said, "Mother tends to be long-winded. Do you mind if I take a rain check on the sandwich you offered?"

"No sweat." It struck Hank that Cat McGillis wasn't the sort of project manager who'd take personal calls on the job unless it was urgent. "I hope it isn't bad news."

"Mom knows I usually eat lunch around this time. I doubt if it's anything serious, but thanks for your concern."

She felt a compelling urge to reach out and touch his arm, to physically show him that she appreciated his concern. Instead, she bounded up the steps and opened the trailer door.

Cold air hit her hot, moist skin like a sledgehammer. "Geraldine, do you think you could raise the thermostat up to zero? It's freezing in here!"

"Hey, don't expect me to suffer a heatstroke just because your mother insisted on talking to you. Not that I blame you for being...miffed." Geraldine fanned her dark eyelashes, which matched her short curly hair. "I wouldn't want to blow a chance at a date with the most gorgeous man on the job site to talk to my mother, either."

Rolling her eyes heavenward, Cat strode to her office. She didn't know which woman was worse when it came to men, her mother or Geraldine. Although there was more than thirty years' difference in their ages, both women considered a single woman who'd reached the ripe old age of twenty-six to be in immediate danger of becoming an old maid.

"Hank Collins is a business associate," she called through the open door.

"Right," Geraldine drawled, her voice filled with skepticism. "Just friends."

From the tone of Geraldine's voice, Cat realized Hank wasn't the only person who didn't believe in platonic relationships. She sighed inwardly as she plopped down in her chair and picked up the phone extension. "I've got it, Geraldine."

"Oh dear, did I hear Geraldine say you broke a lunch date to take my call?" Maude McGillis asked, her voice laced with regret.

"No, Mother. No date. Just a friendly lunch with one of the subcontractors who happens to be a male."

"I thought that nice Bradley Mitchell who you brought out to the lake house might have dropped by to take you to lunch."

"Mother," Cat groaned, mentally bracing herself for the guilt trip her mother was about to lay on her, "has anyone told you that you're about as subtle as a hurricane?"

"Whatever do you mean?"

Cat wasn't fooled for one second by her mother's feigned innocence. "One, you're scolding me for not making an appearance at the family gatherings for the past couple of weeks. Two, you want to know how often I've gone out with Bradley."

"Well, dear, I am the one who referred your name to him for a life insurance policy. It's only natural that I'm interested in how things are progressing between the two of you."

"And I brought Bradley out to the lake because he wanted to sell insurance to my brothers," Cat explained for the tenth time.

When possible, she followed her brother's advice and kept her love life totally separate from her mother. Not because she had anything to be ashamed of, but because all she had to do to get her mother hearing wedding bells was to arrive at the front door with a man on her arm.

"We've all missed you. I was just telling your father the other night that watching my baby daughter leave home and knowing she doesn't have a nice, steady man to protect her is turning me gray-headed."

Cat gritted her teeth, silently praying for tolerance. She'd rather have taken on fifty antagonistic subcontractors than talk to her mother when she was playing the martyr role. Maude McGillis didn't have a gray hair on her head.

Maude paused, waiting for Cat's reaction. When she only heard construction noises going on outside the office trailer, she knew her daughter's jaws were clenched. She'd lived in a male-dominated household too long to be deterred by stoic silence.

"The boys plan on smoking a couple of briskets Saturday afternoon. Why don't you and Bradley join us?" Before Cat could open her mouth to decline, Maude rattled on, "Tell Bradley to dress casually. He looked so attractive in his three-piece suit and starched white shirt, but I felt terrible about the air conditioner being on the blink. You'd think one of your brothers would have it fixed by now, but you know how it is in the construction business. I guess it's the same no matter what business your menfolk are in. On one of the talk shows last week the doctor being interviewed admitted that his kids were the last ones to get their measles vaccinations."

"Mother—"

"Which reminds me, you don't have to worry about the measles epidemic going around. You had it. I remember being worried sick when you broke out in that dreadful rash. I was up day and night, fixing you homemade chicken soup, playing games with you, wiping the perspiration off your brow."

"Mother, I'll be there Saturday," Cat interjected while Maude was forced to pause to catch a breath. Cat knew Maude was on a roll. She'd ramble through every childhood disease known to humanity to get what she wanted.

"You will?"

"I promise. I'll be there Saturday afternoon, dressed casually."

"If you feel uncomfortable asking Bradley to attend a family get-together, I can call him at his office and invite him," Maude pushed. "I'm certain there must be some other sort of policy he could try to sell us."

"No thanks. I'll do the inviting."

"Bradley is such a gentleman. Did you notice how he popped up to his feet every time you entered the room?"

Cat blew her bangs off her forehead with a gust of breath. Bradley had charmed Maude and bored Cat.

"Mother," she interrupted, "I'm in a rush. We'll talk Saturday, okay?"

Her mission accomplished, Maude said cheerfully, "Don't forget to call Bradley. Bye."

"Bye, Mom."

Cat returned the phone to its cradle. She visualized her mother dragging her finger through the air as she chalked up another victory. Resigned to the fact that she'd rather lose a minor skirmish than take a guilt trip, Cat dismissed the image.

Between now and Saturday, though, she'd have to think up a believable excuse for Bradley's sending his regrets. Business, she decided, grinning as she remembered how her brothers had stifled their yawns while Bradley had droned on and on and on about the merits of whole life insurance over term. They hadn't been able to get down to the dock, grab their fishing poles and climb into the rowboat fast enough when Bradley happened to mention how he hated to fish.

"Wish they had let me tag along," she murmured, remembering how she'd had to endure listening to Bradley give his pitch on workers' compensation insurance to her father. Within five minutes, her father's eyes had become wistful, as he absentmindedly listened to Bradley while watching the boys drift from one crappie hole to the next.

But, gauging from the rapt expression on her mother's face, Maude had thought the prize catch of the day was sitting on the back porch. In an uncharitable mood, Cat had to admit Bradley did resemble a fish—red-eyed, from reading the fine print in his competitors' contracts, and cold-blooded, from the feel of his lips when they grazed across her forehead later that same evening.

What does Mother see in him? Cat mused. Why is Bradley's type husband material?

She knew the answer; she'd heard that lecture dozens of times since she turned eighteen. "Marry a man who'll be a steady provider. No layoffs. Paid vacations. Fringe benefits." Maude would hasten to add, "I love Joshua dearly, but I don't want you to have to worry about paying the bills the way I did. Marry *up!*"

Cat's fingers wandered across the word *Goldcoast* embroidered on the flap of her pocket.

She wondered if thwarting her parents by switching her major in college was one of the reasons she continued to let her mother bully her about finding the "right" man. Perhaps being the only member of the family to attend college had made her feel certain obligations.

Cat could vividly remember the day she announced that she'd decided on business administration with an emphasis on construction management as her major. She might just as well have proudly informed her family that she'd bombed Pearl Harbor!

She'd declared war!

With Maude as the self-appointed commander in chief of the McGillis clan, the entire family had retaliated. Every nonviolent tactic known to Maude was used to coerce Cat into picking a "suitable" major. But Cat had stuck to her guns. She had decided that with or without her family's financial or moral support, she had to make this choice for herself.

While she'd been reminiscing, Cat's eyes had automatically moved to the architectural layout of the Lemontree project. Slowly she rose and crossed the room. Each color-coded dot on the map represented the phase of construction each building was in.

In her mind's eye, Cat visualized the completed project. Through the brick-pillared entrance she could see the dark waxy leaves on the lemon trees lining the drive.

Curved concrete streets, sidewalks, green St. Augustine grass and hundreds of Southern Glory azalea bushes would give the complex the impression of a private estate. Clusters of whitewashed buildings with clay-tiled roofs, balconies and private patios would provide the illusion of stepping back in history, when the wealthy Spanish owners of expansive ranches built mansions for their offspring on the same property. It was peaceful and serene, a place where the hectic pace of Houston could temporarily be forgotten.

Cat's fingers danced over the multicolored dots as though she could change them all to green, the color signifying completion. It didn't take magic, only time and hard work. By this time next year, her hard work would make the dream a reality.

Then she'd bring her parents to Lemontree for the grand opening. This would be her first project; it held special meaning for her. They'd know she was responsible for the quality craftsmanship in each building they'd see. They'd be proud of her.

More important, she'd be proud of herself for a job well done.

Maybe then, she mused as she glanced out the window and saw Hank Collins talking to several of his men, maybe then her family would trust her judgment in personal matters. If not, she'd declare World War III before she'd walk down the aisle with a man she didn't love.

Chapter Two

"The snowbirds must have forgotten to close the door behind them at the Texas border," Pedro said, his Mexican accent lyrical as he glanced up at the gathering clouds overhead. "Looks like a blue northerner is coming our way. Good thing it's Friday, huh, boss?"

Hank nodded. Even the threat of rain and a drop in temperature failed to dampen the spirits of his men. Today was Friday, payday. He and his crews had worked ten-hour days to keep ahead of the other subcontractors' crews. They all looked forward to a couple of days of rest.

"My family is going to the beach. You want to come along?" Pedro's hands made a curving motion; his dark eyes danced with good humor. "Plenty pretty *señoritas* in Galveston."

"No, but thanks for the invitation." As often as not Hank accepted his men's invitations to join in their family activities. Although they treated him preferentially,

Hank generally ignored race and class distinctions. "I've got a date with several long-neck beers and a wide sofa in front of the television."

His eyes strayed toward the office trailer. He peeled the corn husk off the homemade tamale Pedro handed him and bit into it. The taste of corn flour, shredded beef and Mexican chilies burst across his tongue.

His mind wandered from thoughts of putting a finishing coat of lacquer on the headboard of the bed he'd been working on in his spare time to Cat McGillis. Lately, she'd been on his mind more than he cared to admit. He'd caught himself going out of his way to walk in front of the office trailer just to get a glimpse of her.

Adolescent foolishness, he silently chided. Next thing he knew he'd be driving by her house like a sixteen-year-old kid with a new driver's license!

He swatted at a fly buzzing around his head and missed. His eyes focused on the trailer door. She'd asked for a rain check on sharing lunch with him. He could grab a couple of tamales and take them to her.

Then what? Stand outside the door while she ate them?

Three days ago he'd made a fuss over stopping by her office to get a couple of glasses of iced tea. Mentally he gave himself a shake by the scruff of his neck. It was okay to erase the dividing line between himself and his men; it was inexcusable to presume Cat McGillis really wanted to share a lunch with him. She was the project manager, for crying out loud, his boss. One wrong move and she could have him worried sick about making payroll.

Hank knew that was just his surface excuse for being wary of Cat. Deep down at gut level, his self-preservation instincts were the cause of his reluctance to scratch the itch she caused each time he got a glimpse of her.

Cat McGillis was the closest thing to a white-collar worker on the job site. The biggest mistake he'd made in his life was thinking a white-collar woman could be happy with a blue-collar man.

Sharon, his ex-wife, had taught him that lesson. The hateful words she'd flung at him were the lyrics to the Texas blues he'd been singing since the day she threw one of her haughty tantrums and stormed out of their apartment.

No, he wasn't about to make the same dumb mistake twice. A high-powered, ambitious woman with hoity-toity ideas about life was the last woman he'd pick to share his hand-carved bed. She'd only complicate his life. Hank didn't want complications. He liked the simple life, working hard, playing hard....

"Too many jalapeños?" Pedro teased.

"Something like that." Hank flashed Pedro a friendly grin, then downed the last bite of his tamale. "I'm going to get a milk from the roach wagon to put out the fire in my belly, and then I'm going to head on down to Building 1 to check out the cabinet work in those apartments. I'll see you later."

"Hey, Mr. Hank, you change your mind about the beach, just give me a call, eh?"

"I'll do that." Hank jackknifed to his feet. His hands automatically hiked up the twin pouches attached to his wide belt. "Don't count on me, though."

A few minutes later, Hank gulped a swig of milk out of the carton as he opened the door of the completed building. Prepared to inhale the scent of fresh paint and new carpet, his nose twitched as it identified an odor that didn't belong in the just completed building.

"Smoke?" he murmured.

Somebody's hide would be tacked outside the front door if he caught one of the workmen sneaking in here to eat lunch and enjoy a cigarette, he thought. Mentally he pictured the framing and carpenter crews he'd left behind eating their lunch under the oak tree. He could account for all his men.

When he heard a sharp noise and heavy footsteps echoing in the empty apartments upstairs, he shouted, "Who's up there?"

Two at a time, he charged up the steps. Milk sloshed out of the carton across his fingers. He paused long enough to wipe the droplets of milk off the carpet, since if he didn't, they'd leave a stain. He'd be the one to catch hell from Cat if he ruined the brand-new carpet.

His head cocked to one side as he heard an outside door slam shut. Whoever it was, he grimaced, he'd blown his chance to catch him red-handed.

As he reached the upper landing the smell of smoke intensified. A curse blared in his mind.

It wasn't burning tobacco he smelled!

He glanced at the four closed doors leading into the units on this floor and prayed he was making the right choice when he lunged toward the nearest one. He quickly crossed from one room to another, following his nose until he reached the back bedroom. His eyes squinted, his throat worked, adrenaline pumped through him as the smoke thickened the closer he came to the source of the fire.

"Son of a bitch!" he yelled when he entered the bathroom off the master bedroom.

Without thinking, he poured the contents of his milk carton on the smoke pouring from the gaping hole beside the toilet, then tossed the carton aside and dropped to his knees in the cramped quarters. Flint Martin had finished the plumbing in this building, but the pipes were still empty of water.

Hank's heart accelerated in his chest. Determined at all costs to stop the fire before it spread, he stuck his hand into the hole. He felt the hair on the back of his hand become singed as he began yanking insulation out from behind the copper plumbing between the walls and throwing it on the tiled floor. The pink glass fibers had melted; the aluminum-coated paper holding the fibers together in long strips was scorched.

Blindly, he felt around the interior of the wall, enlarging the hole by battering his other fist against the drywall. His arm was up to his elbow behind the wall before he began pulling uncharred material from the hole. Checking for warm spots, he felt around the enclosed area until he was certain he'd removed all the smoldering material.

Rocking back on his heels, tight-lipped, teeth clenched, he grabbed the baseboard with both hands and pulled it loose from the wall. He picked through the ashes until he found the source of the fire, the remains of a cigarette butt.

Carefully, he examined the brown paper wrapped around the filter. The only clue to who'd started the fire was a damned poor one, he thought, disgusted. Half the men on the job site who smoked tobacco used this brand!

Hank wiped the cold sweat from his brow on his shirtsleeve as he rose to his feet. Tiny orange embers still lit the edges of the insulation's paper. He ground them beneath his leather-soled boot.

A rash of questions and answers peppered his thoughts as he blackened the embers. Who? The culprit could have been almost anyone on the job site. Most of the men smoked cigarettes.

But why the hell was he smoking in this building? Why did he throw his cigarette in a hole in the wall? Why didn't he drop it in the toilet or the sink? Or grind it out on the floor?

Hank crouched again and peered at the damaged drywall, searching for additional clues. He reached forward and touched the copper coupling that joined two pieces of pipe. One of Flint's men could have been here repairing a leak, Hank speculated. His torch could have accidentally started the fire.

So he threw his cigarette butt in the hole when he heard me shout? That doesn't make sense, Hank thought, shaking his head.

A plumber would have called him for help or he'd have put out the fire himself. Flint wouldn't have been over-joyed about making a deal with the drywall man to fix the hole, but it wasn't something the man would get fired over.

Hank winced as he withdrew his hand from the hole.

Panic must have temporarily sidetracked the pain, he mused, taking a hard look at his callused fingertips and the back of his hand. Beneath the black soot he could see a pinkish tinge to his dark skin. Small blisters had begun to form. He wasn't overly concerned by the minor burns, but he didn't want to take a chance on his good right hand getting infected. He'd need to slap some burn ointment on when he got a chance.

Aware the bottom of his boots were coated with black ash, he sat down on the toilet seat, then took off his boots with his left hand. He didn't need to make a bigger mess by tracking soot on the carpet.

He wasn't satisfied with the possibility he'd come up with as to who'd started the fire. The fact that Flint was his least favorite subcontractor could be the reason he'd automatically jumped to the conclusion that one of Flint's men was responsible for the damage.

Calmly, he considered other possibilities. The man who started the fire could have been one of the drywallers who'd been sent to repair a damaged wall. Or, as he'd first thought, it could have been somebody who'd been sneaking a smoke in an air-conditioned building and had panicked.

As Hank started up the road toward the office trailer to report the fire, he knew he wasn't any closer to putting his finger on who started the fire than when he first entered the building. The culprit could be any one of fifty men.

For that matter, since he'd left the building barefoot with his boots dangling from his left hand, and had made no secret of his being there by putting on his boots outside on the front stoop, more than likely he'd be the person the men would remember seeing near the building at lunchtime.

If he reported the incident and Cat called in the authorities to investigate, he'd be a prime suspect. Silently Hank groaned. He'd be the one at risk of getting on the bad side of the project manager.

He knew he should report the fire, but damn, he didn't need any trouble. Everything in his life was turned around and headed in the right direction for him. He'd be a fool to tempt the Fates. The smart thing to do would be to keep his mouth shut. None of the subcontractors would want the project manager's finger pointing at them, so they'd be more than willing to fix the damage without making a peep.

No, he'd have to tell her. He owed it to his boss to report the incident. She wouldn't suspect him, would she? Damned if he knew whether she would or wouldn't, but he'd be in a hell of a mess if she did!

It suddenly occurred to Hank that even if Cat didn't doubt him, the other men wouldn't appreciate having her watch them with a suspicious eye. They'd probably consider his reporting the fire as snitching on them to stay in Cat's good graces. Hank knew he'd be violating the good-ol'-boy attitude that bonded the subcontractors together. They'd close ranks, leaving him on the outside to fend for himself. Or worse, they'd pull pranks on him and his men that could cost him time and money.

Hank paused when he came to a fork in the road. He looked to the left toward Cat's office, then to the right toward his pickup truck. He could march to the left and take the risk of causing trouble for all the subcontractors, himself included, or he could go right and wash his hands of the whole matter. Neither choice appealed to him.

"What the hell!" he muttered, turning right and ambling toward his truck. "I put out the fire and I can get the wall fixed without a fuss. Why bother Cat with the details? It was an accident. No big deal."

He listened to his decision, half persuaded he was doing the right thing, but not totally. What if another fire cropped up? What if this wasn't an accident? He had to report the incident.

"I'll mention it later this afternoon, when I pick up my paycheck," he muttered. In the meantime, he'd have one of his men clean up the mess and talk to the drywaller about repairing the wall.

Geraldine handed Cat a slip of paper when Cat stepped out of her office with a stack of envelopes in her hand. "I knew you'd skipped lunch to get those payroll checks ready, so I hope you don't mind me fibbing to your mother when she called."

"Mind? Quite the contrary. Bless you!" She read the phone message: Don't forget to bring a date to the picnic at the lake tomorrow. Crumpling the note into a tight wad, she tossed it in the direction of the waste can.

Too curious to be diplomatic, Geraldine asked baldly, "So, who are you taking to meet the family?"

"Cary Grant."

"He's dead."

"I guess that explains why he didn't return my call." Cat fanned the envelopes in front of her face as she pretended to contemplate what lucky fellow she'd call next. "I could give Lee Iacocca or Henry Kissinger a buzz. Mom and Dad would think they were *appropriate* dates."

"Naw, they're too old for you. Why don't you ask—"

"Tom Cruise?" Cat supplied, all too aware of the man Geraldine thought she should ask. It wasn't pure coincidence that every time her secretary opened her mouth Hank Collins's name was mentioned. "He's younger and richer. Maybe I'll give him a call."

"Humph! An actor?" Geraldine said, mimicking Maude's voice. "Actors have less job security than the men who work at the Lemontree. They're always out of work—even during good weather."

Cat laughed. "I do seem to have a knack for picking men Mother would find unsuitable, don't I?"

"Passive resistance?"

"Guilt," Cat admitted. "Mother has never forgiven me for following in the family's footsteps. It's okay for Dad and my brothers to work in the trades, but since I'm the only girl in the family, I was expected to pick a nice, safe job outside of the construction industry. I've told you how Maude feels."

"Yeah, but I think it's time for you to stand up to her."

"That's easy for you to say." Cat chuckled. "I'm still listed among the walking wounded from the battle scars I got from declaring war on the McGillis clan seven years ago. Take my word for it, Maude can change a dove into a hawk when she sets her mind to it."

"You can't go through life pacifying her. She's the one who's insisting that you bring a date along tomorrow. I think you should ask one of the men who works here." Geraldine's eyes dropped to the buzzing telephone. "Consider yourself lucky, Cat. You've just been saved by the bell."

"I'm outta here." Giving Geraldine a sly wink, Cat impetuously twirled in continuous circles toward the door.

"Mrs. McGillis?" Geraldine rolled her eyes heavenward, then glanced at her boss.

Dizzy, Cat leaned against the door, shaking her head and her hands in a negative gesture. "No!" she mouthed emphatically.

At that inopportune moment, she felt the door opening away from her. She shrieked loudly, struggling to gain her balance. Her arms flailed the air like windmills in a storm. White envelopes flew everywhere. Toppling backward, she grabbed for the sides of the door, but missed. Her shoulder blades collided with Hank's muscular chest; his right arm wrapped around her waist.

"Sorry," Hank apologized, placing her back on her feet, but keeping his arm around her waist until she recovered her balance. "I didn't know you were leaning against the door."

Before Cat could sidestep out of Hank's arms and politely thank him, Geraldine covered the mouthpiece with her hand and said, "You-know-who on the end of this line heard your voice and knows you're here. You're going to have to take the call."

While Geraldine spoke, Cat's blue eyes perused the mess she'd made. Frustrated by her clumsiness and her mother's tenacity, at the moment all she wanted to do was bury her face against Hank's chest and bawl her eyes out, which, of course, was the last thing she could do. She'd already damaged her professional image; she didn't need to completely destroy it!

Cat straightened her shoulders. She mustered a polite smile of gratitude and motioned for Hank to go on into her office.

Should she take her mother's call in the reception area, where the subcontractors would be showing up any minute to get their checks, or in her office, with Hank Collins listening to the private battle between her and her mother?

"I'll pick up the pay envelopes and hand them out," Geraldine offered, making the decision for Cat. She pointed to the adjoining room and whispered, "You talk to your mother. She isn't going to listen to me spouting excuses!"

"Right."

Still feeling a little fuzzy around the edges, Cat crossed the room to her office. She needed a clear head to talk to Maude and make it sound for Hank's benefit as though she was conducting business.

To Hank she said, "I'll just be a moment," then picked up the telephone. "Cat McGillis speaking. How can I help you?"

Hank put his hand over his mouth to hide his grin. Geraldine's whispered remarks had been easy to hear through the thin walls.

His grin slipped a notch when he remembered his ex-wife trying to keep a businesslike tone when talking to a customer while he'd been nibbling the side of her neck.

But Cat was as nervous as the animal she'd been named after. He knew she'd jump right out of her skin if he so much as touched her hand.

"You haven't forgotten your promise, have you?" Maude asked peevishly.

Briskly, Cat replied, "No, of course I haven't forgotten. I'll take care of the matter."

"When I couldn't get hold of you at lunchtime, I called Bradley's office to make sure he knew he was welcome to join us. You can imagine how surprised I was when his secretary told me that he's out of town."

"A minor problem. Nothing I can't handle." Cat propped her elbow on her desk and cupped her forehead between her thumb and forefinger. She fervently hoped her performance was making Hank believe she was conducting business. "Don't be concerned. It's nothing I can't take care of."

"But Cat, the boys are considering bringing their girlfriends. You'll be the odd person out."

Not likely, Cat mused. Her brothers would arrive with a dozen weak excuses to cover up their determination to keep their love lives as far away from their mother as possible. Maude scrutinized potential brides for her sons far more closely than Cat considered doing when she made a punch-out list of items that needed to be corrected before a final inspection.

"I don't mind." She preferred it.

"I do mind! You've got to bring someone! Anyone!" Maude pleaded. "Who did you invite?"

"Who?" Cat repeated her mother's question to stall for time.

She peeked below her finger at Hank. The knowing grin on his face convinced her to drop her business-call pretense. Damn his hide, he was actually chuckling!

"Yes, who?" Maude demanded to know.

"Could you hold on for just a second?" Cat had an idea that would solve her immediate problem and simultaneously wipe the smirk off Hank's face. She pointed the receiver in Hank's direction. "Do you like to fish?"

Hank shifted in his chair, away from Cat. Warily he replied, "Yeah."

"How about eating smoked brisket, fresh corn and strawberry shortcake?"

She'd listed some of his favorite foods, but he knew she had to be working up to something. "Maybe," he hedged.

"Since your men are ahead of schedule, you aren't working tomorrow, are you?"

"I hadn't planned on it."

"Good." She put the phone back to her ear. She gave Hank a defiant smile. "Okay, Mother, you'll be thrilled to know that Hank Collins has accepted my invitation for the family outing tomorrow."

"Hank Collins?" Maude repeated. "Who on earth is Hank Collins? I've never heard you mention him!"

Cat hesitated, loving the way Hank's grin had fallen as his chin dropped. She couldn't give her mother Tom Cruise on a platinum platter, but she didn't mind giving Hank an impressive promotion.

"He's my boss, Goldcoast's regional manager. He's in charge of everything we build in the Southwest."

"My, oh my!" Maude gushed with delight. "He sounds important."

The pleased sound of her mother's voice justified telling a little white lie, Cat mused as she gave Hank a once-over with her eyes. She'd have to figure out a way for him to hide those biceps and pecs or he'd never pass her mother's keen inspection.

"He is. Very important." Not wanting to have Maude question her at length, Cat said, "You'll meet Hank tomorrow, Mother. I've got to get back to work. Bye."

Her mother was sputtering questions as Cat hung up the phone.

Before Hank recovered from the double whammy of being given an instant promotion and being nominated her escort to a family function, she said sweetly, "I hope you don't mind accompanying me tomorrow."

"Mind?" Mind. One of them had lost their mind, and he was fairly certain it must have been him. He felt like a brown paper sack filled with nickel-plated nails that had been dropped off a ten-story building. An hour ago he'd balked at inviting her to have lunch with him . . . and now he was having supper with her . . . and meeting her family! How the hell had he gotten himself into this predicament? All he'd done was drop by the office to pick up his paycheck and mention the small fire started by a careless smoker. In less than ten minutes, Cat McGillis had thrown herself in his arms, arranged for him to meet her family and bestowed a job title on him!

"Of course I mind! I've met the regional manager of Goldcoast. Unless I can shrink in height, age fifteen years and grow a paunchy belly, I don't have a prayer of passing myself off as Kent Shane's twin."

"Mother has never met Kent." She scribbled her address on a notepad, tore off the top sheet and placed it on the far side of her desk near Hank. "No problem."

"But you don't expect me to act like I'm your boss, do you?"

"Why not?"

"Because I'm not your boss, and furthermore, I don't want to be your boss. You lied to your mother!"

Cat picked up a pen from her desk and tapped her bottom lip thoughtfully. "Yeah, I did. Are you going to sit there and tell me you never told a white lie to your mother? One that's for her own good? Everybody has done that at one time or another."

"Making me your boss is good for your mother? That's about as clear as the Rio Grande in mid-July."

"Female logic," Cat quipped, refusing to explain. She'd risk hurting his feelings by telling him that her parents would feel a framing subcontractor could never provide the security they wanted for their darling daughter. "Don't worry about it."

"Don't worry about being put smack-dab in the middle of a harebrained scheme? Lady, I can find plenty of trouble on my own, without your help. I don't like being manipulated."

"Mother is the manipulator." Cat grinned. "Don't you kind of like the idea of manipulating a manipulator?"

Out of the blue, it occurred to Cat that Hank's obvious consternation might be caused by a commitment to another woman. She didn't think he was married, but he might have a live-in girlfriend who wouldn't take kindly to his spending the day with her.

Then again, she thought, for all she knew for certain he could be married with ten kids! Just because a man didn't brag about his wife and kids didn't mean they didn't exist. His billfold could be stuffed with pictures of little Collins kids.

"Maybe I acted rashly," Cat said, glancing at his ring finger. He didn't wear a gold band, but men who worked in the trades seldom wore jewelry because it was dangerous. One slip of a tool and the ring finger was gone. Her own father only wore his ring on special occasions. What if Hank showed up wearing his ring? Her mother would have a conniption fit! "Maybe accepting Mom's invitation on your behalf was a bit . . . impulsive."

"Impulsive?" Hank derided. "I'd say that's an understatement coming from a woman who counts the number of nails in a prefabricated wall."

Cat shrugged, but silently agreed with him. Never having asked a man out on a date, she began to consider other ramifications. Who'd drive? Should she offer to pick him up? If she did, should she bring candy or a bottle of wine, the way a Southern gentleman would? Or should she ask him to drive and she'd pay to fill up his gas tank? She couldn't visualize herself at a gas station, filling his tank, while he sat in the driver's seat strumming his fingers on the steering wheel.

And that's only the beginning, she mused, sucking her bottom lip beneath her front teeth and worrying it. Do I open doors for him? Does he help my mother in the kitchen? Who pulls the chair out for whom? Do I bait his hook? Who cleans the fish? Who walks whom to their door? Her mind hit a brick wall when she wondered if she should try to kiss him on the first date.

Reversing the male/female roles made everything damned complicated!

"I didn't consider all the angles," she said, her mind boggling at not having any set of rules to use as a guideline. "I should have thought about it from your angle. You work hard all week. It isn't right for me to take up your leisure time."

"I do enjoy fishing more than watching television," Hank countered. From the way her eyes darted around the room as though she were searching for an escape clause in an ironclad contract, and the way she ravaged her bottom lip, he realized she was as nervous as a cat on a hot tin roof. Her vulnerability touched a responsive chord deep within him. It made him want to calm her jitters by blotting the trace of moisture shining on her bottom lip with his own mouth. His first inclination to stubbornly refuse her invitation changed to a strong determination to go with her.

Cat silently racked her brain for other legitimate excuses that Hank could use to politely refuse her invitation. She found what seemed like the perfect reason. "I guess it wouldn't look good to the other subcontractors if you spent the day with me and my family."

"You didn't plan on inviting any of the other subcontractors, did you?"

"No, but you might mention . . ."

"Brag?" That struck a raw nerve. His thumb thumped his chest as he asked, "Do you think I'd go fishing with you and come back and brag about it to the other men?"

"Don't tell me men don't gossip," she needled. Rather than retract her invitation, she'd decided to let him save face by making him angry. "I work here, remember? I have eyes and ears."

Hank stiffened his arms, put his knuckles on her desk and leaned toward her. "You've got a pert little nose, too, but that doesn't mean you see, hear and smell everything that goes on at the Lemontree."

"Wrong," Cat protested. "No one, yourself included, walks this job site more than I do. Name one thing I've missed."

From his superior height, he stared down into the yellow flecks in her blue eyes. They were shooting sparks at him. Damn! This wasn't an opportune time to divulge anything about the fire, not when they were in the heat of a personal disagreement.

"Do you or don't you want me to go with you?" he demanded, steering the discussion back on course.

"I asked you, didn't I?"

"Okay. I accept!" He snatched the paper with her address written on it off her desk. In three long strides, Hank had his hand on the knob of the connecting door. He lowered his voice to an ominous level. "I just hope we both don't live to regret this little charade."

Cat jumped to her feet. "I'll pick you up around noon," she offered.

"I'll pick you up." He hooked his thumbs in the belt loops of his jeans and puffed out his chest. "Since I'm your new boss, you'd better get used to me making a few of the rules around here." He saw the panic in her eyes and amended his rights. "Off the job site, only."

"I hope I haven't created a monster," she muttered. She still didn't know if he was married. Trying to be nonchalant, she moved beside him. "I just thought of something. You, uh, don't happen to be married, do you?"

"Divorced."

"Divorced." That was a relief. Standing within arm's length of him, feeling his body heat radiating around her, she wondered what kind of fool woman would divorce Hank Collins. "Kids?"

"No kids." He slipped her address into his front pocket while he eyed her from head to toe. "You remind me a lot of my ex-wife."

His parting remark gave him the satisfaction of seeing her chin drop in shock. It seemed fair. She'd had his guts tied in knots for days. Before she could ask him what he meant, he gave her a small salute and said, "See you tomorrow. I'll expect you to be punctual. You wouldn't want to be late for a date with your boss, would you?"

Cat shook her head. "I'll be ready."

Her eyes clouded with bewilderment as they followed his backside as he strode through the connecting door, paused at Geraldine's desk to get his check, then marched out of the office trailer door.

Why is he swaggering like a conquering warrior? she wondered. She'd won the battle of wits, hadn't she?

Against his will, Hank Collins had agreed to pretend to be her boss and go with her to her parents' lake house.

So why, she wondered, is he so cocky? If she hadn't known better, she'd have thought he was the one who'd tricked her into going out with him!

Chapter Three

You remind me a lot of my ex-wife.

Her hair wet, her body wrapped in a thick bath towel, Cat stood in front of the full-length mirror in her bedroom, staring at her reflection.

How? she wondered.

Physically? Was his ex-wife tall, with light hair and blue-green eyes?

Or did he mean the two of them acted alike?

Cat had fallen asleep last night pondering exactly what Hank Collins had meant and had awakened with the same unresolved questions on her mind. She didn't know why Hank's parting remark bothered her, but it did.

She picked up a wide-toothed comb and pulled it through her hair, and found she still couldn't resolve the matter.

She turned to Brute, the ferocious watchdog her mother had given her the day she'd moved into her own town house condominium. Maude had originally planned on buying a German shepherd or a Doberman. The fact that Brute was a pocket-size black poodle didn't affect Maude's choice. A status symbol was far more important to Maude than practicality. Brute's championship pedigree had been the deciding factor in his favor.

"How would you feel if your boss looked like your ex-husband?"

Brute gave the blue rubber ball in his mouth a squeeze, blinked his black button eyes and bounded up onto the pile of lacy pillows decorating Cat's bed. He cocked his head to one side as though her question was of grave importance to him.

"You wouldn't care, would you, big fella?"

Brute dropped his ball, yapped once, then snatched the ball back into his mouth.

"You would?" Cat answered, responding for the dog as she often did. She tousled the kinky pom-pom on the dog's head, then grabbed for Brute's toy. He growled, but he wagged his tail to show his eagerness to play tug-of-war. "You'd love me anyway. You know you would. C'mon, you rascal, give it to me."

She chased him off the bed and around the chair. Brute, jaws clenched, gave muted barks of delight. When Cat gave up and walked into the bathroom to blow-dry her hair, Brute teased her by dropping the ball near her feet.

"Typical male, aren't you, big fella? I know you're trying to tempt me. Forget it. Hank is going to be here shortly to take us to Mom's."

Brute's ears perked up as he recognized a name.

"Yeah, you're going along. Mother would make me 'stand in a corner till the house falls down' if I left you here to guard the premises."

Hearing herself voice one of her mother's outrageous threats made Cat giggle. Like mother, like daughter, she mused. Like ex-wife? Not liking that thought, she made a comical face at Brute.

Bending double, she back-combed her waist-length hair over her head and began blowing it dry. For the hundredth time, she considered cutting it. Something short and sassy, like Geraldine's hair, she thought.

As the long tendrils began to dry and whirl like silken threads around her, she knew she wouldn't cut it—not even if Hank's ex-wife wore her hair exactly the same way, parted on the left and hanging loose down her back.

Cat wasn't going to cut one hair on her head just to please a man. Nor would she change her behavior. She wasn't the least bit conceited, but she was confident in her appearance and her mannerisms. She straightened, tossing her blond mane backward, then began brushing it in long strokes.

She'd tried to be what her parents wanted her to be; she'd failed miserably at the task.

"I can't be what somebody else wants me to be. What I have to show Hank Collins is that no two women are the same. I'm me—take me or leave me."

Hank pulled into Cat McGillis's driveway at ten minutes before noon. Early, he thought, glancing from his wristwatch to her front door. Before he turned off the engine, he considered driving around the condominium project rather than give the appearance of being eager for today's outing.

His dark eyes moved to the bouquet of spring flowers wrapped in green tissue paper. What had possessed him to stop at that corner flower stand and shell out ten hard-earned bucks for flowers?

The same thing that had had him up at dawn, washing and waxing his truck? He'd not only thoroughly cleaned the outside, he'd hauled the thick rolls of architectural plans off the front seat into his garage. He'd scrubbed the black vinyl upholstery and dashboard until he couldn't find a speck of dust.

At the time, he'd justified his actions by telling himself he was searching for the measuring tape he'd lost months before. But he quit lying to himself after he'd showered, shaved and dressed in pressed jeans and a white-on-white shirt, then caught himself returning to the bathroom to splash expensive cologne down the front of his chest.

A man wore cologne for the same reason a woman wore sexy perfume—to attract a member of the opposite sex.

In a flash of stubbornness, he'd recapped the cologne bottle. Good old soap and water suited his intentions. After all, it wasn't as though Cat had invited him because she wanted to be with him. Hell, no! Her mother had pressured her into bringing a man along and he'd been convenient!

He'd been bamboozled into accepting her invitation. Under those circumstances, he didn't want to give Cat McGillis any wrong ideas by showing up smelling like a perfume factory.

The fragrance from the bouquet drew his eyes back to the flowers. What I ought to do, he thought, drumming his fingers on the steering wheel impatiently, is toss those damned flowers in the bed of the truck. One quick spin down a dusty oil-patch road would cure the flower problem and mess up his spotless truck.

He reached for the tissue-wrapped stems, then withdrew his hand. He'd pinched pennies too many years to throw away a ten-dollar bill without reconsideration. He grabbed the bouquet and opened the cab door.

"I'll tell her these are in appreciation for being a nice boss." That sounded utterly ridiculous to him. He swung his legs out from under the steering column, stepped out of the truck and slammed the door. The heels of his boots dragged along the concrete walk leading to the front door. "I'll tell her I brought them for her mother."

Smooth move, Romeo, he silently jeered. She'll think you're trying to score points with her mother, so you can score later with her. Knowing Cat's disposition, she'll shove those flowers in your big mouth and you'll arrive at her mother's house spitting stems!

He preferred eating the flowers, stems and all, to giving Cat McGillis the impression he was courting her. He had absolutely no intention of getting tangled up with another career woman!

Deep in thought, he allowed his feet to automatically follow the walkway to Cat's front door. He had pushed the doorbell button before he solved the battle warring in his head. Chimes ringing brought him back to reality. He shoved the flowers behind him and took three steps backward.

Ready and waiting, Cat opened the door on the first ring. "Get back, Brute! Quit jumping on me, for Pete's sake! Your toenails are scratching my legs!"

From the stunned look on Hank's face, she realized he thought she was scolding him. She scooped the excited poodle up in her arms, chuckled and said, "I meant him, not you."

Hank swallowed, hard. He swung the bouquet from behind his back to a strategic spot below his waist. Cat had an uncontrollable effect on him.

"C'mon in, Hank. I'll hold Brute to keep him from attacking you."

Brute wasn't the only one she held in check when Hank timidly presented her a bouquet of daisies, snapdragons and carnations, with lush green ferns interspersed. Nestled in the center, a fragrant yellow rose reigned as queen.

For several seconds, Cat was speechless. She had to restrain herself from hugging Hank for his thoughtfulness.

"They are beautiful. Thank you."

Hank felt his Adam's apple bob up and down as his throat worked to keep swallowing. Seeing her with her hair unbound, her eyes glistening brightly and her lips slightly parted, he had to shove his hands in his back pockets to keep them from circling her waist to pull her into his arms.

He hated to admit it, even to himself, but the pleasure shining in her eyes made him damned glad he'd brought the flowers and cleaned his truck.

"Ready?" he asked unnecessarily, his voice pitched lower than usual.

Brute pawed the air; he wiggled in Cat's arms demanding release to check out this stranger. Cat stooped and put him on the floor.

"Behave," she ordered Brute before straightening.

Obediently, Brute ran into the kitchen and lay down on the rug in front of the sink.

"Let me put these in water. Why don't you come into the kitchen and fix yourself a drink while I find a vase. The hard liquor is over the refrigerator or you're welcome to have a beer."

"Beer is fine." Badly needing something, anything, to keep his eyes from devouring Cat, Hank opened her refrigerator door. "Long-necks? Great!"

"Dad hates canned beer. Says he can taste the aluminum."

Cat placed the flowers beside the sink, then began rummaging through her pantry. No vase. She tried to think of something she could empty to use. A coffee can? How crude! She could put them in the green plastic pitcher, but that wasn't much better.

Call it pride or vanity or pure cussedness, she thought, I don't want Hank to know it's been a while since a man brought me flowers.

"I can't remember where I put it," she said, as she crossed to the cabinet below the kitchen sink. Out of habit, she sucked her bottom lip beneath her front teeth and worried it. She dropped to her knees and practically crawled inside the cabinet. "I know there's one around here somewhere."

Hank opened the bottle, tilted it to his mouth and drained half the contents in one thirsty gulp. The ice-cold beer loosened his tongue. Appreciatively watching her denim shorts cling to her backside as she swished back and forth, he mumbled, "Nice."

"What'd you say?"

"Oh, uh . . ." His eyes frantically danced around the room while his mind searched for a substitution for "nice." "Rice! Why don't you empty the rice out of the container by the stove?"

"Good idea." Like a crab, Cat reversed out of the cabinet on all fours. "I can't remember where I put the vase."

"You don't have it listed somewhere on a clipboard?" Hank teased.

Cat made a face at him. "My whole life isn't superorganized."

"It isn't?"

Sharon had kept extensive lists in a special organizer designed for time-conscious executives. She had taken tremendous pride in organizing her job, her house and her husband. Hank gritted his teeth. She'd succeeded with the first two, but not the third. After seven years, she'd declared him utterly hopeless. Miraculous Sharon couldn't turn chicken scratch into chicken salad!

"What's wrong?" Cat asked, observing the tautness of his jaw. "Is the beer warm?"

"No. It's fine."

"You're thinking about that white lie I told my mother, aren't you?"

"I wasn't, but it is something we're going to discuss before we get out there. False pretenses cause more problems than they solve." So speaks the voice of experience, he thought, then added, "A man's job title doesn't determine his worth."

"Tell that to my mother." Cat emptied the rice into the coffee can; she rinsed the rice container and filled it with water. "She thinks an executive office means financial security."

"With corporate mergers causing high-level layoffs? My men have more job security than most desk jockeys."

Cat grinned. "You can't confuse my mother with statistics or logic. She made up her mind the day I was born that her 'precious daughter' would never eat Texas caviar while waiting for the sky to clear."

"Red beans and rice? Your father must be in the trades," Hank deduced.

"Yep. And my four brothers." Cat finished arranging the flowers, then turned to face Hank. Holding up her right hand she pressed her forefinger against her thumb. "Dad's a carpenter." Her forefinger moved to her next finger. "Tom's a mason. Luke's in heating and air-conditioning. Russell's a roofer. And James, bless his wayward heart, designs kitchens."

"And you're a project manager. Is there a McGillis Construction Company about to be formed?"

Laughing, Cat shook her head and lowered her hand. "You're being logical again. When it comes to my family and what they want for me, you have to forget sane reasoning. I'm the baby of the family, a girl. I'm supposed to be a teacher or a banker or an accountant. That's why they pooled their nickels and dimes to send me to college. My being a project manager is a sore spot with them. The only way I can redeem myself, in my mother's eyes, is to marry..."

"A teacher or a banker or an accountant?"

"Anyone who wears wing-tipped shoes, has medical insurance and a solid retirement program."

While staring at Hank, Cat decided that the requirements her family felt were of utmost importance were as-inine. Hank worked hard, didn't try to cheat his employer and completed his work ahead of schedule. Few of the "acceptable" men she'd dated had Hank's sense of honor and industry, not to mention Hank's physique.

"Somebody like your boss?"

"You've got it."

Curious, he asked, "What happens when you bring someone like me home to meet them?"

"I don't know for certain. Only fools walk where angels fear to tread." Cat lifted one shoulder in a slight shrug as she watched his dark eyebrows climb higher and higher. "Yeah, I know. I'm a real hellcat on the job, but I'm a confirmed pussycat when it comes to my family."

"You said that, not me."

Hank drained the last of his beer. There had to be some middle ground between being introduced as her boss and being introduced as the framing subcontractor on her job. He tried to think illogically, like her family, but it was difficult. Cat wasn't the only one at the Lemontree who counted the nails in a structural support.

"Is it possible, since you've never dated a man in the trades, that if you took him home your family might not object?"

Cat glanced down at Brute. The tiny dog had his paws over his ears. She bent and picked him up.

"You're right, Brute. Only someone who hasn't met them would venture such a wild suggestion."

"I'm willing to risk it."

"Brave man," Cat whispered into Brute's ear. Secretly she wondered if Hank's suggestion stemmed from bravery or from the fact that he'd be long gone before her family started raising hell. He didn't care about her. She had to remind herself that she had bullied Hank into going along with her. Why shouldn't he be willing to take a chance on her parents' reaction? He knew he'd probably never see them again. "You really do hate false pretenses, don't you?"

"Yes."

"You don't want to be boss for a day—like king for a day?"

Hank grinned as he rolled to his feet. Although he stood several inches taller than her, he said, "Lady, when it comes to the construction business, I'd have to stand on my tiptoes just to be your equal. To be your boss, I'd have to carry a stepladder under my arm."

A warm inner glow lit Cat's golden skin, turning her cheeks pink. "Flattery will get you everywhere."

"You'll tell your folks I'm not your boss?"

"Okay, but don't blame me for what happens," she warned, handing Brute to Hank. She crossed to the refrigerator to get the food she'd prepared for the picnic.

"What's in the bowl?"

"Chicken salad."

Hank tossed back his head and hooted with laughter. Had he finally met a woman who could change chicken scratch into chicken salad? She'd have to force-feed him to get him to take a bite of it.

Brute yapped excitedly, as though, being a male, he understood the insider joke.

"What's so funny about chicken salad?"

"Nothing."

"Why'd you laugh?"

Hank opened the door and held it for Cat to precede him. "I felt like it."

"You hate chicken salad, don't you?" she badgered, unwilling to accept his glib reply.

He really didn't like chicken salad all that much. "It ranks right up there with broccoli, asparagus and spinach," he teased. "My fondest dream is to eat chicken salad and die full. What a way to go!"

"Mine isn't just plain ol' ordinary chicken salad. You'll like it." Her eyes widened with surprise as she sighted his truck. Caught up in his lighthearted mood, she put her hand over her eyes as though the sun shining on the polished chrome dazzled her eyes. "You cleaned your truck!"

"Inside and out."

"Mine looks like it's been parked in the center of a dust bowl. I don't suppose you'd be interested in helping me..." She glanced toward the garage, letting the hint dangle in the air between them. "No, that's too much to ask."

"Help you wash your truck?" Hank opened the passenger door for Cat. He started to put Brute in the back of the truck. "When?"

"Tomorrow?"

Brute panicked; he bared his teeth and growled at Hank.

"Manners, Brute," Cat commanded sternly. "He usually sits on the seat with his head in my lap."

The dog's growl turned into a pitiful whine.

"Smart dog," Hank said, giving Brute credit for knowing the best place in the truck. He could have sworn the dog grinned when Hank dropped him next to Cat. "When I was a kid, I had a hound dog that loved the back of the pickup. At fifty-five miles an hour, his ears would jut straight out to the side. We'd get home and old Jethro would shake his head side to side, flop, flop, flop, then beg to have his ears rubbed." As he shut her door, he added, "Not the smartest dog in the world, but I loved him anyway."

Once he was in the truck, they headed toward Lake Houston. The tape deck played toe-tapping country and western music, Cat's favorite. She rubbed Brute's tummy when he rolled over. His tongue lolled out of the side of his mouth, demonstrating his complete bliss.

"Do you have a dog now?"

"Nope."

"Why not?"

"He broke my heart."

"You're kidding." She watched Hank shake his head and chuckle. "How?"

"A cute little female mongrel came sashaying down the street where I lived . . . and that was the last I saw of ol' Jethro. So much for being man's best friend." He grinned at Cat, looking heart-whole. Cat was a good listener, the kind of woman whom a man could feel easy talking to. That was a side of her personality he hadn't observed on the job site. "Lord 'lmighty, lady, I haven't thought about Jethro since I was knee-high to a grasshopper."

Cat watched his smile compress into a tight thin line. "You don't often talk about what you think or feel, do you?"

He had, once. Sharon had transformed his vulnerabilities into a battering ram and bludgeoned him with them. He'd quickly learned to keep his mouth shut.

"I told Jethro everything. Hell, I even blubbered on his fur when things got bad."

"Lucky Jethro."

Her peculiar comment made him momentarily take his eyes off the highway and glance at her. Brute's head lay on Cat's bare upper thigh. He imagined himself stretched out with his head on her lap, sharing his problems with her. Oh, for a dog's life!

"Funny, I had the same thought about your dog."

Cat stroked Brute's nubby hair. "He's my little buddy, that's for certain."

Smiling, she looked at Hank. She had room in her life for a big buddy, with two legs instead of four. Somebody she could talk to, laugh with and care for. She wondered if Hank had room in his heart for her. She had to admit, albeit silently, she felt a strong physical attraction to Hank that had little to do with friendship.

We have a great deal in common, she mused, and yet, the very thing we do have in common, the Lemontree, could be the one thing that keeps us apart. He wants to keep our relationship on a strictly business level. She suspected the McGillis clan would heartily agree with his noble intentions.

"Why do you bother putting lipstick on your bottom lip?"

"What?"

"You have a habit of worrying your bottom lip when you're trying to solve a problem. What's bugging you?"

Self-consciously Cat licked her lips. "I was wondering about you."

"I'm no mystery man, just a guy earning his living with his hands."

Cat's curiosity made her scratch deeper. "Is your family in the trades?"

"No."

"Just a simple no? C'mon, Hank, open up. I blabbed about my family. Tell me about yours." Going straight to the reason she'd tossed and turned the previous night, she asked, "Why'd you say I'm like your ex-wife? Do I look like her?"

"No." Hank's hands tightened on the steering wheel. He'd been married for seven years and divorced for seven years, but it was still something he couldn't talk about. He was over Sharon. He didn't love her. And he damned sure wasn't going to let another woman get under his skin. He'd adopted a love-'em-and-leave-'em attitude; it satisfied his self-preservation instincts if nothing else. "Is the turnoff up ahead?"

"Yes." Cat could tell he was evading her. Was he hypersensitive about his divorce? To reassure him she wasn't being critical, she said, "You aren't the only man in Texas whose marriage didn't work. According to the statistics I've read, the divorce rate in Texas is about one out of two."

Hank made a right turn, without comment.

"Okay. That topic is off-limits," Cat agreed tactfully. "You could tell me about your family."

"Father, mother, one older male sibling and one younger female sibling. Amen."

Cat heard more than his monotone recitation of the members of his family. Sibling? She recalled other conversations they'd had. Hank Collins had a large vocabulary, far beyond the level of a high-school dropout. There were other clues she'd missed about him, too. The paperwork he completed for Goldcoast was typed. She'd also noticed an accountant's pad stuck under the driver's seat. He was either extremely well self-educated or...

"Where'd you go to college?" she blurted.

Hank swerved the wheel to avoid the center of the road, which resembled a washboard. "Texas University. I dropped out my sophomore year."

"Why?" Getting personal information out of Hank was like pulling hen's teeth—painfully difficult!

"Lack of interest."

That, according to his ex-wife, had been coupled with a lack of drive and ambition. Sharon had graduated, thanks to him, and quickly had realized he was the wrong man to help her climb the corporate ladder of success. She'd pressured him to make something of himself by going back to college and finishing his degree in business administration. She could accept the fact that he'd entered the construction trade out of necessity, but she'd never been able to understand why he continued working with his hands when he could "do better."

His reticence spurred Cat's curiosity. "What was your major?"

"The road needs to be graded."

Cat ignored his second attempt to switch topics. "What made you decide to be a carpenter?"

"The necessities of life...food and shelter." He slowed down to avoid a mammoth hole in the road and shot her a hard look. "I dropped out of college during the construction boom in Houston. Three thousand families a week were moving into the area. There were signs cluttering every construction site from one end of town to the other. Apply here. Bring tools. No experience necessary and *no questions asked.*" He stressed the last phrase in a significant manner, accompanying it with a glare.

Sliding down in her seat, Cat realized her natural inquisitiveness had gone beyond the superficial level appropriate to business acquaintances, and Hank had balked. But as she studied him long and hard through a fringe of honey-blond eyelashes, she had the feeling that Hank Collins needed to talk to someone. He'd bottled all his disappointments and frustrations into a pint-size jar and tightly screwed the lid shut. One good shake, and he'd exploded.

Hank hit the steering wheel with the heel of his hand, disgusted by his outburst. "Sorry, Cat. I didn't mean to bark at you like a wild dog. I guess I'm not used to talking about myself."

"No apology necessary. We're all sensitive about something."

She'd have been happy with the warm smile he cast her, but her smile faded when she heard, "I have to keep reminding myself who's the boss around here."

Chapter Four

"I've so looked forward to meeting my daughter's boss," Maude gushed as she hugged Cat. She gave a nod of approval at Hank's attire and lifted Brute from his arm. Brute lavished wet kisses on her face. "How's my little sweetie pie? You can quit squirming. Yeah, you can run on down to the dock to find Joshua. Excuse me, would you?" She strode to the end of the wraparound porch and shouted, "Joshua, boys, they're here!"

"Tell her," Hank ordered under his breath. "Now!"

Cat heaved a deep sigh. Her mother had taken great pains to impress Hank. The flower beds had been freshly weeded; the wooden rocking chairs lining the front porch had been waxed; the picnic table was decked out with a red-and-white-checkered tablecloth. Pots of hot-pink geraniums and petunias that hadn't been there previously added vivid splashes of color to the grayish, weather-bleached boards.

"They'll be here in a minute. I had them straighten up the boat shed. I swear, every spider in Texas had claimed it as home." She looped her arm into the crook of Hank's elbow. "Lordy, it's getting hotter than sin already. What can I get you to drink? Joshua picked up a bottle of bourbon."

"Water would be fine." Behind Maude's back he motioned for Cat to follow them.

"Iced tea would be better, wouldn't it?" Maude's face lit up with pleasure when Hank nodded. "I just brewed a fresh pitcher this morning. Do you take lemon and sugar?"

"Both. Thanks."

They entered the kitchen with Cat a couple of paces behind them. While Maude fussed over getting a glass, ice cubes, lemon and sugar, Hank looped his arm around the back of Cat's waist. He nodded his head; she shook hers. His fingers pressed against her rib cage to communicate the urgency of telling her mother the truth.

"Later," she mouthed.

"This instant!"

"Did you say instant?" Maude asked, stopping the flow of tea from the pitcher into the glass. "You prefer instant tea?"

"Brewed tea is fine."

Hank took the glass from Maude's fingers, but his other hand remained clamped on Cat's waist, and his dark blazing eyes never left her face. He felt the outside edge of Cat's foot jar against his anklebone. Only then did he notice the ear-to-ear grin on Maude's face. With Cat cuddled against him as though they were Siamese twins joined at the hip, Maude was jumping to her own wrong conclusions.

"What about you, dear? Can I get you something to drink? A diet soft drink?" Before Cat could respond, she looked up at Hank and added, "You don't have to worry about Cat putting on weight. She's the only one in the family who doesn't have a sweet tooth."

Cat wished she could crawl under the table and hide. This was much, much worse than the way her mother had fawned over Bradley.

"I'm not thirsty, Mom." She broke free from Hank's death grip and crossed to the window. She watched the easy camaraderie between her father and her brothers as they approached the house. She had to tell Maude now, before the other members of the family arrived. Casually, oh so casually, she spun around and asked, "Did I tell you Hank and Dad have something in common? Hank's the framing contractor at the Lemontree."

There, she thought, the cat's out of the bag. The look she gave Hank said, I've told the truth. You handle it from here.

"He isn't your boss?" Maude shifted her appalled gaze toward Hank. Through clamped teeth, she gritted, "He's a subcontractor like your father?"

Cat could almost hear her mother's rose-colored glasses shattering on the highly polished hardwood floor. Embarrassed by the abrupt change of attitude, Cat felt her cheeks flame.

Defensively, she stepped in front of Hank. "He's one of the few subcontractors that isn't dealing me a fit."

Hank sidestepped around Cat, prepared to charm Mrs. McGillis out of her prejudice against him. "Did your husband make the cabinets in here?"

Maude nodded stiffly. To her daughter, she mouthed, "You lied to me!"

"I told you what you wanted to hear," Cat silently mouthed back.

"Quality workmanship." He crossed to the counter and smoothed his hand over the semigloss satin finish. "Oak?"

Cat silently groaned. Hank's good intentions were ruined by his bringing up a touchy subject. She gave her mother a duplicate of the glare she'd received herself as a child when she'd misbehaved during church services.

Again Maude nodded. "I wanted pickled oak, but Joshua insisted pink would go out of style in a couple of years."

The screen door slammed behind Cat's father. He nudged his oldest son, Tom, in the ribs. "Looks like we're going to fight the pickled-oak versus natural-stain wars again, boys. Line up and choose sides."

"D-a-d!" Cat stretched the three letters until they sounded like three syllables. "I want you to meet Hank Collins."

"I've been looking forward to meeting you." His callused hand touched Hank's callused hand, and he pumped it vigorously. Joshua introduced Hank to Tom, Luke, Russell and James, then said, "So you're my kitten's boss, huh?"

"No, sir," Hank corrected. He wouldn't make Cat take the heat from the other members of the family. He draped one arm around Cat's shoulders. "I'm the subcontractor doing the framing work at the Lemontree. I do tend to be bossy, but that doesn't have anything to do with how I earn my living."

Cat closed her eyes, waiting, listening, expecting all hell to break loose. She only heard the shuffling of boots, her father clearing his throat, and Hank taking a fortifying deep breath. Her skin became sprinkled with goose bumps as the air turned chilly. At any moment she expected her family to chant in unison, "You aren't good enough for our little Cat!"

"You're just a carpenter?" Joshua said, moving to stand beside his wife.

Hank nodded.

"Well son of a bitch," Luke groaned. "I've been standing over a hot smoker in ninety-degree weather cooking briskets to impress a carpenter?"

Deciding the only way to save the day was to get Hank out of there before the rest of her family voiced their opinions, Cat blinked up at Hank and said, "I know you're anxious to get a fishing pole in your hands. Now that you've met everybody, why don't we go down to the lake?"

Not waiting for Hank's acceptance or her family's approval, she hustled Hank through the back door, down the porch steps, until they were out of hearing range. Humiliated, she was tempted to let Hank go fishing while she returned to the house and read her family the riot act.

"Whew!" Hank wiped the cold sweat off his brow with the back of his hand. He certainly understood why Cat had had to have the truth squeezed out of her. The misery plainly written on her face made him wonder if false pretenses and white lies were perhaps more discreet than the unvarnished truth. To soothe her misery, he joked, "I guess I should have splashed on some expensive cologne after all. From the number of uptilted noses in there, I must be stinking to high heaven. But I guess that's better than having them look down their noses at me, huh?"

"I'm sorry," Cat sincerely apologized. His being nice made her feel horrid. "I'd like to go back in there and yank their noses back in place. You'd think they were high-society muckamucks from the way they acted."

"Nope," Hank dared to disagree. "I'd just say they love you."

"Well, I wish they'd love me a little less!"

While Hank untied the high-powered bass boat from the pier, Cat turned to glare at the house. She could see James, her youngest brother, looking out the window toward her. She heard the rumble of male voices raised in anger.

She made a wide circle with her hand, then pointed behind James. Turn around and get them straightened out, before we come back, she silently commanded. James was the closest to her in age, so the two of them usually stuck together when it came to a showdown with her other brothers. His head disappeared from the window.

She coaxed her lips into a sunny smile, then turned toward Hank. "I don't get mad. I get even. I'll teach them to clan up against you."

"Don't be angry on my account." Hank saw revenge dance wickedly in her eyes and for a moment he almost felt sorry for her family. "I can take care of myself."

"Ha! You only say that because you haven't been on the losing end of a fight in my family. I have. What they've forgotten is that I know where the McGillis's skeletons are hidden." She smiled. "In this particular case, I know where their weak spots are. I'm going to hit 'em where it hurts. We're going to fish every honey hole on this end of the lake. Their Irish blue eyes will turn pea green with envy when we get back with a stringer dripping with crappie and bass!"

"What if the fish aren't biting?" Hank glanced skyward. The sun hit him full in the face, with burning intensity. "It's the wrong time of day, isn't it?"

"Not where we're going," Cat replied with a grin. "Hand me those extra fishing poles out of the rod box under the seat, would you? Better yet, just toss them over the side of the boat. Let my dear sweet brothers swim after their expensive tackle!''

"You're kidding."

"Am I?"

"Uh, Cat, there's revenge and then there's what's known as a death wish." He lifted the seat, grabbed the extra rods, then jumped back up on the dock. "I don't know about you, but I'd like to go home tonight in one piece. In case you haven't noticed, none of your brothers are ninety-pound weaklings."

Full of bravado, Cat laughed merrily. "I'm not afraid of them. A cat always wins when matched up against a pack of mongrels."

"Yeah, but you've forgotten one important detail... I'm the one that you plan to have deep-sixing their rods and reels."

"Hand them to me," she ordered.

"No, I don't think so."

One hand on her hip, she asked defiantly, "Who's the boss around here?"

"It's Saturday." He gestured toward the wide expanse of water behind him. "Unless the backhoe operator dug one hell of a hole by mistake and flooded it, we aren't at the Lemontree where you're the boss." Hank strode into the boat shed and deposited the rods in the nearest corner. "No bosses. Just you and me and a lake full of hungry fish. What do you say we get at it before your brothers commandeer the boat?"

Cat knew when to fight and when to give in gracefully. This was a time for complete acquiescence. She stepped down into the boat, silently vowing to make up to Hank for her family's mistaken judgment.

* * *

A string of crappie later, Hank put his rod in the rod holder, stacked up a pile of flotation seats until they were level with his seat, then stretched out with his hands behind his head and his feet crossed at the ankles.

"This is living," he said, lazily watching the clouds overhead.

"Better than being alone at your place, watching a sports program on television?"

"Mmm."

He looks totally at peace with the world, she mused with envy. "Mind if I join you?"

"Mmm."

"Yes or no?"

"Suit yourself," he replied, but he did lower his right arm for her to use as a pillow. He grinned as she shrugged at his lack of enthusiasm. Actually, he'd been watching her for the past half hour, and his male hormones were popping like gourmet popcorn. With more than one meaning, he advised, "Don't rock the boat."

Gingerly, she moved to the bow. She reclined beside him, extending her cramped legs as if she were a cat who'd been curled up for a long nap. The muscle of his upper arm was rocklike beneath her head. Cat gave a contented sigh.

"Nothing like a hard day of fishing to get life's problems back in perspective," Hank said.

He laced his fingers between hers, giving them a small friendly squeeze. With her next to him, he could nearly forget about her family's reaction, the fire, the daily problems of running his own business. Nearly, he thought, but not totally.

When she returned the pressure on his hand, he had to remind himself that Cat had invited him here to get

Maude out of her hair. He'd just happened to be in her office when her mother called. Convenience and expediency not the attraction he felt for Cat—were the reasons behind her invitation. It was damned hard keeping those facts firmly in his mind when their fingers were linked together.

Turning her head toward him, Cat felt a warmth that had nothing to do with the sun burning brightly overhead when she realized he'd been watching her. With their lips only a breath apart, she wondered why he didn't kiss her. Her heart skipped a beat when his dark pupils flared and his eyes dropped to her mouth.

Kiss me, she silently willed him.

Hank read the expectant expression in her sky-blue eyes. The mere thought of kissing Cat scared the hell out of him. Kissing would lead to intimacy, and intimacy would lead to opening old wounds that were best hidden under a thick layer of scar tissue. He had to protect his heart from being inflicted with new wounds.

Reluctantly, he admitted he could get serious about Cat quickly, too damned quickly for his heart's safety.

Retreating behind the widest barrier between them, he said, "Cat, something happened at the job site that I should have told you about yesterday."

"Not now, Hank." Her thumb traced the blunt edge of his fingernails. She felt the straight cut. Without opening her eyes she knew his nails were immaculately clean. There were some distinct advantages to fishing with minnows instead of worms. "Tell me Monday when my brain isn't in the R and R position—rest and relaxation."

Tempted to take her up on her offer, he paused, thinking of how he thoroughly enjoyed the soft feel of her feminine curves lying next to him. A light breeze blew a silky thread of her hair across his face; he felt it tease the tips of his eyelashes. Only the pad of her thumb lightly circling the sensitive burn on his hand made him avoid temptation.

Cat squinted at his face through sun-tipped lashes when she felt the muscle in his arm contract beneath her head. Intuitively she knew the companionable mood would be shattered unless she let him get whatever it was he wanted to tell her off his chest.

"Okay. Hit me with the bad news." She let go of his hand, rolled to her side and propped her head in her palm. "It is bad news, isn't it?"

"Maybe, maybe not." Without being aware at first of what he was doing, he felt his fingers tunnel through the silky mass of her hair tumbling down her back. He touched the back of her head, then slowly let the strands slip through his fingers. "That depends on whether you overreact or not."

Cat loved the absentminded way he was caressing her hair, as though it gave him great pleasure. It made her want to cup the side of his face with her hand to feel the contrast between his raven-dark hair and the slight stubble of whiskers along his jaw. She wanted to lean forward and touch the sunburned highlights along his brow and cheekbones.

She resisted the impulse, not because of her folks or because he was on Goldcoast's payroll, but because her womanly instincts told her the timing was wrong.

As plain as the nose on her face, he'd told her his work came first. And she remembered again that she reminded him of his ex-wife.

Emotional crumbs were all he would willingly give her. The hungry yearning growing inside her couldn't be appeased with tiny tidbits of him. She wanted all of him, heart, body and soul. She wouldn't allow herself to settle for less.

Welcoming a distraction, she said, "Tell me."

"Somebody accidentally started a fire."

Her half-closed eyes sprang open. "Accidentally?"

She remembered the soiled rags Flint Martin's men had left strewn about in the incomplete buildings. It wasn't necessary for her to close her eyes to envision the look on Flint's face when he'd threatened to pull off the job if he had to do things her way. Maybe Flint had decided not to take the highway. Maybe he'd taken one look at the figure on his paycheck and thought up a nasty plan to get even with her.

"It must have been an accident or vandalism," Hank said reassuringly. "Why would anyone set fire to a building where the work was completed?"

"The fire wasn't in the building you were working in Friday? What building was it in?"

"One."

"One! The interior decorators are scheduled to be in there next week!" Mentally she started to juggle schedules as she spit questions faster than a nail gun with a jammed trigger. "Was the fire in the first-floor apartments? How much damage? How long do you think it will take to repair it?"

"Second floor, rear apartment, in the bathroom off the master bedroom. The damage was minimal. Drywall only." His hand slid from Cat's hair as she moved toward the driver's seat. "I took care of getting the hole fixed and the mess cleaned up."

Cat blew the bangs off her forehead in exasperation. "I wish you'd told me about this yesterday."

"I should have. Hell, I meant to tell you, but I got sidetracked." He raised himself on one elbow. Their eyes met. Relieved that her eyes weren't spitting blue flames because he hadn't informed her, he said, "When I came to the office for my check, I'd decided to tell you about the same time you took the call from your mother."

Remembering the circumstances, she comprehended why Hank had kept his mouth shut; she'd just bullied him into being part of today's fiasco!

Her mind jumped back to the current problem. "Tell me exactly what happened, exactly what you saw," she said as she settled into the driver's seat.

"Okay. One of my men reported some problems with the trim work in one of the kitchens. So I decided I'd check it out. I went into the building, heard footsteps, smelled smoke, located the fire behind the drywall, pulled out the insulation and beat out the embers." He raised the back of his hand for her inspection. "And burned my hand in the process."

"Why didn't you come to me right then?"

He broke eye contact, glancing toward the tree-lined shore. "I felt like an idiot for not catching the person who started it."

"I don't expect you to play cops and robbers, but dammit, Hank, I do expect you to report any vandalism on the job."

"What would you have done if I had told you?"

"Investigated," she replied succinctly.

"Yeah, right." Skepticism in his voice indicated he didn't believe her. "Before I'd been given time to get past the word *fire,* you'd have called the fire department and police. Every man on every crew would have been rubbernecking to find out what was going on. Work would have ground to an immediate stop."

"Are you saying I go off half-cocked?"

"No. I'm saying you're so damned conscientious about your work that you don't allow room for accidents. C'mon, Cat, admit it. Would you have thought about how easily a fire can get started? But you've been around job sites all your life; you've probably seen or heard about some accidental fires."

"I wasn't responsible for putting them out. There's a great big difference between being a kid tagging along with her brothers and being the project manager."

"True."

"I need to find out who started the fire."

"True again, but face it. The chances are slim or non-existent. I asked around. Nobody knows anything about it other than a couple of guys who remember seeing me on the front stoop putting on my boots."

Cat leaned toward him. To erase forever any doubt in her mind, she bluntly said, "You didn't have anything to do with this."

"Only what I've told you."

"I'm sorry you hurt your hand, but frankly, I'm damned glad you arrived on the scene when you did."

Professionally, she couldn't tell Hank that she'd been instructed to "get tough" on the subcontractors' billing because Goldcoast had a temporary cash flow problem. General office went over her cost sheet with a fine-tooth comb. She had to justify every penny spent.

But she did say, "To underbid the other general contractors Goldcoast cut the profit margin to near nothing. I not only want to prove myself as a project manager, I'm also trying to bring this project to completion below bid. Costly delays are going to look bad on my record and cause problems for Goldcoast."

Hank grinned as he reached over and covered her hand with his. "I've got my reputation and my bank account on the line, too. Goldcoast isn't the only company that wants to avoid any and all complications.''

"You mean me?"

He nodded, smiling at her. "You aren't a simple woman, someone I'd pick up, sleep with and forget the next morning.''

"You're right. I'm not interested in one-night stands.'' His honesty must be contagious, she mused, wrapping her fingers around the heel of his hand. "Think about it, Hank. We have a lot in common, both on and off the job. We're both independent, self-sufficient, and we don't want anybody sticking their nose in where it doesn't belong. Yeah, I caught the message you sent about me prying into your personal life,'' she admitted. "I don't know about you, but there are times when I'd enjoy having someone to talk to, other than family. How about you?''

"You're management. I'm labor.''

She shook her head. "We both want to reach the same objective. Doesn't that erase the invisible line between us? Don't you like me?''

Hank felt his heart jump. "Do you think I'd bring flowers to a woman I didn't like? Yeah. I like you. What about you? Do you like me?''

"I wouldn't have invited you here today if I didn't like you,'' she replied, matching his honesty. "I'd have come alone.''

For a moment they studied each other, both of them realizing that what they felt was more than simply liking each other. Whatever the plateau was between liking and loving, they were both balanced precariously on it.

Chapter Five

James shifted from one foot to the other while he watched Cat and her new boyfriend idle up to the dock. He caught the rope his sister threw him, muttering over the low hum of the engine.

"It's about time you showed up. Nothing quite like dropping a time bomb and leaving me behind to listen to it ticking, is there, sister dear?"

Determined to ignore her family's lack of hospitality and to remain cheerful, Cat pulled the string of fish from the lake. "I can hardly wait to show these to the rest of the McGillis clan!" she gloated.

James eyed their catch. "You didn't."

"Didn't what?" she asked, her blue eyes rounded with mock innocence.

"You took a complete stranger to the places where we've seeded Christmas trees for the past twenty-five years. The Three Mean Musketeers are going to cremate the Gruesome Twosome for a stunt like that!''

Cat chortled with glee. She hopped up on the dock, then turned to explain the nicknames to Hank.

"James and I dubbed Tom, Luke and Russell the Mean Musketeers—Mean, Meaner and Meanest, because they were obnoxious meanies when we were kids. In retaliation, they named us the Gruesome Twosome."

"I imagine they've been calling me worse names," Hank replied as he tied the back rope to the ring on the pier nearest him.

"Sticks and stones can break my bones," Cat chanted, pointing toward James.

"But words make great fodder for humble pie?" James completed.

"Doesn't rhyme, but our minds are still on the same wavelength," Cat replied. She nudged him in the ribs. "I don't suppose I could coerce you into helping Hank and me clean the fish?"

"What happened to the rule, 'He who catcheth 'em, cleaneth em'?" James gave Hank a helping hand out of the boat. Under his breath he said for Hank's ears alone, "She detests gutting fish."

Enjoying the banter between brother and sister, Hank took the string from Cat's hand and moved toward the cutting board and hand pump built at the end of the dock.

"I'll cooketh them for your dinner tomorrow night," she offered.

"Naw, sis, I'd rather watch you clean them," James tormented. He moved beside Hank. "You'd think with her double-edged, sharp tongue she could clean a fish with one slice."

"That's enough, sweet James. Don't tell all the family secrets in the first five minutes you talk to Hank, please."

"Why not? You did."

"You aren't telling me Cat McGillis is squeamish, are you?" Hank asked, joining in the fun.

"I could clean those fish faster than James, if I wanted to."

"Believe me, she won't want to." James turned from Hank to Cat. "Men's work, right?"

She was saved from thinking up a smart retort by the sound of the screened door banging shut, drawing their attention to Brute, who came running onto the dock. His whole rear end shook as he wagged his tail, jumping off all four paws, begging Cat to pick him up.

"What's that I see on your whiskers, Brute McGillis?" Cat demanded, picking a fleck of brown goo off his whiskers. "Don't try to lick off the evidence. Who's been feeding you chocolate icing?"

Brute looked at Hank and barked.

"Don't fib to me, you little stinker." She set him down on the dock and lightly swatted his behind. "You'd better get it out of your system or you'll be banned from the bedroom, shut in the laundry room."

James grinned at Hank. "You don't have problems digesting chocolate, do you?"

"James!" Cat protested. "How'd you like to take a long walk off a short pier?"

"How'd you like to go for a swim right along with me?" James shifted his feet to a balanced stance, fully expecting his sister to throw a body block against him at any moment. "She'll do anything to get out of cleaning fish!"

Hank stepped between the two of them. "I'll clean the fish. Cat, you go get a plastic bag filled with ice. James, you just keep talking. You're a real fountain of information." He winked at Cat.

"You heard the man. Scat, fraidy-cat." James picked up a fillet knife off the cutting board. With a sigh of resignation, he said to Hank, "I don't mind cleaning her share of the mess. I'm used to it."

To let Cat know he'd been kidding about pumping James for information about her, he said, "Did I hear someone mention you design kitchens, James?"

Cat felt like joining Brute, who was sprawled out at the edge of the bank eating grass. The thought of going up to the house made her stomach churn. She imagined that the Mean Musketeers and her parents were seated at the kitchen table deciding what tactic they would use to dissuade her from dating Hank.

They'd never believe her if she told them Hank wasn't interested in her. To them, she was irresistible. Was it any wonder, she thought, she'd reached the ripe old age of twenty-six without getting married? What man in his right mind would give her a second look with her brothers glaring at him?

For Hank's sake she had to come up with a plan that would make them treat him with the respect he deserved.

Tom, Luke and Russell were as hardheaded as Missouri mules. A swift clout on the head with a two-by-four was the only thing she could think of that would get her brothers' attention. And she wasn't certain she had the strength in her arms to make that effective.

Her parents were hopeless, too. Nobody was good enough for their baby daughter. Except for Bradley, she reminded herself, and dismissed him as an unpleasant afterthought.

"So what am I going to do?" she muttered.

She hated bucking her family, but she had to take a stand. Given a choice, she'd much rather have been taking a stand inside the walls of the Alamo, watching the

Mexican army approach. Her odds of winning would have been better.

She straightened her shoulders, took a deep breath and marched up the steps. To bolster her courage, she whispered, "Hank Collins would be worth fighting for!"

"Thanks for having your daughter invite me, Mr. and Mrs. McGillis." Hank would have been lying if he'd said he enjoyed their hospitality. Cat tugged impatiently on his arm as he added, "James, you have my phone number. Let's get together and go over those plans we discussed."

Cat had gone through the family ritual of giving each of her brothers a peck on the cheek, but in protest against the silent treatment they'd given Hank, the hugs she'd given her parents were less than wholeheartedly enthusiastic.

Hank, bless his heart, had acted as though eating dinner with five mute, deaf and blind people was an everyday occurrence. He'd set a good example that was difficult for her to follow. Long before she helped her mother serve the promised strawberry shortcake to the men, Cat had considered jumping up on the table to dictate a few ultimatums to them.

The rebellious urges she'd controlled for the past three hours surfaced when Hank opened the truck door. She knew her family remained lined up on the porch watching them.

"Play along with me, please," she whispered.

She stepped up on the running board and wrapped her arms around Hank's neck. Her eyes sparkled with promise. "I'm declaring World War III, right here and now!" she murmured. "Care to be my ally?"

She felt him tense from shoulder to thigh. Momentarily she feared he would jerk away from her. She hadn't expected his wariness to be stronger than her desire to show her family she didn't give two hoots for their opinion of Hank. She breathed a quick sigh of annoyance that she hoped would shatter his cynicism.

A slight shudder shook him, then he wrapped his arms around her.

"This is one hell of a way to retaliate," he said, finding the feel of her enticing.

One kiss, he thought, one kiss from Cat could soothe the damage her family had done to his hard-earned self-confidence. She'd taken the initiative; he masterfully took control.

She'd never known a man could take such care with a kiss. She'd imagined a hot, torrid meshing of lips. When his tongue lightly traced over her naked bottom lip, then flicked across the lipstick on the twin peaks of her upper lip, she recalled his mentioning her bad habit. Had he wanted to kiss her then?

Hank captured her lower lip between his teeth, silently communicating for her not to worry. He drew it inside his mouth, gently sucking it until he felt her need for revenge altering, transforming into a need for him.

Cat moaned, a deep, throaty sound that signalled the surrender of her original goal. Her tongue met his. She tasted the sweetness of strawberries blended with his own special flavor. The sweet taste of revenge was bland compared to the rush of raw, consuming passion his kiss evoked.

"Enough?" he asked, his lips moving against hers.

"They've gone inside." The porch light flashing on and off beside the front door had nothing to do with her reply. Hank Collins had the power and finesse to make her forget her principles. It scared her to think she could easily, quite easily, be convinced that love and lust weren't one and the same.

Brute strutted to the edge of the seat cushion, put his front paws on Hank's arm, looked up at him, yawned, then gave a shrill series of yaps.

Both Cat and Hank chuckled.

"I swear, I can almost hear Brute saying, 'Knock off the mushy stuff, fella. My stomach is upset and I'm pooped. Take me home.' There's no mistaking what he wants, is there?" Hank scooted the pooch to the center of the bench seat. "You're a pint-size nuisance, dog."

"Don't pay any attention to him, Brute," Cat countered, sliding in beside Brute. "You're a super watchdog." After Hank shut her door and circled the front of the vehicle, she tacked on, "You have to admit, Brute knows when to watch and when to bark. He was very quiet while you were kissing me." And he knew to bark when I was in danger of getting lost in your kiss, she thought.

Hank let his keys dangle in his hand while he sorted through his thoughts. He'd enjoyed kissing her, especially when she'd forsaken her cockeyed reason for inviting his kiss. It had only taken seconds for him to abandon his reasoning, also. One kiss had made him hungry for more. He'd had to move away from her to avoid disgracing himself!

He stuck the key in the ignition. With a flick of his wrist the powerful engine hummed. Slowly, he followed the parallel ruts that circled an oak tree in the front yard. His headlights swept across the length of the house.

"You know how Brute's eyes glow when bright lights hit them?" Cat asked. "It's a good thing human eyes don't do that."

"I'll bite. Why?"

"The front window, lit with six pairs of red eyes peeking from behind the curtain, would have inspired both of us to start singing Christmas carols."

Hank grinned at her. "They want to protect you, too."

"With good reason," Cat muttered.

"Meaning?"

"It's a good thing you can't read my mind as easily as you read Brute's," she drawled. A woman could easily become addicted to his brand of sweet kisses.

Hank steered with one hand and with the other reached for the knob to turn up the volume on the radio. He felt a sinking sensation in the pit of his stomach. Damn! He was falling for Cat McGillis. He couldn't. Not without her knowing the worst about him.

"Your favorite song?" She recognized the lyrics. They told the story of a man's search for love in the wrong places. Her heart soared sky-high, but hit an air pocket when Hank fiddled with the tuning knob. "I liked the first station," she said.

"The Astros are playing tonight. I might be able to catch the last couple of innings."

"Is that a polite way of telling me I'm prying again?"

"There's the station." Hank listened for the score. "How 'bout that? They're winning."

She was tempted to reach over and turn the damned thing off. How could she listen to a ball game when what she wanted to hear was every little detail about Hank's life before she'd met him? Judging from the hard line of his jaw, he wasn't about to discuss his private life.

Okay, Cat thought, I'll be flexible. I can play by your rules. "Dad mentioned he has extra tickets to the game tomorrow afternoon...."

"It's a sellout, so it'll be televised."

She couldn't blame him for his curtness. She wasn't anxious for a repeat performance of today's fiasco, either. Her hands knotted together on her lap as she glanced at Hank. He appeared to be intently listening to the game as he dodged ruts in the road.

She could try to break down the visual and auditory barrier he'd erected, but her experience with her brothers told her that probably wouldn't work. Her brothers would just have told her to shut up. Hank would be more polite; he'd probably resort to one-syllable replies.

She nibbled her bottom lip and took another glance at Hank. For a fraction of a second their eyes met. Abruptly the realization came to her that usually she preferred to listen to the radio than try to carry on small talk. Just as abruptly, a second realization hit her. The only reason the radio bothered her now was because she would rather listen to Hank than to some stranger spouting baseball statistics.

That, and she hated the way Hank hid his feelings behind an emotional brick wall. She hunched down in the seat, pretending to listen to the game as avidly as Hank was. She wouldn't touch the damned radio!

She had squelched her impetuosity; that was what was getting her into trouble. No more invitations to family get-togethers. No more kisses. No more hinting for future dates. She'd let him take the initiative, and she'd put a curb on her wayward tongue.

Hank pulled into her driveway. She grabbed Brute and hopped out of her side of the truck before Hank could assist her. As she strode toward her front door she said, "Thanks for an eventful day. Once again, I'm sorry my family is overly protective of me."

Brute whined and squirmed in her arms. He jumped the instant her hold slackened. "Don't run off, Brute."

Twenty-five feet separated Cat from where Hank leaned against the front fender of his truck. She absolutely, positively and unequivocally would not take one step toward him.

"You have a job to do tomorrow," Hank said, wiping one finger along the dusty hood of his truck. "Actually, two jobs."

"Go check out the fire damage and what else?"

"Wash your truck, then wash mine?" He grinned as her expression changed from puzzled to pleased. "That's the two I had in mind. Who knows? If you get up early and work fast, maybe we'll be finished in time to catch the televised game."

"I like lots of soapsuds."

While Hank watched, Cat squeezed liquid detergent into a five-gallon pail, then put her finger over the nozzle of the hose to increase the water pressure. She dropped a rag into the billowing white foam.

When she suggested he help wash the truck, he hadn't been certain if she did so because hers badly needed a thorough scrubbing or if she was hinting at their spending Sunday together. It took only one backbreaking hour of unloading the tools from the truck bed to discern her invitation stemmed from necessity.

He couldn't fault Cat for not toting her share. He'd had to bodily stop her from heaving Goldcoast's pipe fitting machine to her shoulders. "I can do it," seemed to be her motto; he'd heard her mutter the phrase on several occasions before he removed the object from her hands.

"I'll wash, you rinse," she said, offering him the easier job since it was her company truck. The reckless spark in his eyes made her reconsider handing him the hose. "It would be childish for you to spray me."

"Yeah, it would," he agreed. The oversize, hot-pink T-shirt and cutoff jeans she wore did make the idea tempting. Water splashed off the concrete onto his bare feet. Suds dripped, lightly plopping onto her foot from the rag in her hand. "And equally childish for you to spray me."

Her wrist flicked upward; the green hose snaked, spewing water closer to his big toe. A teeny bit more, she thought, chuckling, and she could drench him. He'd go for the hose; she'd pelt him with the soggy rag, then run for the hills.

"Don't think about it." He inched toward her, ready to grab her wrist. "You'll never make it to the other side of the truck."

Cat stood her ground. The closer he came, the higher the water went up his bare leg. Unless he stopped, water would be tunneling into his belly button within seconds, without her having to move the hose upward at all. Whirling toward the truck, she aimed at the truck's cab.

"Fraidy-cat, like James said?"

Quick as a scalded cat, she threw the soapy rag in the direction of his voice and started to make a mad dash around the tailgate. She'd have made it, too, if her hair hadn't whipped against his chest.

She heard him make a tsking noise as he gently reeled her backward. She could have pulled away; he barely had hold of her hair.

"I still have the hose!" she squealed, laughing at being, literally, caught by him.

"Drop the hose."

The laughter she heard underlying his command made her want to tempt the Fates. She pivoted and, following his orders, dropped it—down the front of his shirt.

He instantly freed her hair. She carried out her original plan and ran to the opposite side of the truck.

"Son of a biscuit eater, that's cold!" he yelled, but the corners of his eyes crinkled in mirth. As though he had all the time in the world, he lethargically unbuttoned his shirt, shed it and tossed it aside. "Bubba said the *H* in your name stood for Hellcat! James was wrong! You aren't afraid of anything, are you?"

Cat giggled. She'd scoffed when she heard her nickname on the job site. There were worse names to call a woman in a job usually held by a man.

Mentally she measured the distance between the front of the truck and the garage. I might make it, she thought. That plan went awry as she watched Hank stride to the front of the truck.

She circled to the back. Face turned upward, she saw a spritz of water arching over the truck bed. She ducked. It pelted her back. She'd have to stay low and watch his feet, she realized.

"Cold?"

Chuckling, she decided to use a maneuver that always worked on her brothers. She stood up and marched toward him, silently daring him as he'd dared her. Men loved the hunt; they hated having the quarry walk right up to them.

She bowed her head, feigning remorse, crossed her fingers behind her back and said, "Sorry."

He'd admired her mettle, until she opened her mouth to spout a fake apology. Knowing he'd tormented her into dousing him, he'd been prepared to forgive her. But, he thought, this is one time the lady should have kept her mouth shut!

Cat lifted her head and opened her mouth to explain exactly what she was sorry for, the way her brothers invariably demanded, and felt her face being thoroughly washed. She barely had time to shut her eyes, much less her mouth.

"Hank!" she sputtered. "You're drowning me!"

"I'm sorry," he mimicked. "Didn't your mother ever wash your mouth out with soap when you were a kid, for fibbing?" He tossed the hose on the ground. "Should I use the soapy rag?"

She raised her hands in case he intended to carry out his threat. "You asked for it!"

"Sure, I did, little hellcat," he replied good-naturedly. "I distinctly remember begging, 'Please, soap up my kisser, then hose me down!' Funny, I can't quite remember if I said that before or after you asked for your shower."

"Your eyes speak louder than you can yell."

Cat bent over and wrung the water out of her hair. When she looked up, his hot black eyes were telling her secrets she doubted she'd hear from his lips. Her thin T-shirt was fused to her skin. She could feel her nipples, rigid from being soaked in cold water, pointing up at him. She lowered her arms, self-consciously crossing them over her chest.

"I'd better change. Why don't you go rustle through the closet in the guest bedroom? You ought to be able to wear something one of my brothers left behind."

"Get out of here, Cat." While you can, he thought. The two of them, undressed, only a hallway apart... Hank wiped his eyes to blank out the mental image of the natural outcome. "You go ahead. It's going to take two washings to get your truck clean. I'll do the first scrub-down."

She's getting to you, ol' boy, he mused. Energetically he began scouring the roof of the cab. She hadn't faked her shyness, of that he felt certain. If she'd brazenly met his stare, he'd have been inside the town house, in her bed, in her . . .

Again, he stopped his libidinous thoughts. His hand moved the cloth in small circular motions over the smooth paint. Her skin would be soft, supple beneath his hands. He'd stroke her, slowly, sensuously, until he heard small kitten noises coming from the back of her throat. His shoulder muscles flexed as he imagined her fingers raking across them.

Water splashing up in his face brought him back to reality. She didn't want him, not that way. She'd offered friendship. By arriving on her doorstep this morning, he'd accepted her offer.

"Dammit, man. Get your mind on your work! In ten minutes, she'll be out here chewing your ass for doing a crummy job on her truck!"

He doubted that, but verbalizing the idea served its purpose. In earnest, he began scrubbing layer upon layer of grime from the truck. He hoped to hell the chore would thoroughly exhaust him. Physical labor, he silently chanted. Work her out of your system. He'd done it before when Sharon left him.

"What's that old saying?" he muttered between clenched teeth. An ounce of prevention is worth a pound of cure. Yeah, that's the one.

"Which old saying?" Cat asked, thinking he'd seen her standing beside the truck. She'd changed clothes faster than a quick-change artist because she was afraid Hank would lay a strip of tire rubber backing out of her driveway if she didn't hurry.

Hank stiffened his arms as he tried to think of a reply. "Nothing. I was just thinking out loud."

"Friends bounce their thoughts off each other. Tell me what you were thinking about." His smoldering dark eyes traveled over her dry navy-blue top and matching shorts. "No fibbing or I get to wash your mouth out with soap."

"Sharon, my ex-wife. I was thinking about her."

Sharon! Is that who he thinks of when he looks at me? Cat had to swallow twice to diminish the size of the lump forming in her throat. She wanted to delve deeper, but she had knocked her head against the stone barrier Hank surrounded himself with once too often to ask questions.

Scrubbing an imaginary spot off the paint, he said, "I guess I ought to tell you about my marriage to her."

"Only if you want to."

"She's a part of who and what I am." He tossed the wet rag into the bucket of dirty water as he jumped over the side of the truck bed, landing next to Cat. He'd never talked to anyone about Sharon or his marriage. As he tried to organize his thoughts, he took Cat's hand and led her to the front steps of her porch.

Her hand felt warm, smooth to his touch. In contrast, his were puckered from being in the water. His thumb moved across the hills and valleys of her knuckles as he decided the only place to start was at the beginning.

"At nineteen, I thought Sharon was like a Christmas angel that had dropped off a tree into my arms." His eyes met Cat's, then quickly swerved away. "We had all these dreams that had nothing to do with reality. I'd work until she finished her degree and then she'd support me while I finished my degree."

"Your parents wouldn't help with tuition once you married?"

"No. Their not helping financially was supposed to be a deterrent. My parents and Sharon's parents only agreed on one thing—marrying young would wreck our futures. Her parents repeatedly told her that I'd never amount to anything."

He pinched the bridge of his nose between his thumb and forefinger. "I was so damned young and cocky. I thought all I had to do to get a job was show up and be hired. You can imagine what a shock it was when I found out that nobody wanted to hire an inexperienced kid."

"But you found work," Cat said, "in the trades."

"Yeah. Minimum-wage jobs." His shoulders hunched forward as he recalled the pittance he had earned. "To make a long story short, the bill collectors arrived at the front door and love flew out the back door. We scraped through financially by me working as a carpenter's helper during the day and delivering pizza at night."

"Did she work?"

Hank shook his head. "Once or twice she talked about getting a job at a fast food joint. But like an arrogant kid, I discouraged her. My pride kept telling me that a real man supported his wife. I didn't need her help. I was hell-bent on proving to her parents that I could take as good care of Sharon as they could. All I wanted Sharon to worry about was making the dean's honor roll . . . which she did. Before the end of the first year, we were more like roommates than husband and wife. Hell, I worked sixteen hours a day. By the time I got to our apartment, I was too exhausted to talk to her, and she wasn't interested in what I had to say anyway."

Cat's heart wrenched for him. "Did she graduate?"

"With honors. I slept through her graduation ceremony." He grimaced and dryly added, "I wish I'd been able to sleep through the celebration afterward. Have you ever wanted something with all your heart, and then when you get it you ask yourself, 'Is this all there is?' "

Cat nodded.

"Hell, to be truthful, I was probably jealous of her. I was dog tired and I felt ancient compared to her friends at the party. They talked about this class and that class, this professor and that professor, and I drank one beer after another. And then, the crowning blow came. It was one of those awful moments when the whole room is noisy, then everyone takes a deep breath and there's a lull in the conversation. That's when one of Sharon's girlfriends spotted me and asked if I'd put the pizzas in the kitchen." He laughed without mirth. "Even in my drunken haze, I recognized her as one of the Friday night regulars."

Her heart ached for Hank. She wanted to reach out and touch him, but she kept her hands to herself. She had the feeling none of the good ol' boys had bothered to listen to Hank.

"You should have seen the horrified look on her face when I told her I was Sharon's husband. Later, after the bash, I couldn't even describe the girl to Sharon. I'd only seen red. I was hurt and frustrated and angry, and I was spoiling for a fight. I wanted Sharon to have to experience my humiliation. I needed to be consoled for being the only one at her party without a degree."

"That's understandable," Cat dared to murmur.

"Is it? Sharon didn't think so. Not after she'd giggled her way through a bottle of champagne. Bubbly juice loosens the tongue. I found out what she thought of me in no uncertain terms."

Hank winced. A cynical smile twisted his lips into a grisly smile. "She quoted her parents. Can you imagine that? Only with one slight variation . . . her opinion of me was much lower. Not only was I a social embarrassment to her, I'd never amount to anything. I'd always be crude, rude and socially unacceptable. Putting me through school would be a waste of money. I'd never get a job with a Fortune 500 company like she had."

His eyes leveled on Cat. "Ironically, by then I knew she was partially right. I had lost interest in going back to school. The thought of being cooped up in an office being a desk jockey was actually repulsive to me."

Cat strongly empathized with his feelings. They were two of a kind when it came to their work.

"Up until then, I hadn't thought much about who I was and what I wanted to be. I'd been marking time. It never occurred to me that the calluses on my hands, the clothes I wore and the way I spoke were truly a social embarrassment to her."

"You had nothing to be ashamed of. You did an honest day's work for an honesty day's wages. You were still the man she'd married."

"No, I wasn't. If either of us had had a lick of sense, we would have ended it right then and there. I felt...angry... humiliated...cheated. And so did she. Subconsciously, we both probably knew we were poison for each other, but we were too stubborn to admit defeat. She kept hoping I'd change, and I kept hoping she'd go back to being the way she was when I first met her. It took five years of zapping each other with insults before things finally broke."

His shoulders sagged as though they carried the weight of the world. His eyes dropped to the ground. "I was so damned mad that when she filed for divorce I considered suing her for alimony. Isn't that a hell of a thing for an able-bodied man to do?"

"You wouldn't have been the first man to do it. There's been many a woman who's filed for and been awarded alimony after she put her husband through medical or law school."

"What price tag should a man put on his self-respect? I wouldn't be able to look at myself in the mirror without puking if I knew she'd paid for it." He lifted his shoulders. "I'll say this for her bad-mouthing me. It inspired me to work harder, faster, to be frugal with my money. I swore there'd come a day when she'd look at me and wish she'd stuck by my side."

"You still love her, don't you?"

"Hell, no." He watched Cat raise one eyebrow. "Try the flip side of the coin. I hated her."

"Past tense?"

"Long past. She's happily married to an attorney, and I thank my lucky stars for my own good fortune. I don't think it's likely that she'll call me to build an apartment project for her husband's investment portfolio, but if she did? She'd be just another customer."

Cat knew better. Sharon's shallowness had left an indelible mark on Hank. She'd broken her vows and her promises. Sharon had taught him a lesson he'd taken to his heart. Hank Collins distrusted women, all women.

No longer could Cat hold back from showing her sympathy. She needed to hold him; he was a man who desperately needed a woman's soft touch. It should have occurred to her, as she put her arms around his waist and swept her hands up his back, that her hands were as callused as his.

She should have thought of how her family's treatment must have hurt him. And she should have remembered he considered her to be like his ex-wife.

As he folded her tightly against him, her only thoughts were of giving comfort. He'd been treated shamelessly. She couldn't change his dismal past; she could only hope she'd brighten his future.

Chapter Six

"I've watered half of Houston, but your truck still needs a wash job," Hank said, loving the compassion she'd given him, but beginning to feel awkward about sitting on her porch steps holding her. "We've got my truck yet to do, too."

"And a ball game to watch," she added. Reluctant to let go of him, she hugged him tighter. "We could skip washing the trucks. They'll only get dirty tomorrow."

"The baseball game won't start for another hour."

"We could just relax on the patio," she suggested. "I've got a double-wide hammock. We could talk some more, get to know each other better."

Hank wanted to accept her attractive offer. He liked the idea of lying close to her, getting to know her better. But he shook his head. "Uh-uh, sweetheart. I'm all talked out. Your caring hands make me feel like a man who's in intensive care after open heart surgery. I'm feeling better for getting this off my chest, but I need some recovery time."

"Okay." Cat stepped back; her hands trailed down his shoulders and arms, until they reached his hands. She raised them to one side of her face and rubbed her cheek against his knuckles. "I'm glad you opened up to me, Hank. Very glad. I'm always here if you need me. Remember that in the future, would you?"

Hank smiled his acceptance into her blue-green eyes. "We'd best get started or we will miss the game."

For the next companionable hour they slaved over the trucks. Hank did the gritty work; she cleaned the interior of the cabs. He applied a coat of wax; she spit-polished the chrome bumpers. While he organized her hand tools, she rolled up the hose.

"If the construction industry takes a nosedive, we can apply at one of the car washes. Nobody is going to recognize my truck tomorrow. It looks terrific," she bragged, pleased by how well they'd worked together and the results of their labor. "C'mon inside. Do you like Tex-Mex food?"

"A lot better than chicken salad," he teased.

Unoffended, she asked, "How would you know how my chicken salad tastes? Yesterday, you avoided it like you thought you'd get ptomaine poisoning from it."

"Next time, I promise I'll hold my nose and taste it." He looped his arm across her shoulders and headed through the garage toward the kitchen entrance. "Just to prove my sincerity, if you want to call Ninfa's Restaurant for a take-out order, I'll go get it."

He opened the door, and she led the way into the kitchen. Brute scampered up to her, tail wagging, ball between his jaws.

"Brute, would you please inform Mr. Collins I not only fix superb chicken salad, I also fix terrific nachos supreme?"

Brute barked a succession of short, muffled yaps.

She opened the refrigerator door and handed Hank a beer. Before he'd arrived, she had grated the Monterey Jack cheese and diced tomatoes, onions and green peppers. She'd even gone to the trouble of making guacamole, homemade picante sauce and spicy chili.

"See? I have the makings ready. Why don't you get the blue cleanser off your face while I throw them together?"

Squatting, Hank picked up Brute. "She seems to have everything under control as usual, huh, pup?"

"You're still welcome to borrow some of my brothers' clothes if you want to. They'll never miss them." Especially since they won't be here until they learn how to act like gentlemen, she silently mused. Unwilling to dwell on a sour note, she began removing covered dishes from the refrigerator. "Put Brute down and he'll show you the way to the guest room."

Doubtful, Hank glanced down at the midget-size dog. "He's not only a watchdog, he's the perfect host, too?"

"You don't believe me? You owe him a doggy bone if he takes you straight into the spare room and brings me his leash. Fair bet?"

"I'll owe the pooch a doggy bone if I'm wrong. He's smart, but he's also part of your family. What do I get if he escorts me straight to my truck?"

"Lunch?"

"Uh-uh. You've already offered that as payment for my truck-washing services. A project manager ought to know you can't pay a man twice with the same check."

"Truc." Cat cradled Brute in her arm, petting his head to make him drop the ball. She considered offering Hank a doggy kiss, but vetoed the idea. If there was any kissing to be done, it wouldn't take place between Hank and Brute! "You decide. Make it easy on yourself, though. Brute is well trained."

Hank's eyes instantly dropped to her mouth. A kiss would be a reasonable penalty. But he'd be taking a cold shower if he let his mind dwell on kissing Cat. He shrugged. "I'll think of something."

"It's a good thing I have faith in Brute. It takes heaps of trust to enter into a bet without knowing the forfeit in advance." She rolled her tongue in her cheek. "You have to tell me what you decided, even if I win, right?"

"That's fair."

She wrenched at the ball. Brute refused to drop it from his mouth. "Okay, tough guy." She lifted one floppy ear and whispered, "Show him your stuff. Go get your leash, big fella."

Brute's paws churned the air in readiness, before his toenails touched the kitchen tile.

"Just follow him," she instructed Hank, grinning with confidence. "You're gonna lose."

Hank darted after Brute. Once out of her sight, he scooped the poodle up off the floor and continued down the hallway. "I'm gonna win this one," he said to himself, chuckling, delighted Cat had overlooked making any stipulations.

Brute whined as they passed the first door.

"Don't worry. You'll get your doggy bone. All I have to do is figure out what's safe for me to ask for. I know what she thinks I'll ask for. For both our sakes, I'll have to think up something else."

* * *

Humming aloud, Cat removed the nacho ingredients she'd prepared from the refrigerator and set them on the counter. She put the chili in the microwave to heat. As she set the timer, she glanced toward the kitchen door.

Brute should be back by now, she thought. She'd trained him to put his leash in the guest room closet when she'd grown tired of searching the house for it. Second to going to the lake, he loved strutting around the neighborhood.

So where was he? She couldn't claim a victory unless Brute came back to the kitchen dragging his leash.

"Brute," she called softly. She tilted her head, listening for a muffled bark followed by the sound of the leash being dragged across the floor. "C'mere, fella. Bring me your leash."

Perplexed, she walked from the kitchen to the hallway. Brute never failed her. Only a closed door would prevent him from finding his leash.

Or...

Hank Collins stopping him? Scoundrel! She grinned, glad she hadn't made strict stipulations on their wager. Should she return to the kitchen and pretend she hadn't caught on to his devilish prank? No, she decided, remembering how he'd soaked her when she faked an apology.

"Oh, Hank," she called, progressing toward the spare bedroom. She rapped on the door. "You can let go of Brute. You win."

She heard a playful growl coming from the other side of the door.

Stinkers, both of them! They've been playing ball while I've been waiting for them.

"Ready or not, here I come." She twisted the knob and pushed the door open. Her heart slammed against her ribs.

Stretched out on the bed, Hank held the ball three feet off his chest, with Brute's teeth clamped in the rubber. The pup swung back and forth like a trapeze artist in a circus.

But that wasn't what caught and held her attention. Hank had changed his jeans, but evidently her brother's pair had been too snug in the waist. The snap was open; the zipper was down a few teeth more than an inch.

What was it Geraldine had called Hank? Hot? Not descriptive enough, Cat decided. He had her internal thermometer climbing to the boiling point.

"He just won't give up, will he?" Hank said, shaking his wrist. "Stubborn little cuss. He must get it from his mistress."

Her mercury went up another degree. Mistress? Why had he chosen that word instead of owner? Did he realize the effect he had on her?

Mesmerized, she walked closer to the bed. "Lunch is ready."

"Don't tell me you've conveniently forgotten about our bet." Casually, he patted the side of the bed with his free hand as though he were lying on her sofa in the living room. He dropped the ball to his chest. "Sit."

Both Brute and Cat followed his command.

Hank folded his arms behind his head. "I've been playing with Brute while I thought about what would be an appropriate forfeit. A million dollars would be nice."

"That's fair? A doggy bone versus a million bucks?" A curtain of hair fell across her face as she looked down at him. She pushed it over her shoulder with one hand. "Would you settle for an out-of-state lottery ticket?"

"I said it would be nice. That isn't what I decided on. I just wanted you to know I'd given this careful consideration."

"And?"

His hand moved to her hair, twining it around his wrist, drawing her face closer. "I decided I wanted something . . . soft, silky."

"You want me to cut my hair and give it to you?" she asked, being deliberately obtuse. Her position grew increasingly awkward. She nudged Brute off Hank's stomach and leaned across him.

"Uh-uh. Something warm and cuddly."

"Yeah?"

"Something that would learn to love me . . . unconditionally."

"Me?" she whispered, her lips a scant inch from his mouth.

Hank paused. "Brute."

For a second Cat's mind didn't register when he meant. Was he calling her dog or naming the forfeit? To clarify her muddled mind, she repeated, "Brute."

"Yeah. I don't have a dog. You're the one who said I needed a friend."

From the tone of his voice, he sounded utterly sincere. She tried to stiffen her arm, but his hand clamped on her bent elbow. Her stare skipped from Hank's mouth to his eyes. They were closed. She couldn't tell if this was a joke or not.

"You can't have my dog. That's like asking me for my firstborn child!"

"No dog?" His lips tilted up at the corners. "Then I'll have to think up something of equal value to you, won't I?"

"Open your eyes, damn you. I can't tell if you're putting me on or..."

He opened his eyes, but at the same time he grabbed her waist and twisted her across him until her head and shoulders were on the pillow next to his. He tapped her bottom lip with his forefinger.

"I was kidding. Don't pout. You're the one who taught me how to verbally waltz someone up a primrose path."

"I'm not sure I appreciate your sense of humor on an empty stomach." Disappointment that he'd wanted her dog instead of a kiss made her cross. He hadn't danced her up a primrose path; he'd paddled her canoe up a well-known creek without a paddle. "The chili is getting cold."

Hank chuckled. "So are you. It's getting decidedly frosty in here. Tell me, Cat, what did you think I'd ask for?"

Turnabout is fair play, she mused. "Something hot and moist."

"Uh-uh." His chuckles turned to low laughter. "You aren't going to try my own trick on me, are you?"

She arched her back and gave him a sultry smile. The tip of her tongue skittered across her teeth. "Something...exciting, heart-stopping."

"No! I'm not falling for it." He started to roll toward the edge of the bed, but she wrapped one arm under his shoulder and whispered something that got his full attention. "What do you mean...something you've never given another man?"

Spry as a jungle cat, she removed her claws and bounced off the bed. She paused at the door, turned and winked at him.

"Nachos and the baseball game. That's *all* you're getting from me! Oh, and incidentally...gotcha!"

* * *

Monday morning Cat arrived at the job site extra early. Hard hat in her hand, she climbed from her truck. As she strode toward Building 1, she felt somewhat irresponsible for not driving by the job site yesterday to check out the fire damage Hank had reported. Dropping by the Lemontree on Sunday was part of her regular routine. She considered herself to be on call seven days a week, twenty-four hours a day.

So did Goldcoast Construction, she thought. They'd hold her accountable if anything slowed down their schedules. She'd dreaded doing it, but she had had to relay the information back to them.

She could rationalize her absence with a dozen weak excuses. Mentally, she reviewed them. From what Hank told her, there weren't any clues as to how the fire had started. The damage had been repaired, at no cost to Goldcoast. None of the men she considered prime suspects would be there on Sunday for her to question. Last and weakest, the truck had needed to be scrubbed.

None of the excuses satisfied her. Plain and simple? She'd let Hank and her family interfere with her job. She silently resolved to focus her energies back on the Lemontree.

Hearing a truck's engine, she glanced over her shoulder. The sight of Hank's black truck heading straight toward her weakened her resolve. True, she should have checked out his report earlier, but evidently taking a couple of days off had energized both of them. Her heart quickened; she grinned and waved at him.

He drove up beside her. "I knew you'd be here bright and early this morning," he said, shifting the truck into park. "Feeling guilty?"

"As a matter of fact, I am."

"Don't. After I left your place last night, I decided I'd take a spin through the project." He cut the engine, then pointed toward Building 1. She stepped backward as he opened his door. "You can quit chewing your bottom lip. The damage has been repaired. No harm done."

She jangled the keys hooked to the front loop of her jumpsuit. "How'd you get in?"

"The sliding patio door in the rear apartment."

Cat scowled. She'd have to beef up the security. "Somebody left it unlocked?"

"No. I popped off the stationary door."

"It wasn't screwed into the frame?"

Hank shrugged. "They usually aren't. Patio doors are a burglar's best friend."

"Not on this project." She unclipped a pen from her breast pocket and made a notation on the top page of her clipboard. "I can't have every Tom, Dick and Harry roaming through the completed buildings. It's a wonder the appliances haven't been stolen!"

"Lighten up, Cat. Not everyone knows that trick. You didn't."

"Any other tricks of the trades I don't know about?"

He grabbed her elbow to keep her from stepping on a board with two nails spiking upward. "Like avoiding a trip to the emergency room by not walking while you're taking notes?"

"I'm usually more careful. Thanks." His large hand shifted, cupping her elbow, steering her clear from danger. She could smell his after-shave lotion. Much as she liked his protectiveness and the woodsy fragrance, she shook her arm free. "I'll watch it."

Hank raised his hand, shaking his fingertips as though he'd held them too close to a fire. "Touchy this morning?"

"Nope." The sun had risen on the horizon. She had to squint when she looked up at him. "Some things are nice enough to be habit-forming. What would my boss think, or the other men on the job site for that matter, if it looked as though I needed help getting around here?"

"No problem." Her mild rebuke stung. Sharon had always worried excessively about appearances. "Next time I'll let you walk on the nails."

"That's why wearing boots is required."

She raised her eyes to his bare head. Blue highlights glistened beneath the rays of sunlight. He'd left his hard hat back in his truck. She hated to remind him, but dammit, it was her job.

Hank saw her look and read her thoughts. "I'll get it when I get my tools. The odds are I'm fairly safe from mishap just walking through a finished building."

"Now who's being touchy?"

"I just don't want you cold-shouldering me because you think I'll take advantage of our friendship by breaking the safety rules." He stopped on the bottom step of the entry. "If it'll make you happy, I'll go back and get the damned thing right now."

"Happy?" Cat chuckled as she reached for her keys to unlock the door. His wearing a hard hat had nothing to do with her happiness. The feel of his arm lightly resting on her shoulders as they watched the baseball game, his lips grazing her forehead before he left last night—those things made her insides tingle with happiness. "No, on a happiness scale of one to ten, I'd say your wearing a hard hat scores less than a two. However, I would feel less remiss in my job if you did. I didn't make the rules, Hank. Goldcoast does pay me to enforce them, though."

She opened the door for herself, not waiting for Hank to open it for her.

Hank bit his tongue to keep from saying, You're management, I'm labor. You enforce the rules, I follow them. Unintentionally, he'd stepped over the fine line between being her friend and being employed by Goldcoast.

He turned on his heel and called over his shoulder, "I'll see you later. I've got work to do, too."

Cat watched him jog toward his truck. She was left with the distinct impression that he wasn't pleased with her.

"Hank!"

She didn't know what she'd say, but she couldn't let him leave without making an effort to mend the breach caused by her being his boss. He stopped and slowly turned toward her. From his stance, legs spread and one hand on his hip, she instinctively knew he wasn't going to let her make amends easily, even if he realized she hadn't had a choice.

"Yeah?"

"After work, maybe you'd like to drop by my place?"

Hank hesitated. Being friends with Cat McGillis was going to be tougher than he'd thought. Experience had taught him to roll with the punches, but the impact of her light reprimand had hurt more than he'd expected. His instinctive sense of self-preservation made him want to run far and fast, to get away from a severe blow to his pride.

"Maybe," he answered, noncommittally.

"You still haven't collected on the bet I lost," she said, hoping to remind him of the fun they'd had yesterday. He neither moved a muscle nor spoke a word. Feebly she smiled. "Have a good day."

"You, too."

"Not likely," she mumbled, viewing the tiff she'd just had with Hank as a bad omen of things to come. You could have bent the hard hat rule, she told herself.

She strode up the steps and to the back apartment. Her eyes traced the ceiling, automatically checking for changes of texture or color. It appeared to be perfect, unlikely to fall down on her head.

She fumbled with the keys, her fingers shaking as she inserted the key into the lock. Twisting the key to the left, she murmured to herself, "Rules are inflexible, like glass. They don't bend, they only break." But in Hank's case, if making him follow the rules was right, she'd rather have been wrong, just this once.

Sniffing for the odor of smoke, she crossed to the back bedroom and into the bathroom. Fresh paint and new carpet, she thought, identifying the smells.

"Once?" She shook her head. "What happens when he breaks a different rule? What happens if his framers build the Leaning Tower of Pisa? Do you make special allowances because they're his men?"

"No."

Startled by the sound of a voice other than her own, Cat jumped. Hand over her thudding heart, she said, "You scared the bejeezus out of me!"

"Sorry." Hank swiftly moved beside her and fastened his hands on her arms. After she'd disappeared into the building, he'd figuratively stepped out of his boots and into hers. The toes pinched. Selfishly, he had been preoccupied with his own feelings. "For scaring you, and for being an ass about the hard hat. I was being oversensitive."

Delighted she wasn't the one going to him to explain her action, she said, "Apology accepted."

"I overheard what you said about my crews erecting buildings that lean to one side. I don't expect you to approve any shoddy work my men do." He added, "You were only doing your job. It's asinine on my part to presume on our friendship. I know how I'd feel if you started asking me to do work for free."

She raised her fingers to his lips. "Hank, it's okay. You only overheard one side of the conversation I was having with myself. I feel ridiculous wearing a hard hat in here, too."

"Can I change my 'maybe' to your invitation to an enthusiastic 'yes'?"

Her hard hat bobbled backward as she nodded. Hank caught it before it fell off her head. His hand slid to the back of her neck, drawing her closer to him.

"I'd like to start this day over," he said, his voice husky.

"Me, too."

"Good morning, Cat."

Her minty breath fanned his face as she replied, "Hi, Hank."

"Did I tell you how pretty you look? You have the perfect figure for wearing a jumpsuit."

She felt their knees touch, then the silver buckle of his belt between her ribs. The pressure of his hand at the base of her neck raised her heels off the floor.

"Are there any rules about a subcontractor kissing the project manager in your procedures manual?" he asked, checking to make certain he wasn't violating company policy.

"The rules... were written... before they hired a female." She took quick gasps of air to quell the rush of hot blood percolating through her system.

"So, there isn't *any* job-related reason why I shouldn't kiss you in the privacy of an empty apartment?"

She realized her hands were on his shirtfront when she felt the cotton fabric wadded in her hands. "Hank, are you going to kiss me or not!"

He did, but wisely. Lightly. He felt a tremor race through her.

Tonight, he promised as he tilted his head to brush a kiss on the opposite corner of her parted lips, tonight he was going to feel her tremble in his arms again. He understood his own needs enough to know he had to stop or the fires of anticipation he felt would ignite into a passion that wouldn't be appropriate on the job site.

He relaxed his hold on her nape, and said, "Let's check out the fire damage."

Her eyelashes opened wide in stunned surprise. That wasn't a kiss! She'd expected a kiss that would curl her toes, singe her hair... make her heart beat wildly in her chest! Compared to the kiss she'd given him Saturday, this one wasn't much better than the one Brute had given her before she left home!

Hank peeled her fingers off his shirt. His hand slipped to her wrist as he led her toward the bathroom. "See? It's fixed. Nobody would know there was a fire in here."

She honestly made an effort to focus her eyes on the place where he pointed, but she was still in a daze.

"What's wrong?" he asked when she didn't respond. Maybe her keen eyes were better than his. He stepped closer to the wall and bent at the waist to get a better look. "I can't tell where it's been patched, can you?"

His rear end was perched temptingly in the air. Cat had all she could do not to give him a good swift kick!

He did notice a small bump. A nail must have backed out of the drywall. He tapped the lump to draw her attention to it. "Another trick of the trade I learned when I was hanging drywall was to use screws instead of nails. Then this won't happen."

He straightened and saw the golden flecks in her eyes shooting sparks. He assumed her anger was directed toward the arsonist. "Like I said, I wish I'd been in here sooner. Anybody could have started the fire."

"Right," she agreed. "Any suggestion on how I go about catching a man who starts a fire and walks away from it?"

"I still believe it was accidental."

"And if it wasn't?"

"The chances are pretty slim you'll be able to nab him."

Cat knew they were talking about two different kinds of fire, but she promised, "I'll catch him next time."

"You be careful. If someone did purposely start it, he had his reasons and he's probably dangerous. I know you're dedicated, but Goldcoast doesn't expect you to put your life on the line. Promise me that you'll come and find me, that you'll let me help you."

Smiling, Cat patted the side of his face. "I will. That's a promise you can count on."

For the remainder of the day Cat had to struggle to keep her mind on her job. Her frustration should have ebbed. Instead, it grew each time she caught a passing glimpse of Hank. At noon, while she and Geraldine split a salad, she watched him sitting under a tree, eating lunch with his men.

"There ought to be a rule in the manual that covers half-naked men running around the job site," she grumbled.

"Uh-uh, boss lady. You're not cutting my fringe benefits! Make the men wear shirts and it'll cost Goldcoast a bundle."

"I thought you were in favor of equal rights for women." Cat stabbed a cherry tomato on her fork. "Can you imagine what would happen if we strutted around like that?''

Geraldine rolled her eyes as though the idea was ordained from above. "My wildest dreams come true. Since you brought up the subject, is Hank Collins as . . . hot as he looks?''

"Hotter," Cat said, biting into the tomato. A trickle of juice spurted down her throat. "Everything you've ever fantasized.''

"C'mon, Cat. The salad is enough . . . you don't have to feed me a line of bull. A man can't be hot the way I mean hot, not at a family picnic.''

"No, really, Hank Collins is hot, hotter, hottest.''

"I don't know if you're fibbing or not. You were fairly open with me about Bradley, but why wouldn't you be? All he ever did was talk . . . about insurance.''

"Fibbing gets me into trouble. You should have seen the look on Mom's face when I told her Hank wasn't my boss.''

"Skip the boring part. Get right down to the nitty-gritty. Tell me what you did when you weren't under . . . your parents' close supervision.''

Cat grinned. Geraldine just cut herself out of the best part, she mused, remembering how Hank had kissed her while her entire family watched.

"Fished. Washed the trucks. Watched television.''

"I guess it's all relative to what you're used to, but I'd classify those activities as tepid to lukewarm," Geraldine scoffed. "Let me tell you about my date with Ron. Have you ever heard the rumor about saxophone players having . . . hot lips? Whooee! Whoever started that rumor knew what they were talking about!''

"Great kisser, huh?''

Cat's frustration mounted as she compared Hank's first kiss to the others she'd received. He'd gone from passion to platonic in twenty-four hours.

"I don't want to make you feel bad, but Ron is the kind of guy who can tie a knot in a cherry stem with just his teeth and tongue. I'll let you imagine what else he can do with them."

"Hmm." Hank could probably tie a short thread of silk with his tongue. He had the ability and the know-how, he just didn't. Why? It wasn't as though she'd been fending him off while he kissed her. To keep Geraldine talking, she asked, "Can do or did?"

"See this?" Geraldine flipped back the collar of her jumpsuit. Purple marks trailed down her neck, disappearing beneath the fabric. "Passion marks."

"Where's he from, Transylvania?"

"Pennsylvania." Geraldine giggled. "He's in medicine."

"A doctor? You could have fooled me. Those look like vampire tracks! You'd better let me get a closer look." Cat leaned across her desk. "Yep, he sure did. I think you donated a pint of blood."

Geraldine swatted at Cat's finger. Both her eyebrows were raised toward her widow's peak. "How many times have you given blood . . . and enjoyed it?"

"I'm not sure that's hot, but I have to admit that it's something I haven't experienced." *Nor do I want to,* she silently added.

Glancing toward the window, Geraldine said, "Maybe I should introduce Hank to Ron."

"No, thanks. Hank gave at the Red Cross," Cat quipped, grinning from ear to ear.

"Ha-ha. Very funny." Geraldine spoiled the condemning tone in her comment by laughing. She picked up her paper plate and pitched it into the trash can. On the way back to her desk, she paused long enough to say, "Men aren't inhibited about sex, like certain women I know. They discuss it openly. That's how they get from luke-warm to hottest. Think about it."

Cat did think about "it." By quitting time her frustration level was at an all-time high!

Chapter Seven

"Hilda Catherine McGillis, you turn off your telephone recorder this instant and pick up the phone. I know you're there! You can't be at the Lemontree. It's after dark!"

Cat listened to the playback on her telephone message recorder while she unloaded groceries into the pantry. With Hank due at any minute, she barely had time to whip together a dip for the snacks she'd bought and get the brownie mix into the oven.

"Better to return the call now than when he's here," she muttered, neatly folding the brown paper sacks to recycle as trash sacks.

Brute pattered across the kitchen tile with his leash in his mouth. He dropped it at her feet and gave an imperious bark.

"Gimme a break, Brute." She picked up his leash and put it on the dinette table, simultaneously reaching for the portable phone. "Go play with your ball. I can return Mother's call, mix the dip and get the brownies in the oven, but I can't take you for a walk at the same time."

Whining, Brute put his front paws on her leg.

Cat dialed her parents' number. "Don't beg. You had a quick run while I went to the mailbox. I'll take you for a walk before I go to bed. I promise."

The pitiful look Brute gave her had Cat thinking of ways to do three things at once.

"McGillis residence."

"Hi, Mom. I just got home." She spooned the sour cream into a mixing bowl. "I was at the store when you called. What's up?"

"I wanted to talk to you about that little stunt you pulled Saturday evening."

"The stunt *I* pulled?" Cat had difficulty believing her mother dared to criticize her behavior. "What about the McGillis clan ganging up on me?"

"No one ganged up on you."

"Okay, not me," Cat conceded. "You ganged up on the guest that you insisted I bring out there. He's still suffering from frostbite."

"He shouldn't be. The steam on my windows still hasn't evaporated. Your father kept flipping the light switch. You knew we were watching."

"Just one question, Mom." Cat crossed to the can opener to open the can of crabmeat. "Was the steam on the inside or the outside of the window?"

"Young lady, don't you be sassy with me. This is your mother you're talking to."

"And this is your quarter-of-a-century-old daughter talking to you."

Several long seconds of dead silence gave Cat time to drain the liquid from the can, stir the contents into the sour cream, add a splash of dry sherry and sprinkle paprika on the concoction.

She'd back down if this argument pertained strictly to her behavior, but not while Hank was involved. Her family had behaved dreadfully.

"All of you owe Hank Collins an apology." She heard her mother gasp, but she dared to continue. "You can't pick and choose my friends, Mother."

"I only want what's best for you."

"Then let me make my own mistakes, please." She savagely tore off the top of the brownie mix.

"Why? If I saw you racing toward the edge of a cliff, do you think I'd keep my mouth shut? What kind of a mother do you think I am?"

Cat skimmed the directions on the back of the box, turned and set the temperature on the oven. "You're the best mother a girl could have, but you are also overly protective. Good grief, how can you compare going over the side of a cliff with taking Hank fishing?"

"Falling. You'd fall off a cliff. You're falling for Hank."

"Mother, the results wouldn't be the same."

One third of a cup of water, one egg, shortening to grease the pan, she mentally recited, scurrying from the cabinet, to the refrigerator, then back to the counter.

"Both would be disastrous. You need a man in your life that brings a paycheck home twice a month. Somebody reliable. Somebody who won't get laid off during the bad weather or injure himself on the job. Do you think I want you to worry about paying the monthly bills like I did? Is it wrong to want a better life for my only daughter?"

Cat cracked the egg on the side of the bowl and stirred it into the contents from the pouch. "You love Dad. Doesn't that count for something?"

"That's precisely why I'm talking to you now, before you get involved. It's just as easy to fall in love with a nine-to-five man, like Bradley, as it is to love a carpenter."

"Okay. Since you're so wild about boring Bradley, why don't you divorce Dad and marry him?"

"That's utterly ridiculous," Maude sputtered.

"Mom, we're finally in total agreement. I won't insist that you marry him if you'll do the same for me."

Another lengthy pause gave Cat time to pour the batter into a baking pan and slide it into the oven. She set the timer.

"Now, I love you, Mother. I don't want to do anything to make you unhappy, but I've got company coming—"

"Hank Collins?" Maude injected.

"As a matter of fact, yes, Hank Collins. I appreciate your concern, but you all are going to have to let me lead my own life."

"We'll see about that, young lady."

Cat sighed. Both of them were stubborn, neither was willing to compromise or be compromised. Continuing this conversation would only cause more bad feelings.

"I have to get off the phone, Mom, or I won't be ready when he gets here."

"Ready for what?"

Her mother was the last person she could talk to about her immediate plans. Maude's reaction was predictable. First, she'd be shocked. Then, she'd rush into the living room and wake Cat's father, who'd be sleeping on the sofa by now. Her father would break speed records to arrive at his daughter's house; his trusty shotgun would be loaded, ready to defend his daughter's honor. No, Cat mused, she didn't need a blueprint to figure out what would happen.

"I have to shower and change clothes. We'll talk again, soon. I do love you. Dad, too. Give him a hug for me. Bye."

She hung up the phone without feeling a twinge of guilt or regret. As she cleaned up the cooking utensils, she leaned forward to smell the flowers Hank had brought to her. The one and only thing her mother had been right about was her falling for Hank.

She smiled, at peace with the realization. She only hoped and prayed he was falling for her, too. He felt something for her. She had to look on the bright side or the minor uncertainties she felt would blossom into major doubts.

Tonight, she had no room for doubts. He'd said sex stood in the way of their being friends. By sunrise, she'd have that problem solved.

Brute jumped up on a dinette chair, snatched the leather handle of the leash in his teeth and leaped to the floor. Circling Cat's feet, he coiled her ankles in chain.

"What do you think you're doing, pooch? Stop that!" Cat watched Brute sit on his haunches and lift his front paws. "Oh, I see. You think since I was standing here, doing nothing, that you'd take me for a walk, huh?"

He jerked the chain.

"Sorry, pal," she said, unwrapping her ankles, "I have to take a shower and change. You're going to have to be patient." Freed of the chain, she tugged on it. Brute growled, shaking his end. "Let go of it. I don't have time to play tug-of-war."

He shook his small head, refusing to relinquish his leash.

"Pit bulls don't have anything on you, do they? Lightning could strike the pom-pom on your tail and you wouldn't let go. I give up. You keep it." She dropped her end of the chain. "But that doesn't mean we're going for a walk!"

Relentless, Brute followed her into her bedroom. He sat at her feet while she stripped off her clothes and let them drop to the floor. He sniffed her underwear, then curled up on her jumpsuit and stared at her.

Cat knew how to get him out from under her feet. She strode into the bathroom, turned on the water faucet in the shower, squatted and asked, "Want a bath, big fella?"

Brute scooted his rear end in reverse, backing away from his mistress's hand as she reached for him.

"No?" She straightened, pointing to the steaming hot water pelting the back of the shower stall. "Follow me in there and you'll get one, like it or not."

Dissuaded, Brute hung his head and disappeared into the bedroom.

Cat removed the pins from her hair. As she shook it loose, she poked her head through the doorway and called, "Stay out of the closet!"

To her chagrin, she saw him innocently stretched out on the heap of clothes she'd left in the middle of the floor. She'd had to pitch too many teeth-marked shoes in the trash can to take a chance on his staying there, however. Brute was a true Texan. He had no qualms about following the motto, Don't get mad, get even. She glanced at the bifold doors; they were closed. She made a mental note to pick up her work clothes.

Twenty minutes later, she'd showered, washed her hair, blown it dry and arranged it in loose curls at the crown of her head. After ousting Brute off his impromptu bed, she picked up her Goldcoast jumpsuit and tossed it in the clothes hamper.

Wearing only a pair of lacy red bikini panties she crossed to her closet. She reached to the far side, searching for an outfit she'd impulsively bought but had lacked the nerve to wear. Her fingertips skimmed over the hangers until she felt the flimsy plastic the sales clerk had put over it to keep it from wrinkling.

"There it is, Brute," she said, with a triumphant smile as she pulled the fire-engine-red jumpsuit from the closet and stripped off the plastic.

She held it up for close inspection. High-necked, sleeveless, hemmed below the ankle, from the front only the dynamite color and silky fabric hinted at the explosive impact the designers had had in mind when they fashioned this ensemble.

Cat grinned as she swished the garment around. "What do you think, puppy?"

Brute lifted his head and yawned. The way the backside of the jumpsuit plunged in a deep V from shoulder to waist didn't interest him.

"Simple, elegant—" her smile took on Cheshire-cat proportions "—designed for desire!"

Quickly, she slipped into the garment. Her hands smoothed it over her waist and hips. Shoes, she thought, returning to the closet, reaching to the top shelf and pulling down a shoe box. She crossed to the bed, remembering the dent in her pocketbook these strappy pieces of red leather and spiked heels had made. As she slipped them on her feet, she admitted they were worth every penny she'd paid for them.

A dab of perfume later, she twirled around in front of the full-length-mirrored wall in her dining room. Brute, imitating her, stood on his hind legs and spun around, too.

Only the leash dangling from his mouth spoiled the effect by tangling around his spindly legs.

"You're a rascal, Brute McGillis. No way are you going to let me off the hook, are you?"

She glanced at her wristwatch. Seven-thirty. Neither she nor Hank had set a specific time for him to be at her place, but she figured that by the time he showered, shaved and ate it would be around eight o'clock. That gave her half an hour to keep her promise to Brute. Better now than later, she decided.

"Give me the leash. I'll take you for your walk."

Hank gave up ringing the doorbell. She could be in the shower, he thought, and can't hear the bell. He shifted the sack he held to his left arm and rapped on the door. As he listened for movement inside the condo, he poked his forefinger beneath his starched collar and eased it around in an effort to loosen the tie strangling him.

Brute ought to be raising holy hell, he thought, but he could hear only a faint beeping noise from inside and a breeze whispering through the pine needles high over his head.

Wherever she'd gone, she'd taken Brute with her.

He'd seen her truck leave the Lemontree at six o'clock. He glanced at his watch. So where could she be at quarter of eight, with her dog?

Having observed her treat Brute like a precious child, he quickly deduced that she wasn't out shopping. Pets weren't allowed in the stores and she'd never leave him alone in the truck. That ruled out the grocery store, too.

He tried the door handle to see if it was locked. A gentle push swung the door wide open. Hesitant to walk in, he called "Cat? Are you here?"

The heavenly scent of chocolate and the incessant beeping of an oven timer drew him inside. She had to be somewhere in the neighborhood, he mused, piecing together the clues of her whereabouts. She wouldn't take Brute, leave the door unlocked and something in the oven unless she planned on returning soon.

He set his package on the credenza in the hallway and crossed into the kitchen. The oven was the same make and model as his own. He tapped his finger on the keyboard to stop the timer. Peeking through the glass in the oven door, he felt his mouth water as his eyes honed in on brownies, his favorite dessert. He hadn't eaten since lunch.

"I'd better get them out of there," he muttered, as he unhooked a pair of quilted mittens from the magnets clinging to the door.

His stomach growled. *Since I saved them from burning,* he reasoned, *Cat won't mind if I snitch a little piece.* He set the pan on a stove burner and removed a knife from the butcher's block.

"Hot," he mumbled, using his fingers to balance a healthy wedge of brownie on the knife.

He raised the knife to his mouth and took a small nibble. The instant the heat hit his tongue, he starting billowing air in and out of his mouth. He should have waited until they'd cooled!

"Hank, are you in here?" Cat called from the outside door. She unsnapped the leash from Brute and it dropped to the floor beside him. "Go find Hank, Brute."

Unable to speak, Hank dumped the remains of the brownie in the palm of his hand and drummed the knife handle on the counter.

Brute cocked his head in the direction of the kitchen. But, trained to put away his leash in the spare bedroom, he picked it up and scampered off in the opposite direction from the noise.

"Must be some truth in that old saying about old dogs and new tricks," Cat muttered.

Lithely rising, she spied the paper sack on the credenza. Hank must have put it there, she thought. Curiosity made her consider scooping it into her arms, but she decided against the idea. How could she strike a seductive pose in the doorway with a sack under one arm?

Her lips turned up into the warm, welcoming smile she'd rehearsed while she brushed her teeth. She'd also practiced a sultry Mae West imitation: "Hiya, big fella. Is that a gun in your pocket or are you just happy to see me?" She'd decided against that. The last thing she wanted him to do was laugh at her.

She completely forgot to pose when she reached the kitchen door and saw Hank standing with his back to her at the sink, gulping a glass of water. She'd heard women were attracted to eyes, shoulders and buns, not necessarily in that order. The well-fitting charcoal-gray slacks Hank wore made her modify her idea about being an "eyes" woman.

Sounding breathy, but not phony, she said, "Hi, Hank."

"I hope you don't mind me . . . helping . . . myself."

He'd started speaking before he turned around and saw her. Damn, he silently swore, she isn't just attractive, she's a blond bombshell! His scorched tongue gingerly raked across the roof of his mouth. He'd swallowed a glass of water, but his mouth was as dry as the Texas Panhandle.

"I'm glad you came in and made yourself at home."

She noticed his red tie, the knot casually loosened below his open collar; she wished her mother could see him. He was a man who could wear dress clothes with the same case as he wore jeans and a T-shirt. His black loafers were polished better than the wing-tipped shoes Bradley wore.

Her breath caught in her lungs. She seemed to have lost the power to force it out as he lazily moved toward her. Suddenly an unexpected calm settled over her.

This, she knew, was what she wanted, what she needed.

Slowly, she turned full circle. She wanted him to feel the full force of how she'd changed her appearance just for him. When he stopped at arm's length in front of her, they stood unsmiling, studying each other.

"I made a mistake when I bought you something at the mall," he said. "I noticed a pair of unusual dangling earrings as I walked by the jewelry counter. I wish I'd bought them."

She felt the tremor in his fingers as his hands circled her throat. "I don't need gifts, Hank."

"I've tried to be your friend."

"I know."

"But I've wanted you." His thumbs rotated where her pulse point throbbed irregularly beneath her pale skin. "I wanted you this morning when I kissed you. It took every ounce of my self-control not to kiss you the way I wanted."

"The way I wanted," she repeated. In high heels, she hardly had to tilt her head back to invite his kiss. "Kiss me the way we both want."

"Cat, sweetheart, I won't stop with kisses."

She smiled. "I hope not."

"What about Brute, your vicious guard dog?"

He's nervous, she realized, wondering why. His eyes no longer met hers.

"He usually naps after his evening walk. Hank?"

"Yeah?"

"I'm nervous," she candidly admitted. The only way she could think of to eliminate his nervousness was to bring it out into the open. "Are you?"

"Yeah," he said again.

She placed her hand over his and brought it to her lips as she backed through the kitchen door, leading him to her bedroom.

"Why?"

"You deserve better than a man like me." The one thing he hadn't told Cat about his ex-wife was the remark Sharon had made as she stormed out the front door never to return: You're a bum lover, too! "I'm not the world's best lover."

"Good."

"Good?"

"I've been worried about my lack of experience. You've been married. That gives you an advantage." Open up, Hank, please, she silently begged. Whatever is wrong, give me a chance to make it right.

He paused at the threshold of her bedroom. It would be dastardly to think of Sharon or say her name in the sanctuary of Cat's bedroom.

Taking a deep breath, he blurted, "Sharon said I'm a bum lover."

She let her deep concern for him show on her face while she searched for the right thing to say. She realized what a disastrous effect a woman could have on a man. Sharon had made Hank doubt his self-worth and his sexuality. For an intense moment, she hated his ex-wife more than he could possibly have hated her.

"Spite? I imagine she said it so you'd be afraid of caring for another woman. Maybe it was her means of holding on to you . . . or, no pun intended, it was her way of hitting below the belt."

She worried at her lip when he remained silent. There must be something else she could say to ease his mind.

Or do.

She linked her smallest finger to his forefinger and stepped into her dimly lit room. With her other hand, she unzipped her jumpsuit. She barely had to shrug her shoulders for the silk to slither to her waist.

"It's how you feel about making love to me that's important, Hank."

His eyes slowly moved from their linked fingers until they swept over her. She was so damned beautiful it made him ache with longing. He closed his eyes to keep from charging into her.

"What if..." he whispered, then had to clear his throat. "What if she was right?"

"Love, we can worry ourselves to death with what-ifs. Everything is a risk. What if you and I make love and it turns out to be the most breathtaking experience you've ever had in your life?"

"What if it isn't? For you, I mean."

"Then we'll try, try again," she answered, loving the prospect. "We won't give up until it is breathtaking."

"I'm not the one taking the risk, Cat. You are. Why? Knowing what your parents think of me, what my ex-wife thinks of me... why do you believe differently?"

She stepped from the pool of flaming red silk and moved close to him. Softly, barely above a whisper, she said, "Because I believe in how you make me feel. You make me feel...alive...feminine...desirable. You make me feel good about myself. I care for you, Hank Collins."

Still unsure of himself, but knowing he'd be making the biggest mistake of his life if he denied both of them what they wanted, he slowly lowered his lips to hers. He wanted to love Cat McGillis, intimately, because she made him feel good. And he realized he hadn't felt wholly good about himself for years.

Cat sweetly returned his kiss until she tasted passion's tartness when his tongue parted her lips. He was like a man dying of thirst who stood knee-deep in clear water. At first he seemed almost afraid to drink from her lips, to quench his thirst. But once he realized she wasn't a mirage, he couldn't get enough of her.

Her hands freed his shirt from the waistband of his slacks. Gliding her fingers up his spine, she drew the thrust of his tongue deeper into the contours of her mouth. Her fingernails lightly scratched the corded muscles along the hollow indent of his spine; he arched her against him, hard.

His mouth left hers, trailing moist kisses across her cheek, down the side of her neck. His hands settled low on her hips, squeezed lightly, then slowly inched up to the sides of her breasts.

"Lord, woman, who'd believe you feel and taste better than you look?"

"One of us has too many clothes on," she gasped as the taut fabric of his shirt prevented her fingers from gliding across his shoulder blades. Her hands slid to his stomach, but it was impossible for her to unbutton his shirt from the wrong side. "Help me."

His right hand went to his tie, which he swiftly removed, then moved down the front of his shirt. With a jerk, a shrug and a toss, his shirt was gone. Within seconds, his slacks and undershorts were also on the floor.

Scant seconds seemed like hours to him. His mouth fastened onto hers again; his body fitted to hers. He lifted her into his arms, carrying her to her bed. Gentleness was swept aside as quick heat and urgent need sent a shaft of desire surging through him.

Cat had neither expected nor wanted gentleness. His tough, lean hands moved roughly over her. His mouth trailed over her, communicating his hunger. She quickly learned that he made love as he framed buildings—with hard-driving fervor and intensity. Cat moaned with trembling pleasure when his fingers found her nipple; her back arched off the soft pillow. He flicked his tongue over her sensitive nipple with such finesse, coaxing all the sexuality in her into play. Hot and wet, his lips, teeth and tongue gingerly played with it until it hardened more. Then he paid the same loving attention to her other breast while continuing to fondle and knead the soft globe he'd thoroughly familiarized in his mind.

Her fingers tugged in his hair with the same intensity his mouth suckled her breast. Her teeth made tiny dents in her lower lip as her head restlessly twisted from side to side. When she felt his mouth crisscross against the flesh covering her rib cage, she reflexively bent and raised her knees as her toes dug into the coverlet beneath her. She grabbed handfuls of his hair and held his head, feeling her heart would surely burst, it slammed so hard and fast in her chest.

His head continued to move lower and lower.

"Hank...Hank..."

Her cry contained both desire and panic. His tongue licked a feverish path along the lacy edge of her panties; his hand covered the slight mound at the juncture of her thighs. Her knees pressed tightly together to stop his sensuous foray.

"It's okay, sweetheart. I'd never do anything you didn't want." His touch became feather-light as the heel of his hand rotated against her. His fingers touched the soft, springy hair of her womanhood.

She began to move with the circular motion of his hand, a woman's instinct making her hips arch slightly, enticing and inviting him as his words soothed her fear of the unknown. Her inquisitive nature had cost her her virginity while she was in college, but as she had warned him, she was inexperienced. She wanted to please him, and yet the thought of him kissing her there was the ultimate intimate invasion. She wasn't ready for that.

Before she realized what he was doing, he had deftly slid the last wispy barrier of clothing between them off her hips and legs. His hand stroked the calf of her leg, the ticklish spot behind her knee, the sensitive skin of her inner thigh.

He levered himself up beside her so he could watch her face as his fingers parted the petals of flesh protecting her womanhood. He heard the kittenish sound he'd longed to hear purring from the back of her throat as the tip of his finger gently slid into her. Sleek, hot, wet. The ecstatic expression on her face wordlessly told him of the pleasurable sensations bombarding her.

Selfishly, he wanted to watch her climb to the pinnacle of rapture, holding her there in readiness for him. He'd been without a woman too long to expect his body to sustain the fevered pitch of his passion. Although her hands caressed his shoulders and chest, he held his hips away from her. One sweet touch and he knew he'd explode, ruining everything, proving everything said about him to be true.

Cat arched her neck as tiny explosions ignited deep inside her. Her eyes blinked open. She could feel herself pulsating against his hand. She tried to speak, to tell Hank what was happening to her, but passion robbed her of her

IT'S FUN! IT'S FREE!
AND IT COULD MAKE YOU A
MILLIONAIRE

If you've ever played scratch-off lottery tickets, you should be familiar with how our games work. On each of the first four tickets (numbered 1 to 4 in the upper right) there are Pink Metallic Strips to scratch off.

Using a coin, do just that—carefully scratch the PINK strips to reveal how much each ticket could be worth if it is a winning ticket. Tickets could be worth from $10.00 to $1,000,000.00 in lifetime money.

Note, also, that each of your 4 tickets has a unique sweepstakes Lucky Number…and that's 4 chances for a **BIG WIN!**

FREE BOOKS!

At the same time you play your tickets for big prizes, you are invited to play ticket #5 for the chance to get one or more free book(s) from Silhouette. We give away free book(s) to introduce readers to the benefits of the Silhouette Reader Service™.

Accepting the free book(s) places you under no obligation to buy anything! You may keep your free book(s) and return the accompanying statement marked "cancel." But if we don't hear from you, then every month we'll deliver 6 of the newest Silhouette Special Edition® novels right to your door. You'll pay the low subscribers-only price of $2.74* each—a savings of 21¢ apiece off the cover price! And there's *no* charge for shipping and handling! You may cancel at any time.

Of course, you may play "THE BIG WIN" without requesting any free book(s) by scratching tickets #1 through #4 only. But remember, that first shipment of one or more books is FREE!

PLUS A FREE GIFT!

One more thing, when you accept the free book(s) on ticket #5 you are also entitled to play ticket #6, which is GOOD FOR A GREAT GIFT! Like the book(s), this gift is totally free and yours to keep as thanks for giving our Reader Service a try!

So scratch off the PINK STRIPS on all your BIG WIN tickets and send for everything today! You've got nothing to lose and everything to gain!

Here are your BIG WIN Game Tickets, worth from $10.00 to $1,000,000.00 each. Scratch off the PINK METALLIC STRIP on each of your Sweepstakes tickets to see what you could win and mail your entry right away. (SEE OFFICIAL RULES IN BACK OF BOOK FOR DETAILS!)

This could be your lucky day - GOOD LUCK!

THE BIG WIN
LUCKY NUMBER

TICKET 1
Scratch PINK METALLIC STRIP to reveal potential value of this ticket if it is a winning ticket. Return all game tickets intact.

1S 391987

THE BIG WIN
LUCKY NUMBER

TICKET 2
Scratch PINK METALLIC STRIP to reveal potential value of this ticket if it is a winning ticket. Return all game tickets intact.

3C 388830

THE BIG WIN
LUCKY NUMBER

TICKET 3
Scratch PINK METALLIC STRIP to reveal potential value of this ticket if it is a winning ticket. Return all game tickets intact.

9Y 400181

THE BIG WIN
LUCKY NUMBER

TICKET 4
Scratch PINK METALLIC STRIP to reveal potential value of this ticket if it is a winning ticket. Return all game tickets intact.

5X 390967

FREE BOOKS
AUTHORIZATION CODE

TICKET 5
We're giving away brand new books to selected individuals. Scratch PINK METALLIC STRIP for number of free books you will receive.

130107-742

FREE GIFT
AUTHORIZATION CODE

TICKET 6
We have an outstanding added gift for you if you are accepting our free books. Scratch PINK METALLIC STRIP to reveal gift.

130107-742

YES! Enter my Lucky Numbers in THE BIG WIN Sweepstakes and when winners are selected, tell me if I've won any prize. If PINK METALLIC STRIP is scratched off on ticket #5, I will also receive one or more FREE Silhouette Special Edition® novels along with the FREE GIFT on ticket #6, as explained on the opposite page.

(U-SIL-SE-03/91) 235 CIS ACGX

NAME _____

ADDRESS _____ APT. _____

CITY_____ STATE _____ ZIP _____

Offer limited to one per household and not valid to current Silhouette Special Edition® subscribers.
© 1991 HARLEQUIN ENTERPRISES LIMITED.

PRINTED IN U.S.A.

Carefully detach card along dotted line and mail today!

Play your BIG WIN tickets and get everything you're entitled to—including FREE BOOKS and a FREE GIFT!

If game card is missing, write to: Silhouette Reader Service, P.O. Box 1867, Buffalo, NY 14269-1867 voice. Her lips parted; only a harsh guttural groan passed through them.

Wildly, desperately, her fingers dug into his hips. Hank echoed her groan, then moved between her parted legs. His tongue thrust into her mouth mimicking the thrust of his hips as he surged deeply inside her. She locked her arms around his neck, surrendering to a pleasure so acute it brought with it a hint of pain.

He stroked her, building her passion beyond anything Cat had imagined possible. She tried to breathe, but the hot air she exhaled made the air too thick for her lungs when she inhaled. She thought she'd peaked, and yet her pleasure only increased.

When she thought she'd surely black out from lack of air, the tiny pulsations she felt earlier exploded in hot, irresistible waves that spread delicious fiery sensations to the far extremities of her body. Her scalp tingled; her toes curled. Her fingers stiffened, then splayed across his buttocks. Her lungs heaved air into her, but her eyes squeezed tightly shut as she catapulted into a world of solid darkness.

Chapter Eight

Cat contentedly curled against Hank. With a small sigh, she clung to the memory of how she'd felt while he made love to her. Smiling, she tried to remember a time when she'd felt such inner peace, and her mind slid back to Saturday mornings when she was less than ten years old. In the twilight zone between deep sleep and being fully awake, she would lightly doze, anticipating nothing but pleasure to fill the day. There had been no clipboard, no schedules, no completion dates confronting her then.

Her hand trailed over Hank's arm; its weight across her body reminded her of the security blanket she'd clung to as a child. She snuggled closer to absorb the warmth radiating from his skin. Her eyelids lazily fluttered open.

She looked directly at Hank's face. His eyes remained closed, but she sensed the same feeling of contentment in him as she observed a small smile tilting the corners of his mouth upward. The sharp lines that often bracketed his mouth as he clamped his lips together had vanished; his brow was smooth. He looked younger than he did an hour ago.

She felt younger, as though she could accomplish difficult feats with a mere flick of her wrist. She felt good, inside and out.

"How long have you been awake?" Hank asked, his voice thick with sleepiness.

His fingers idly roamed over the curve of her hip and up to the side of her breast. He stretched one leg, then the other. As though they'd slept together for decades, he bent his knee, tucked his heel behind her legs and drew her closely to him.

"Not long."

"I didn't mean to fall asleep on you. Bad bed manners, huh?"

She knew he needed assurances from her. She was only too willing to give them. "You were wonderful, Hank. At the end of our lovemaking, I truly thought I'd died and gone to heaven."

"You scared me for a minute or two. Your body stiffened, then you went totally limp. I thought I'd hurt you."

"Hurt me?" Cat grinned at him. Her fingers smoothed over his puckered brow. "It was the most glorious sensation I've ever experienced."

He grinned, a bit smugly. The tears he'd repressed until Cat had forced him to confront them began to slowly dissipate. Maybe, with Cat, he wasn't a bum lover.

His stomach chose this inappropriate moment to growl. "Hungry?"

A little ashamed of the impolite rumblings that only increased in volume, he answered, "Yeah. I skipped dinner. One bite of brownies and a glass of water seems to be causing a protest." He glanced in the direction of his belly button and rubbed his hand over his stomach. "Shut up, stomach. I'll feed you later."

"I don't think it heard you. I can still hear it." She languidly rolled to her side of the bed. "I skipped dinner, too. How do you feel about junk food, brownies and a tall glass of milk?"

His stomach gave a record-setting growl, answering for him.

"Hey, wait a minute." He caught her wrist, tugging her across him. "Food isn't the top item on my priority list."

"What is?"

"This." He buried his fingers in the loose waves of her hair. One by one he removed the hairpins, tossing them in a pile on the bed. When her hair hung like rippling skeins of silk ropes over her shoulders and down her back, he said, "And this."

He brushed his lips over her love-swollen mouth, kissing her much as he'd kissed her that morning. "I didn't realize it until today, but I'm beginning to think I'm a man of great fortitude."

"Oh?"

"Mmm. If I'd been weak, I'd have made love to you this morning. Or again right now. It takes one hell of a strong man to resist temptation."

"Or a man on the edge of starvation," she teased. "We'll see how much...fortitude...you have later. Hmm?"

"Promise?"

Cat nodded, then gave him a quick, hard kiss. "You can bet on it."

"I can't nail shingles to thin air," the roofer complained, glaring at Hank. "Come Thursday my men are gonna be sittin' around playin' pinochle."

Buck Jones, the insulation man, nodded. "I thought the trusses were supposed to arrive yesterday."

Mesmerized by the motion of Cat's hand as she took notes on her clipboard, Hank barely heard the conversation. He'd purposely chosen to sit on the folding chair farthest from her desk during the weekly meeting. Considering how the subcontractors were squeezed together, shoulder to shoulder and butt to butt, the heat and the odor of sweat should have made him forget the tantalizing memory of the perfume she'd worn in bed last night. It didn't. He pictured her hands holding him as tightly as she held her pencil. His powers of concentration on the concerns raised at the meeting were blown to hell and back.

"Hank?"

His mind struggled to snap back to attention when Cat spoke his name. She'd kept her promise to him. The second time they made love she'd shouted his name at the height of her ecstasy.

"What about the roof trusses, Hank?"

Cat had noticed that Hank appeared preoccupied. She had the same problem. She'd deliberately kept her eyes glued to her notepad to avoid focusing them on him.

"I called the lumber mill in Georgia," Hank replied, forcing his thoughts back to business. "According to the secretary, they had a minor problem prefabricating the trusses to meet specifications, but their trucks are on the road. I expect them to arrive this afternoon."

"It's a good thing your crews are fast," Buck commented. "What about you, Flint? Are those slowpokes of yours gonna have the pipe sticking through the roof or do you plan on installing the flashings after I put the roof on?"

"Hell, no, man." Taking umbrage, Flint tilted his chair on its back legs and roared, "That's your job."

"My men will do it if the late arrival of the roof trusses causes a problem," Hank volunteered.

Flint made a rude noise. "Your men do a fine job sawing lumber and hammering nails, Hank. But if those flashings around my pipe don't keep the rain out of the attic, you and me both know who the little lady sitting behind the desk is going to come to when the drywall crashes down on the carpet." His thumb pecked the front of his chest. "Me, that's who. I'm the one Goldcoast will back-charge for the cost of repairing it. You know how these general contractors like to keep every nickel of the subcontractor's retention if they're given an excuse."

Every head in the room nodded in agreement, except Hank's and Cat's. Goldcoast held fifteen percent of the contracted price until the completion of the work, just in case inferior workmanship caused the sort of problem Flint mentioned. For many of these men, that money represented their profit. The weekly payments only kept their cash flowing.

All eyes focused on Cat when Bubba said, "Goldcoast has a reputation for dipping into that money."

"Have any of you been back-charged?" Cat asked, neither defending Goldcoast nor denying Bubba's claim.

Since this was her first job as a project manager, it was the first time she had been in charge of recommending when it was appropriate to deduct money from a subcontractor's retention. She didn't know Goldcoast's policy, and until this meeting she hadn't heard rumbles about the company's reputation.

"Not yet," Bubba replied, assuming the role of spokesman for the grumbling men. "But you sure don't mind redlining our bills."

"Goldcoast expects and pays for quality workmanship, completed on schedule," she replied, letting her eyes move around the semicircle of disgruntled men. "I suggest each of you fulfill your contract and then none of us will have to worry about the fifteen percent retention, will we? You'll be paid according to the agreement."

"What's this I hear about Goldcoast losing their ass on the Dallas job?" Bubba Clark asked. "I heard from another electrical contractor that you guys are having financial problems."

Cat caught Bubba's implication that Goldcoast might use the money from this job to pay the losses on another job. From the side glances passing between Bubba and Flint she guessed Bubba had been checking on work to see if Flint could make good on his threat to hit the highway if she cut his bills again.

"Anybody have a Goldcoast check bounce?" she asked.

Some men shook their heads, and several said, "No."

"Then that's another bridge we'll cross *if* we come to it." She glanced down at the agenda attached to her clipboard. "I have several items that I'll speak to you individually about, but there's one problem that concerns all of you. There was a fire last week in Building 1."

She closely observed the men's reactions, searching their faces for telltale signs of guilt. The men who'd taken part in repairing the damage wore bland expressions; the others appeared surprised and curious.

She raised her hands to stop the barrage of questions being hurled at her. "When? Friday, at noon or shortly after. Where? Apartment G, in the bathroom. Minor damage occurred, but it's been repaired. Had I been notified, Goldcoast's insurance company would have paid those of you who fixed the wall."

She observed the tile and drywall men shake their heads. "Since I wasn't informed, I'll expect you to submit a bill and I'll do what I can to see that it's paid. In the future, I expect to be informed in a timely manner."

She pointed her pencil at the man who installed the windows and patio doors. "I want screws put in the bottom part of the frames in all stationary patio doors throughout the project."

She moved her pencil to include all the subcontractors. "I want any fire-hazard materials disposed of on a daily basis. And I want each of you to make certain your men aren't sneaking into the air-conditioned buildings to take their breaks or eat lunch."

Because her mind played a trick on her, flashing a picture of Hank and his men eating lunch under the oak tree, she dropped her eyes to the blurred page on her clipboard.

She hesitated, focusing her eyes, then read directly from her notes. "Each subcontractor is contractually obligated to submit proof of insurance to the general office. For any of you who have neglected to take care of this detail, Geraldine has offered to send your document in the express package that goes out Thursday. Any subcontractor who doesn't have it in by the following Thursday will have a hold put on his check. Any questions or comments regarding this item will be handled on an individual basis."

She looked up and rose to her feet. "Unless there are other matters concerning everyone that need to be aired, I think we've covered today's agenda."

None of the men paused at her desk, Hank included. Oddly, that was a relief and a disappointment. She would have welcomed a friendly exchange, and yet she'd been the one to readily agree to keep their relationship "strictly business" while at the Lemontree.

After the room emptied Cat collapsed into her chair. The meeting had gone fairly well, she thought, taking all things into consideration. At least no one had left openly hostile.

Mentally she compared the meetings she ran to other meetings she'd attended. She'd been an assistant project manager for the past two years; she'd seen the comradeship between her boss and the men on those jobs. During the weekly meetings one boss she'd had would scream, throw papers and ridicule the men, but the minute the meeting ended someone would crack a joke and everyone would laugh. Most of them pumped his hand and slapped him on the back when they left.

It bothered Cat that she couldn't seem to strike a congenial rapport with the men. She hated to admit it, but sometimes she thought the men on this job expected her to fail, not only expected it, but were willing to toss stumbling blocks in her path so she wouldn't succeed.

Why? Was it being a woman in an all-male environment that set her apart? Because she was a female, did they expect her to conduct meetings as though they were weekly social events? Or was it just her, personally? What did they want from her?

She made an honest effort to be fair. She informed them of what Goldcoast expected and followed the rules. She seldom raised her voice, much less ranted and raved. No, she didn't pass out coffee and doughnuts, nor did she flutter her eyelashes when she delivered bad news. She had a feeling she would be the butt of a thousand jokes if she did.

She had to establish a neutral territory, somewhere between being flirty and being a hellcat.

Her mind strayed to Hank calling her "hellcat," the way he made it an endearment instead of an indictment. They'd been at her front door. She'd thanked him for the crystal vase he'd given her and teased him about bringing a deck of cards to teach her how to play gin rummy. He'd teased her about making love to a woman when he didn't know her real name. When she'd whispered her name in his ear, he'd said he preferred to call her "my little hellcat."

Cat sighed. Daydreaming wasn't getting the items on her checklist taken care of. She needed to walk the buildings before the sun became unbearably hot. The delayed arrival of the roof trusses gave her a legitimate opportunity to go and talk to Hank.

She was a woman who seldom missed a good opportunity.

Standing at the pay telephone, Hank dropped several quarters in the slot and dialed the number of the lumber mill in Georgia. Chances are, he thought, I'm wasting my money, but it's better to spend a couple of quarters than to worry myself to death.

He glanced down at the mouthpiece when the phone rang and rang and no one answered. That's strange, he mused. He glanced at his watch. Eleven-fifteen. There was an hour's time difference between Texas and Georgia. Maybe the lumber mill was one of those rural companies that completely shut down the office during lunch.

His cheeks puffed as he inhaled, then he blew a gust of air through his lips. He clicked the cradle; change noisily spewed into the coin return. In case he'd dialed the wrong number he redeposited the coins and tried again.

Since this was his first job as a subcontractor, he'd lacked the capital and the credit rating necessary for the lumber supplier to be willing to give him credit. To get the job, he'd agreed to have Goldcoast make his checks payable jointly to Butler Lumber Mills and himself. In the construction business, this practice wasn't unusual. With contractors going in and out of business like the changing of the tides, many suppliers preferred to have the checks made out jointly. This way the supplier was assured that he'd be paid for the materials.

Hank had signed last week's check and express-mailed it to Butler Mills. Usually an express envelope containing his share arrived at the Lemontree by Tuesday noon; that money was what he used to make this week's payroll for his men and his own personal paycheck. As he listened to the phone ring, he could only hope the person responsible for answering the phones wasn't the one responsible for deducting the sum he owed the mill and sending the remainder of Goldcoast's check back to him.

He hung up the telephone and retrieved his change. Still no answer, he thought, vexed. He'd have to try again later. In the meantime he'd pick up his express envelope at the office.

His heart lurched as he anticipated seeing Cat. After the morning meeting, he'd had difficulty keeping his hands to himself when he'd heard a few off-color comments regarding how she'd conducted the meeting. She'd been called everything from "hard-nosed bitch" to "Goldcoast's lackey," with a few "hellcats" sprinkled in the conversations.

He knew Cat would not appreciate his defending her reputation with his fists. He'd settled for making a couple of cutting remarks. Flint and Bubba had smirked and dubbed him Cat's "golden boy."

Hell, he couldn't care less what those two nicknamed him. The entire job would run more smoothly if they'd pack up their tools and men and go to another job.

Hank opened the office door and stepped into the cool interior of the trailer. "Hey, Geraldine. How's it going?"

"Better now that . . . you're here."

He wasn't flattered. Geraldine treated every man on the job as though he were a potential bed partner. When he talked to her she always had an unsettling habit of pausing before she completed a sentence.

A shiver ran down his spine. The perspiration running down his back felt like droplets of ice water. The temperature had to be thirty degrees lower than outside. He moved out of the blast of cold air blowing toward Geraldine.

"Has the express mail arrived?"

"Yep. But you didn't get anything."

Hank glanced through the open door into Cat's office. The metal folding chairs had been stacked against the wall. She wasn't at her desk. Double disappointment, he mused.

"If you're looking for the boss lady, she's outside sweltering in this god-awful heat." Geraldine twisted a lock of her curly hair with one finger and winked. "She might be looking for you, handsome."

Hank played dumb. "Oh? Anything in particular?"

"Nope. Just checking out your—" her eyes darted from his shoulders to his feet and back again "—work. My, my, you do look hot."

"It's more than ninety in the shade out there." He chose to ignore her roaming eyes and the pause she'd made. "I'm hotter than hot."

Geraldine chuckled. "You won't get any argument from me. Cat mentioned you liked to . . . fish?"

There it is again, Hank mused. That damned pause. She makes going fishing sound synonymous with water-bed polo!

"Yeah, but they wouldn't be biting today. Too hot."

Geraldine let loose her lock of hair, fluffing the ends until it tangled with her other curls. She uncrossed her legs, then crossed them. Her toe swung in his direction. "They're probably doing... other things."

Other things? Hank thought. Like what? Swimming? This had to top the chart for being a strange conversation. Geraldine made him feel like a goldfish being pursued by a barracuda! What a man-eater she was!

"I'd better get back to work. I'll check back with you later about the letter."

"You do that, sweetie. I'll look forward to seeing you... later."

Outside, Hank leaned against the door. He wiped the cold perspiration off his forehead. Obviously Cat must have mentioned their going fishing. From the way Geraldine acted, he wondered what else they'd discussed.

By late afternoon what Cat had told Geraldine was the least of his worries. Pedro, his lead carpenter, had been accidentally knocked off a scaffold; he fell thirty feet and landed on hard-packed dirt. Hank took one look at the dilated pupils of his eyes and called an ambulance. At the hospital, his diagnosis was found to have been correct. Pedro did have a mild concussion and wouldn't be able to return to work for a week.

Hank had meanwhile placed several unanswered calls to Georgia. He couldn't figure out what was going on at Butler Lumber. He even checked his calendar to make certain May 5 wasn't some obscure holiday. He'd also made three trips to the office to see if his check from Butler had arrived in the afternoon delivery. It hadn't. Cat had asked him about the delivery truck carrying the trusses. He couldn't blame her for being irritated. She had been nice about it, but nevertheless irritated. He knew it sounded as if he were stalling, but he couldn't give her an explanation because he couldn't get the lumber mill on the telephone! And, to round out an absolutely hellish day, he found a six-inch nail protruding from a flat tire on his truck when he was ready to drive home.

He arrived there at eight o'clock, wishing he was the one who'd fallen off the scaffold. Too weary to think about cooking dinner, he'd stopped at a fast food restaurant for carryout hamburgers.

Physically and mentally depleted, he entered his apartment, kicked off his boots and sprawled facedown on the couch. He lay there, not thinking, not moving, not feeling a damned thing.

A couple of hours later, he rolled over and stared groggily up at the ceiling. Time was the only cure for his problems. Pedro would heal; the lumber mill would answer the phone; his check would arrive.

Hank chuckled as he remembered bragging to Cat of being a man with great forbearance. Well, ol' buddy, he thought, you'd better use some of your patience tonight because you don't have any other choice.

He reached over his head to the end table, picked up his sack of cold food and the remote control for the television. He realized how long he'd slept when the late news program came on.

Sitting upright, he unwrapped the cheeseburger. It looked as pathetic as he felt. Another night he might have microwaved it. Tonight he ate it without noticing it tasted like sawdust doused in ketchup.

On the television screen, acres of trees, trucks loaded with prefabricated materials, abandoned equipment and a sawmill empty of workers caught his attention. He turned up the volume.

"Today in Crossroads, Georgia, lumberjacks, mill workers and office personnel entered their second day of a strike against the Butler Lumber Mills."

The camera focused on a tall, burly man carrying a picket sign. "Hang 'em from our trees!" he shouted.

The announcer continued. "While it is generally believed that the strike is related to money issues, a spokesman for Butler Mills has so far refused to comment."

Hank felt his stomach twist. He dropped his sandwich on the end table and reached for the telephone. The broadcast had given him the answers to the questions Cat had asked. She'd been irritated; now she'd be furious.

"Cat?"

"I saw the report." She wrapped the coiled telephone cord around her forefinger. She could tell from the strangled tone of Hank's voice he'd realized how the strike would affect his work at the Lemontree. "Do you think there's a chance the trucks left the mill before the strike?"

"I doubt it. Could you call Goldcoast's payroll department and see if the check issued last week has cleared the bank? If it hasn't, have them stop payment and issue another check made out solely to my company."

"Hank, you signed an agreement with the mill. Goldcoast has a copy of it on file."

"What you're saying is you don't think Goldcoast will stop payment on the check."

The tip of her finger had turned bright red; she unwound the cord, thinking how many small contractors like Hank were going to be choked out of business by the strike.

"Legally—"

"It'll take years to go through the court system. Butler has my money and the trusses I paid for! Dammit, Cat, I need those trusses now!"

She had to help him find a solution, for both their sakes. "I can call Kent Shane and have him consult with the legal department. Maybe there's a loophole somewhere in the contract you signed."

"And in the meantime, what am I going to tell the roofer?"

"His men haven't finished Buildings 4 and 5. That gives you a week or so. Would it be possible for you to get credit with a local lumber company? Just for enough trusses to keep ahead of the other trades?"

"I tried that before I went to Butler. You know this is my first big project. I don't have a credit record or a bank balance large enough to cover this. I couldn't get the local companies to go for the cosigned check agreement."

"Maybe we're overreacting. Let's see what Butler Mills does. I'm sorry I can't think of a simple solution."

"Well, I'm sorry for the problems this is going to cause you."

"It isn't your fault, Hank."

"That isn't what your boss will say. There's a nonperformance clause in the contract I signed with Goldcoast. If I don't figure out a way to get roof trusses on those buildings, you may be the one who has to kick me off the job."

Silently Hank wondered what she'd do in that case. Would she stand by him or Goldcoast? Would she set her professional ambitions aside to stand by him? Insecure and vulnerable, he held his breath waiting for her reply.

Cat wanted to make false promises. Telling him what he wanted to hear was nothing more than a white lie. He badly needed to be reassured. Sadly, she shook her head.

"We'll think of something before that happens. There has to be a way out of this."

"Yeah. We cut down the pine tree in my backyard and build those trusses ourselves. Do you think they would miss a few trees around your condo complex? How about the ones out at the lake?"

His sarcastic questions gave Cat an idea. Her father might be able to help Hank. He had hundreds of business contacts in Houston. He also had a warehouse filled with leftover lumber he'd collected from projects he'd worked on.

"I've just had a brilliant idea. I can't promise anything, but maybe my father can help."

"C'mon, Cat," Hank groaned. "Your family hates me. They'll applaud when you hand me my walking papers! It'll prove I'm not good enough for you. I appreciate your offer, but offhand, I don't think that idea is feasible."

"Right now, it's my only idea. Do you object to my approaching him?"

"Let me sleep on it. Okay?"

"Hank, I'll do everything I can to help you. You believe that, don't you?"

"We'll both do our best. G'night, Cat."

"G'night, Hank."

Hank hung up the phone. Blindly, he stared at the television. His entire body felt numb. He dreaded going to work in the morning. Bad news traveled fast on a construction site. The Lemontree's "golden boy" was in trouble. Big trouble.

"It isn't his fault the mill went on strike," Cat said, her voice calm, but her insides tied in knots. She had come up with another idea after she spoke to Hank. "If you won't stop payment on the check, will you release the retainer on the work he's completed?''

"Goldcoast can't do that for one subcontractor without doing it for all of them," Ken Shane, the regional supervisor, replied.

"We don't have to tell the other subs. The only ones who'll know are you and me and Hank."

"And the accounting department. And my boss. And his boss. That many people don't keep secrets. Think about the other guys, Cat. At one time or another most of them have had money problems. They aren't dumb. Even if someone doesn't tell them, they'll figure it out. When they do, they'll be the ones demanding that you place a similar call for them."

"If that happens, I'll handle them. They squawk when I have to cut their bills, too, but I do it. Don't I?"

"Okay, let's pretend no one finds out. Think about this strictly from Goldcoast's viewpoint. What happens if we give Mr. Collins his retainer on the other buildings, he spends it, and he still can't complete his contract? What do we do then?"

"He'll finish the project. His work is excellent. He's a good man."

"Cat, we don't run a charity organization. Think about why general contractors hold fifteen percent of subcontractors' paychecks. If the subcontractor can't finish his contract, Goldcoast has to be financially prepared to pay another contractor more money. This isn't a nonprofit organization."

"But Kent, I'm not asking you to give the man charity, only fairness! Justice!"

"Life isn't fair, Cat. If he wants justice, let him sue Butler Mills. Incidentally, if Goldcoast stops payment on a legally authorized check, Butler will sue us."

"In other words, Goldcoast is going to stick their hands in Hank Collins's pockets by keeping monies he earned, and find another framing contractor?"

"At this point, Mr. Collins is still in compliance with his contract. Thirty days after he hammers his last nail in a piece of wood, we'll have someone there to take his place."

Kent paused, then said, "Let me give you some friendly advice, Cat. Don't get involved. Do your job as you've been doing it... coolly, efficiently, competently. You're a woman breaking new ground. Don't be softhearted or softheaded. Bluntly speaking, don't screw up, if you get my meaning."

She did. And she didn't like his innuendo. When it came to business, she was clearheaded. "I'd do this for any subcontractor who did his job and got a rotten break."

"And I'd refuse to help them, too. When you've been in the construction business as long as I have, you'll have seen dozens of *good* framers nail themselves to the wall financially. You'll stop worrying about covering their butts and protect your own. Like it or not, that's the way this business is, Cat. Take my word on it. I expect you to continue to thoroughly document Hank Collins's performance record."

Without his saying it, Cat knew that when the time came, Kent also expected her to mail the registered letter informing Hank he had ten days to comply with his contract.

"Oh, one more thing, Cat. This can't go any higher. I was the one who recommended you be promoted to project manager. You blow it and I've got a black mark on my record, too."

"It would be pointless." Of all the men she'd met at Goldcoast's general office, Kent was her only hope. "He doesn't know I placed this call on his behalf."

"A man has his pride. Take that away from him and there isn't much left. I'll be talking to you later in the week."

"Yeah. Bye."

Cat hung up the phone and leaned back in her chair. Kent usually called her once or twice a month. He's following his own advice, covering his butt, she mused. Although she'd considered Kent her mentor, she realized if she made the wrong move, he'd ditch her as easily as he'd ditch Hank.

Through the window, she watched Hank crossing toward the pay telephone. She got up and moved to the window to watch what happened. She deduced from how he slammed the phone in its cradle that no one had answered. When he turned toward the trailer and appeared to be looking at her window, she motioned for him to come to her office.

Unless he'd thought of another option, the only one left was for her to call her father. Would that be stealing his pride? she wondered. Men were so damned peculiar when it came to their fragile egos.

Through her open door she called to Geraldine, "Tell Hank to come on in to my office."

"Do I get to listen at the door?" Cat's secretary teased. "He might start chasing you around your desk...if you're lucky."

"Please, not today, Geraldine. I have a splitting headache."

Geraldine pulled out her bottom desk drawer and produced a bottle of aspirin. "Double strength. Does your headache have anything to do with Hank's problem with Butler Lumber Mills?''

"How'd you know?"

"I'm the lady who puts the checks in the envelopes, remember? I also watch television. One and one add up to a splitting headache."

"You haven't mentioned this to anyone, have you?"

"No, but it's been mentioned twice to me. Once on the parking lot when I was getting out of my car, and—"

"Did you want to see me?" Hank asked, not realizing he'd interrupted Geraldine.

Cat searched his face. His dark eyes looked haunted and tired. He'd shaved, but nicked his chin. His full lips were clamped into a tight line. What she saw made everything inside her ache for him. And there wasn't one damned thing she could do to ease her pain or his, without trampling on his pride.

"Yes." She slid her hands nervously up and down the side seams of her jumpsuit. "Could you come into my office for a minute?"

Silently Hank followed her. He'd thought about her offer to approach her father. Hell, he'd worn a path on the carpet at the end of his bed pacing back and forth. By dawn, he'd drawn one conclusion: he couldn't let her help him.

He closed the door and leaned his head against it. "No."

"No?"

"I won't let you go on your hands and knees to your family to help me."

She drew in a shaky breath and perched on the corner of her desk. She had to convince him not to let his stubborn pride get in the way of completing this job. "Dammit, Hank, you have to let me help you—"

"No, I don't." He snorted a laugh, without humor. "It's sort of ironic when you think about it. Two women in my life, both ambitious, both powerful, both successful. I hated one for not helping me, for destroying my faith in myself—" his eyes were full of pain as they leveled on Cat "—and the other generously offers her help, but I can't accept it because the results would be the same. I'd end up doubting my own worth. And you'd end up hating me because you had to buckle under to your family to do it. No, Cat. Thanks, but no thanks."

Cat gnawed on her bottom lip; her face drew into a worried frown. She knew how important it was for him to solve this problem on his own, but she couldn't keep her mouth shut when she had an easy solution available to her. "Dad has more than enough lumber in storage to build those trusses you need."

"No."

She could play on his sympathy, telling him it would look bad for her professionally if he complicated her job by being unable to finish his contract, but she realized that would be despicable.

Hank crossed the narrow room. He cupped her face between his rough hands. "I have to get this problem straightened out by myself, Cat. How can I care for you if I can't take care of me?"

"Do you care for me, Hank?"

"You know I do. I could pack up my tools, pay off my men and ride out of here if I didn't. I could find another job. Maybe not as a subcontractor, but I could support myself. It's caring about you and my reputation that keeps me here."

She caved against him, letting his strong body support her. She laid her cheek against his shoulder and drank in his scent. His arms clamped around her shoulders, holding her securely close to him. His lips gently, fleetingly kissed her temple.

"I'll stand by you, Hank, whatever you decide."

Chapter Nine

The kiss that followed her declaration was sweet and savage, filled with hope and despair. His mouth twisted over hers, dominating her as he forced her lips to part. She yielded to him. His hips thrust forward and ground into hers as though he could physically leave his imprint on her. She accepted him. She understood his frustrations and fears. They were her own.

Hank's lips gentled as he came to his senses. He'd taken his frustration out on the one person who was clearly backing him. Apologetically, he sweetly nuzzled her mouth, ending his kiss as he usually began them. He lifted his mouth, then gently wiped her moist lips with his thumb.

Cat wanted to make love to him more than she wanted to breathe. She burrowed her nose against his neck, afraid of saying or doing the wrong thing.

"Can I come by your place tonight?"

"Yes. Please," she whispered.

Fully clothed, standing in the middle of her office, not moving a muscle, she felt more intimate with him than when they'd made love. She knew both of them were thinking so intensely about the act of physically becoming one that mentally they'd mated.

Hank mouthed her name into her hair. He couldn't foul up and lose her, he told himself. He'd shrivel up and die if he did.

Minutes passed and neither of them stirred. They stood there, each of them holding on to the present, almost afraid to part and face the future.

Piecemeal, first his thighs and hips, then his torso and finally his hands moved away from her. He had closed his eyes, memorizing this moment. It would be his only sustenance during the long hours from morning to nightfall.

A heartbeat later, Cat was alone.

Flint, Bubba and the news media had something in common, Cat thought, snapping off the evening news. All of them were having a field day with Butler Lumber Mills's problems. Sitting Indian-style on the sofa with a microwaved frozen dinner on her lap, she poked her fork into the aluminum foil, wishing she could have poked the knowing grin off Bubba Clark's face.

As she'd walked through the buildings to check on the work completed, she'd spotted Flint and Bubba slapping each other on the back and pointing toward the building where Hank was climbing in the open rafters. They barely managed to contain their snickers when she separated them, taking Bubba to the side wall of Building 3 to show him the chafed wires leading into the circuit box.

"I'll tape 'em."

"You'll pull out the slack leading into the box and check the coating," she corrected. "If it isn't frayed, cut this part off, add connectors and I'll check it before you leave this afternoon." She watched his chest expand as he puffed up to argue with her. "This is a fire hazard. It'll never pass inspection."

"It'll be tomorrow before I can free up a man to get to it."

"You scheduled the inspection for tomorrow. I don't want electrical current put on in this building until the wires are repaired. Got it?"

"Don't go cuttin' my bill. The inspector will pass it."

She'd seen the electrical inspector and Bubba together. The inspector might pass a blind eye over Bubba's work while they swapped jokes, but her eyes were wide open.

"You heard me," was all she had said.

Cat took her half-eaten dinner into the kitchen. It irked her that Bubba had the nerve to make fun of Hank's difficulties while doing slipshod work himself. She scraped the food out of the foil into the garbage disposal and flipped the switch.

Over the grinding whir, she heard the phone ring. Hastily, she turned off the disposal and darted to answer the phone. She offered a silent prayer that it wasn't Hank calling to cancel coming over to her house. He'd still been working when she left the job site.

"McGillis residence."

She heard her father's chuckle. "Your voice sounds just like your mother's when you answer the phone."

Maude has brought in the big guns, Cat mused, displeased. When her mother couldn't get what she wanted, she coerced her father into speaking his piece.

"How are you doing, Dad?"

"Fine, just fine." Joshua didn't beat around the bush, but went straight to his reason for calling her. "While I was at work today, I heard a rumor I thought you'd be interested in."

"I know all about Butler Lumber Mills, Dad."

"You mean that strike going on in Georgia? Honey, that's not a rumor, that's a fact. I'm calling about Goldcoast. I heard they're only a couple of days away from being kicked off that big project they have going in Dallas. Any truth in it?"

"I don't honestly know. I talked to Kent this morning and he didn't mention it."

"He wouldn't. Not if they're soaking up the cash flow off of the Lemontree to get them out of trouble in Dallas."

Silently, Cat groaned. If the rumor going around held an ounce of truth, that could explain why Kent adamantly refused to release Hank's retainer. Goldcoast could find another subcontractor at the same price they paid Hank, and use the thousands of dollars they'd held back from him to keep their cash flow moving.

The doorbell pealed. "Hang on a second, Dad, I think Hank is at the door."

"Good. I want to talk to him about a rumor going around about his company."

"Dad, I don't think this would be a good time to discuss it. He knows how the McGillis family feels about him without having salt rubbed into his wound."

Brute barked, running between the kitchen and the front door.

"Hush!" she called to him. She put her hand over the mouthpiece. "Come on in, Hank! I'm on the phone."

"You don't have to yell, daughter."

"I didn't mean you." She heard the door open and close accompanied by Brute's excited yaps. He charged into the kitchen with a rawhide dog bone clamped between his teeth. "I was yelling at Brute."

"Is Hank there?"

"Yes."

"Put him on the line, would you?"

She glanced up, unsure of what to do, as Hank stuck a double-dip chocolate ice cream cone under her nose. She said into the mouthpiece, "Hold on a second." She looked up at Hank. "It's Dad. He wants to talk to you."

Reflexively, his hand drew the ice cream cone away from her. "Did you call him after I told you not to?"

"No!" she whispered. "He called me. I haven't said a word about your business to him."

Hank traded the cone for the phone. "Yes, sir."

Licking the edges where the ice cream had melted, she watched Hank's expression. Much to her dismay, she couldn't hear what her father said.

"Yes, sir. She is."

"Is what?" she mouthed.

"He wants to talk privately to me." Hank paused, listening to Joshua. "He says if you're too nosy to leave the room . . . he'll call me later at my apartment."

Shaking her head, her eyes dared Hank to tell her "nosy" father that he wouldn't be home later. Realizing it was wrong to make Hank take the brunt of how her father would react, she let her eyes drop to her bare feet.

"C'mon, Brute. The men are going to trade secrets."

She had to grin after Hank stopped her by grabbing her arm and planting a swift, hard kiss on her mouth.

"I'll be in the living room, Dad, with the television turned up real loud," she said into the mouthpiece. She couldn't stop herself from giving her father the same warning she'd heard when she was a teenager. "Don't do anything I wouldn't do."

"Sassy-mouth," she heard in reply.

So help me, she thought, plopping on the sofa, if Dad asks Hank if he has honorable intentions, I'll kill him!

Too curious to concentrate on a game show, she leaned her head back until she could catch faint murmurings of the telephone conversation. She heard a string of "yes, sirs" from Hank's end of the line, which told her nothing.

She fidgeted for a couple of minutes, then called, "I'm going to take Brute for his walk."

Hank did more listening than responding. Houston was a major metropolitan area, but the accuracy of the rumors Joshua repeated proved what Hank had always suspected, that the construction industry was strictly small-town, with everybody knowing everybody else's business.

"There's a recorded message on the phone at Butler Mills, right?"

"Yes, sir." Hank could repeat it word for word. *Sorry, we are unable to process your call due to a work stoppage. Please be patient. Leave your name....*

"Did you have a cosigner agreement with them?"

"Yes, sir."

"So you're stuck with no lumber and no money."

"Yes, sir. That sums it up."

"Cat's mother, the boys and I had a get-together last night that might be of interest to you. Between the five of us, we've pretty well got the trades covered. The boys have often talked about pooling our know-how and our money to start up a small general contracting company. Nothing big and fancy, just a family operation. Well, I hate to admit it, but I'm the one who's been dragging my feet. Guess at my age, a man starts feeling entitled to slow down, spend his days fishing instead of chasing the buck. Know what I mean?"

Uncertain of what he'd be agreeing to, Hank chose to keep silent.

"At any rate, James brought up the idea of you substituting for me . . . doing the framing and carpentry work."

"Mr. McGillis, before you continue, I think you ought to know that every cent I have is tied up at the Lemontree."

"That's natural for a contractor, son. But let's step back a minute and see if me and the boys can help you with those roof trusses you need. Being a carpenter myself, I trained them. None of them followed in my footsteps, so to speak, but a nail gun fits into their hands real good. I figure between your men and my boys, you all could take the specifications sheet and build your own damn trusses. That's how we did it when I was young— stick by stick."

Hank rubbed his fingers wearily across his forehead. Cat had told him about her father stockpiling lumber. He wondered if she'd told her father about his difficulties, against his request to let him take care of his problem on his own. There was only one way to find out.

"I have one question, sir, and I need the truth. Did Cat put you or your sons up to making this offer?"

"No." Joshua chuckled. "Maude said you'd ask that. She's a fine woman, my Maude. Seems to understand the boys, but she can't boss Cat around like she does them." He lowered his voice, in case his daughter stood near Hank. "Cat's fur would stand on end if she knew about this so I'd appreciate your not mentioning it. Every once in a while I ask one of the men where I'm working to drive me by the Lemontree just to see how things are going. A week or so ago, one of Butler's trucks was blocking the entrance. I just put one and one together and figured you might be in trouble."

Hank had the feeling Cat wasn't the only one Joshua McGillis had been checking up on when he rode around the job site. It pleased him to know his reputation must have left a good impression on Cat's father, but when it came to business deals, he wasn't one to leap into something that appeared to be too good to be true. Besides, he liked being his own boss.

"I didn't expect an answer tonight," Joshua said, after a long pause. "I don't want you to think I'm pressuring you into something 'cause of Cat. The timing just seemed right. I have the lumber you need to get you off the hook, and you have the experience and know-how the boys need to get me off the hook. Seems like a fair deal to me."

"It's not that part of the deal that worries me."

"You worried about my sons?"

Hank grimaced. Here comes the kick in the pants. "They weren't exactly friendly last weekend."

"Well, to be honest with you, Cat's name was mentioned in our little discussion."

Here it comes. Before Joshua could mention the drawback to accepting the McGillises' offer, Hank said, "They want me to stop seeing Cat, right?"

"I won't lie to you, Hank. That stipulation was mentioned."

Without a second thought, Hank succinctly said, "No deal."

"You don't want to negotiate?"

"Not when it comes to Cat."

"She's more important to you than those roof trusses you desperately need?"

"Yes, sir, she is."

"He flat turned me down," Hank heard Joshua say to someone in the background, then he chuckled. "Well, young man, why don't you give it some more consideration, then come out to the lake house Saturday and we'll talk about it? One of us might've changed their minds by then."

"I won't."

"You're as stubborn as my daughter, huh?"

"About this? Yeah, I am."

Joshua paused, as though listening to what was being discussed in the room. Hank overheard James crow with delight, "I told you he'd never go for it."

A few seconds later Joshua said, "Well, Hank, we'd still like to have you drop by on Saturday."

"With or without Cat?"

"With or without Cat?" Joshua repeated for the benefit of those privy to only one side of the conversation. "You'd better bring her along. We'd appreciate it if you wouldn't mention the...uh...you know, the details of our offer. Cat acts like a feline with her tail set afire when we stick our noses in where she thinks they don't belong."

Not wanting to be the cause of the rift widening between Cat and her family, Hank said, "I'll only tell her about the first part of your offer, sir."

"Don't misunderstand. It's not that we object to you personally. We've all just had an idea in our minds about...hell, I'm digging a trench with my own mouth. Could you put my daughter back on the phone? Maude wants to speak to her."

"She's taken Brute for a walk."

"Hmm." In an undertone, Joshua added, "Probably just as well Maude doesn't talk to her. Give her a hug for me. We'll be talking to you Saturday."

Hank hung up the phone, wondering if he'd turned down his last chance to save his business. He strode to the front door, stepped outside and looked up and down the street for Cat and Brute; they were nowhere in sight. He wouldn't let himself think about trading his relationship with Cat for a pile of timber!

As he went back into the living room, he considered the ambiguity of Joshua's offer. Did the McGillis clan think he was good enough to be a business partner, but unacceptable for their daughter and sister? While Joshua had been checking out his reputation, had he also uncovered what a mess he'd made of his personal life? That he'd been married? Divorced?

Hank's hand knotted at his sides. He couldn't blame them for considering him a poor risk. Here he was, a divorced man on the brink of financial disaster and showing a personal interest in the youngest member of their family. No, he couldn't fault them for being wary of him.

They weren't the only ones who were wary. Much as he cared for Cat, taking a chance on commitment to her still scared the hell out of him. Was he a fool to consider building a life with a woman who was as ambitious, as driven for power and success as his first wife? Four or five years from now, would she make it to the top and look back at him and wonder what had possessed her to marry him?

He glanced around her living room in an effort to distract himself from his painful thoughts. Like Cat's office, the room was small, but neat and uncluttered. Bold green-striped fabric on the sofa matched the draperies. The same forest green was in the background of the floral print on her occasional chairs. Unclenching his hands, he ran them over the lacquered coffee table. The fruit-wood stain matched the headboard in his garage that he'd temporarily abandoned working on. An oil painting of a seascape, a collage of family pictures and a few potted plants completed the decorations.

He picked up the frame that held a collection of family snapshots. A picture of Tom, Luke and Russell, posing as Mean, Meaner and Meanest, made Hank grin. His finger touched a photo of Cat looking about five years old, proudly holding up a small bluegill. Another of Cat and James as teenagers, with their arms looped across each other's shoulders, drew his attention. For several moments he studied a recent snapshot of her parents holding up a twenty-fifth wedding anniversary cake.

Mentally he tried to put his picture into the frame, but it didn't fit; there was no room for him in this closely knit family. He put the collage of photos back where it belonged.

What the hell am I doing here? Cat has her job, her family, friends. There isn't a thing I can add to her life, other than trouble.

Halfway to his feet, he heard the front door slam. Brute barreled into the living room, made a quick trip around Hank's feet with his leash, then darted toward the spare bedroom.

"Hey!" Lithely, Hank caught the leash's handle before the chain tightened around his ankles.

"It's a new trick he taught himself. When he wants somebody to go with him, he wraps his chain around their feet and tugs on it." She turned to scold Brute, but he'd dropped his end of the chain and picked up the rawhide bone Hank had brought him. "I'm hoping that bone will save me the cost of several pairs of shoes. Brute seems to like it."

Her eyes searched Hank's face. She hoped he'd volunteer the reason for her father asking to speak to him.

"Your dad heard about my problem with Butler Mills. He made me a business offer."

"Honest, Hank, I didn't call him. I swear I didn't."

"You don't have to get out the Bible, Cat. Your dad heard through the grapevine that I was doing business with Butler Mills. He asked a few pertinent questions, which I answered truthfully, then offered me that stockpile of lumber you'd mentioned."

"Hank!" Cat squealed, overjoyed. She hugged him with all her might. "Your problem is solved!"

"Maybe." His arms circled her shoulders. "Your brothers came up with the idea of forming a business partnership."

She snuggled against him. "They've been trying to talk my father into that for the past couple of years."

"So he said."

"I think he's more interested in retirement than starting up a new business." She looked up and grinned. "He wants you to take his place?"

"Something like that. We didn't go into details over the phone. They want us to come out to the lake house Saturday."

"Well? What do you think?"

"I think your hair smells lovely." His thumb stroked her cheek, then the edge of her hairline. With her in his arms, it was nearly impossible to think about any partnership other than theirs. He knew he wasn't doing her any favor by staying, but he couldn't let go of the one good thing in his life. Not yet. "It's so soft."

She began to protest. She wanted to know all the wonderful details, but Hank drew her closer, silencing her objections. Cat knew she could slip out of his arms, but why would she? She was right where she wanted to be. Relieved that her father had given Hank a viable solution to his problem, she only wanted to communicate, by hanging on to him, how she felt about his becoming part of her family's business.

He lowered his head until their lips touched. Hers parted. Suddenly, she couldn't get enough of him. She felt his weight shift as he cradled her intimately against his hips. His tongue danced with hers and he lifted her higher into his arms. Her breasts dragging across his shirtfront sent a rush of heat to the tips of her toes, which no longer touched the floor.

Her last sane thought was that she loved having a physically strong man. She moaned softly as she felt his arousal pressing against her; one of his hands slid down her back to her hip to hold her there.

She peppered tiny kisses along his jaw; he immersed his face in the fragrance of her hair and perfume by kissing her arched neck. He needed to possess her, to make her his. He wanted their passion to take him to a place where lumber and family and divorces didn't matter. He wanted the sun rays of her love to burn through the hazy fog of anguish threatening to engulf him.

She moved against him. He groaned and fastened his lips on her mouth. He kissed her long and deeply, his head tilting first to one side and then to the other. But kissing failed to quench his need to possess all of her sweetness.

He lowered her to the sofa and knelt beside her. His eyes held hers as he unzipped the front of her jumpsuit. "Work clothes and lace," he murmured.

"I didn't have time to change," she whispered, explaining why she still wore the Goldcoast uniform.

She made fast work of unbuttoning his shirt. Vaguely she wondered how he'd had time to go home and change clothes. Hows and whys and wherefores were the least of her interests. Her hands pushed his shirt down his shoulders, then her fingers shook with delight as she spread them through the masculine hair on his chest.

Hank sensed her unasked question. Later, he mused, he'd tell her he kept an extra set of clothes in his truck. He unclasped her bra, pushing it aside. For now, the feel of his own callused fingers rasping against the velvety softness of her breast captured his tongue, making it impossible for him to speak. He stroked her to give her pleasure, hell, to give him pleasure.

He heard her broken sigh as she raised herself to let him remove her garment. She remained suspended above the sofa pillow as though silently asking him to nuzzle her breasts while he quickly dispensed with his clothing. Moving beside her on the wide sofa, he lowered his head; his mouth dipped, kissing one breast then the other.

"Better than a double dip of ice cream," he whispered, while his tongue licked and nipped the pinkish-brown tips of her breasts. His hands slid down to her hips, tucking her against him. "Much, much better. I'll never forget the way you taste, never."

Restlessly, Cat shifted beneath him, knees bent beside each of his hips, wanting the strength of his body to press against her. No, more than his strength, she wanted to hold his hard maleness against the cradle of her femininity.

We fit together so beautifully, she thought, her knees hugging him to her. She began to move with the age-old rhythm of desire as his hands moved over her body, sure, confident, rediscovering her.

She explored him with the same confidence, boldly taking him into her hands; the tremor that ran the length of his body as he fought for control gave her a mysterious sense of power. A kiss here, one there, could make his heart pound; another, lower, made his pulse race faster. And she knew he had equal, if not greater, power over her.

Hank clenched his teeth. The hot moistness of her tongue making circular motions around his navel drove him wild. He could feel himself touch the soft vulnerable skin beneath her chin. Abruptly, he pushed her shoulders back against the armrest, then guided himself into her.

Twilight bathed her skin in a golden hue; the same light washed over him, changing his tan to a reddish bronze. For a timeless moment, they were as still as statues intimately entwined, both of them wanting to capture this sublime feeling forever in their memories.

Hank began to move. Cat watched his face change from an expression of wonder to one close to pain. His taut hips rose and fell rhythmically as he plunged deeply, withdrew, stroked lightly, then delved again deeply inside of her. His rhythm increased its pace, tormenting her until her eyes could no longer watch him. They closed tightly as she concentrated on the exquisite sensation building inside of her.

Reaching the summit, she experienced a higher level of rapture than the first time they'd made love. She hadn't thought that humanly possible.

With Hank, anything and everything was possible.

Chapter Ten

"You are going to accept their offer, aren't you?" Cat asked. She had her arm across the back of Hank's shoulders while he drove to the lake. He'd carefully avoided discussing the reason for their going to her parent's house. "It doesn't look like the lumberjacks at Butler Mills are likely to throw down their picket signs."

"The one big guy ought to quit and get a Hollywood agent. He's had more coverage this week than the President! I read somewhere that we'll all have fifteen minutes of fame during our lives. I think the Friendly Giant in Georgia has taken my share."

"No he hasn't," Cat refuted, lightly nudging him in the ribs. "You're going to make the front page of the *Houston Post* tomorrow if you don't answer my question."

"Did anyone ever tell you that you're too nosy for your own good?"

"Yes." Her thumb and forefinger spread to headline size. "'Collins Tortured into Talking. See obituaries for further details.' That's the caption, mister."

Hank chuckled. Keeping one hand on the wheel, he squeezed her knee with the other. Her leg jerked.

"Boy crazy, huh?"

Threats hadn't worked. She cuddled closer. She nipped his ear and said, "Only you drive me crazy... and you're no boy."

"Cat, you have no shame."

"What do you mean?"

"One tactic won't work, so you've switched to another. Has it occurred to you that I can't give you a definite answer because three of your four brothers have barely spoken to me?"

"Yes." She flashed him a cheeky grin. "But I dismissed it as irrelevant. You couldn't find four men who work harder than they do. And, when Mother isn't misdirecting them, they're good guys."

"Coming from their younger sister, I'd say that's a good recommendation... if I didn't know how you occasionally tell people what they want to hear because you think it's good for them."

"You're never going to forget that, are you?"

"Nope. But, if it will make you happy, I'll tell you that most of what I've heard from your father sounds interesting."

"Most?"

"Okay. If it will make you happy, I'll tell you I'm ready to sign on the dotted line anything they put in front of me."

"You wouldn't mean it, though, would you?"

"Nope. No more than I plan on ever being your boss."

"What if I'm part of the package deal the McGillis family is offering?"

Hank slowed down and stared at her for a second. Had Cat somehow gotten her father to change his offer?

"Are you?"

"Can you think of anyone better qualified to supervise the overall operation of the McGillis-Collins enterprise?"

"You're overqualified. What your father mentioned would be small potatoes compared to Goldcoast."

"You wouldn't mind?"

"It'd be a little late for that. In case you've forgotten, you are my boss." Hank shrugged. "Professionally, I don't have problems with a qualified woman being the top executive."

"I wish the Three Mean Musketeers were as open-minded. At least with you joining the Gruesome Twosome, the odds in my favor would be higher...three for, three against. Dad would have to step in and arbitrate." She gave Hank a speculative glance. "You would vote in favor of the idea, wouldn't you?"

"Whoa, sweetheart! I'm not a voting member yet. You're getting ahead of yourself."

"You will be soon," she replied in a sassy voice. She only had to worry about her mother influencing her father's vote. Optimistically, Cat thought Maude might like the idea of the whole family working together. Cat pointed to the turnoff. "There's the lane. I can hardly wait to get there."

A sinking feeling chewed at Hank's insides. What if the McGillises were adamant about their stipulation? He'd given his word he wouldn't tell Cat about it. They'd put him in a lose-lose situation. She'd be madder than hell when he refused the offer, and he wouldn't be able to defend his action. He felt as though he'd tied his hands behind his back, with his own tongue!

The entire week Cat had tried to sway his opinion in favor of the partnership. Quietly, he'd gone about trying to find another source of lumber. There had to be a way over, under, around or through this problem; he simply hadn't found it.

Hank circled under the oak tree, parking beside the other trucks. "Well, here goes nothing."

"How about a kiss for good luck?"

"A hot, steamy kiss?" Hank teased.

Cat glanced through his side window. Hands folded across her chest, Maude stood on the porch next to Joshua. Her brothers were in full view, seated at the picnic table. She noticed none of them had brought his girlfriend. All four sets of blue eyes stared at the truck.

"On second thought, I think I'll take a rain check. No point in antagonizing them." She winked at Hank. "I'll antagonize them later when I nominate myself as president of the newly formed company."

Hank waved at Cat's family, greeted them, then circled the front of the truck and opened the passenger door. "Cat McGillis, whatever happens I want you to know that I care for you."

"The feeling is mutual." Not out of defiance but out of love, she changed her mind about showing affection for him in front of her family. She kissed him full on the lips, then brought his hand to her lips. "They might as well get used to seeing how I feel about you."

"Good to see you, Hank," Joshua called, striding toward them. "Why don't you come on down to the boys' out-of-doors office and we'll talk while Cat helps her mother finish things up in the kitchen?"

Glancing toward the porch, Cat noticed her mother hadn't unfolded her arms. Her foot tapped impatiently on the wooden slats. It struck Cat as mighty peculiar that her father oozed glad tidings and her mother looked as though she'd been snacking on fishing worms.

Dreading a confrontation with Maude, Cat stammered, "Uh, Dad, I thought I might go with you two and hear what my brothers have to say to Hank."

Joshua lowered his voice to keep it from carrying any distance. "I'd appreciate it, daughter, if you'd go pacify your mother and let me take care of the business matters. You can add your two cents into the negotiations later."

"Something tells me I should have worn my hard hat," she muttered under her breath to Hank. "I'm definitely entering a dangerous area."

"You don't need one," Joshua teased. "When the man up above assembled you, he yelled, 'Heads,' and you thought he yelled, 'Beds' and asked for a hard one."

"Family joke," Cat explained to Hank. To her father she said, "Pardon me if I've heard it too many times to laugh."

Hank barely managed to keep a straight face. Had they been alone, he'd have made an additional comment about her preference for hard mattresses, too, but he wisely decided her good-luck kiss was enough provocation for one day.

"Now, Hank," Joshua said, "about that little deal we talked about on the phone. Did you bring the specification sheets with you? The boys want to have a look at them."

Cat tagged along behind them for a couple of steps until her father cast her a dirty look over his shoulder. Then she slipped her hands in the back pockets of her jeans and slowly ambled into the house.

"You took your own sweet time getting here. How many stops along the way did you make?" Maude asked.

"Counting the stoplights or just counting the eight or nine times we had to stop coming down the lane?" Cat quipped, thinking her mother hadn't wasted time giving her a welcoming hug.

"You should have made it ten." Maude threw the dish towel she'd been wiping the counter top with into the sink. "Your father and I have been married going on thirty years and we've never necked in front of you kids."

"It's not too late. Why don't you march outside and give Dad a big smackeroo?" Cat suggested. "It might put you in a better mood."

"Kiss him?" Maude gave an indelicate snort. "I haven't spoken to him since Wednesday night."

After Dad spoke to Hank, Cat silently deduced. Not a good omen. Her dream of Maude standing on the sidelines, cheering for her children as they bedazzled the construction industry, began to fade.

"What can I do to help?" Cat asked.

"Stop dating that man," Maude baldly replied.

"Mother, I meant here in the kitchen."

"Nothing. I took care of everything." She glanced at the kitchen floor. "Where's Brute?"

"I left him at home. Somebody overdosed him on chocolate last time we were out here. He had sugar withdrawal all week."

"Phooey! I only gave him a tiny bit of cake."

Cat crossed to the window to see how Hank was doing. "And my darling brothers each gave him a tiny bit and Dad gave him..."

The men had crowded into the bass boat. "Where are they going?"

"James installed an electronic fish-finder on the boat. I imagine everyone has gone for a test drive to see if it works."

"It's a lovely day outside. Why don't we join the men? I've never seen one of those electronic gadgets."

"The front porch will do." Maude marched toward the front door. "The men won't appreciate your disappearing with Hank again. C'mon, child. The fresh air out here may clear up those rose-tinted sunglasses you're wearing."

"Are we going to continue fussing and fighting with each other?"

"No." Maude put one hand on her hip and shook her finger at her daughter as though she were a preadolescent. "You're making it real hard for me not to say 'I told you so.'"

She has to get out whatever is stuck in her craw, Cat mused. Her attempt to make light of her situation was only infuriating Maude. She followed her mother out of the house and eased into one of the rocking chairs on the porch.

"You told me what?"

"For years I've been telling you to find a nice, steady, reliable man."

I have, Cat thought, rocking back and forth, chewing on her bottom lip to keep silent.

"Nine to five. Paid vacations. Benefits. Someone who can give you security." Maude spoke to Cat, but her eyes were on her husband. "It isn't easy trying to raise a family while the bill collectors are pestering you on the phone." She looked at her daughter. "Oh, I know what you're thinking, young lady. Why didn't I get a job or have fewer children? Well, I wasn't qualified to do anything other than work at a fast food restaurant or sell pantyhose, that's why. I couldn't have made enough money to pay for a baby-sitter. That's also why I wanted you educated. I didn't want you to feel ... trapped.''

Cat lifted her feet to the edge of her chair and wrapped her arms around her folded legs. This was a side of her mother she'd never seen. She wondered where she had been while the bill collectors were ringing the phone off the wall.

"Not that I regret having you kids," Maude inserted. "I don't regret doing without because of you all. But, when you were born, I promised myself I'd be a springboard for you, lifting you higher than I was. I wanted you to have the pretty clothes I missed having. I wanted you to have a steady job, a nice place to live. I wanted you to have every chance I didn't have. I wanted you to be happy, that's all.''

"Mother, you can't live your life through me. I feel badly that you've sacrificed and I've been a disappointment to you. I know you resent what I do for a living, but it's what I'm good at. You said you wanted me to be happy. Don't you realize I'd be miserable cooped up inside, pushing a pencil, or trying to teach a bunch of kids who'd rather be outside playing?''

Maude shook her head. "I know you're happy. That's why I quit harping on the subject of you working for Goldcoast. Unless you butt heads with the bosses, you do have some security. It's your hoping for a future with Hank Collins that worries me sick. It's like watching history repeat itself and not being able to stop it.''

"It isn't the same. I'll never be trapped because I can always earn a good living.''

Maude chuckled without mirth. "Oh, yes, daughter. I can see you five years from now, trudging around a job site, pregnant, with a couple of kids trailing after you. Will you be happy then?''

"I won't have children until I can afford them." Her mother's raised eyebrows made Cat add, "I can always work in the general offices, bidding jobs, or purchasing materials."

"Fine. What happens when there's a building slump? You can't plan or order materials for what isn't going to be built. Are you going to pick up your family and move hither and yon, looking for work? That's what your father did. Don't you remember him being gone for months at a time?"

"I remember Dad coming home and how happy you were."

"Don't confuse happiness with relief."

"I remember being a teenager and thinking how you two were like honeymooners."

Maude's eyes rose to the roof of the porch. "And I remember that nine months later Tom had a new baby brother and finally a baby sister."

"Mother, you make it sound like every time you and Dad went to bed together you had a child."

"Only because back then it seemed that way. Thank goodness it's different now." She laid her hand on Cat's arm. "But some things are the same. You think the sun rises and sets on Hank Collins. That's how I felt about Joshua. You think both of you are invincible, nothing bad will ever happen to you. Your dad and I thought so, too. But it's an illusion. That's how young people in love view the world." Her grip tightened. "Honey, in one week Hank has gone from being on top of the world to facing the prospect of going broke. Construction work is one monstrous roller coaster ride. It's scary. Believe me, I know. I've been in that seat."

"Hank is good at his trade," Cat replied defensively.

"So's your father. That doesn't put him in the driver's seat."

"But you're being completely unfair. It isn't as though Hank was doing lousy work. You can't blame him for the lumber mill having labor problems."

"I don't. I didn't blame your father when the general contractor he worked for went bankrupt. Or when the gravel haulers went on strike and he couldn't put up the lumber because there wasn't a slab of concrete to build on. Or when he threw his back out of whack and was laid up for a month. None of that was his fault." Her hand moved up and down and around sharp curves. "It just happens in this business. The roller coaster keeps rolling and you hang on for dear life. I don't want that for you. I want you to have control of your fate."

It won't be that way for us, Cat silently argued. We'll have setbacks, but they'll only be temporary.

Maude sighed. "I know you're sitting there thinking everything is going to be fine. Butler Mills's shutdown is only a temporary setback. It isn't, love. It'll happen over and over and over. Only the names will change. Next time it could be the manufacturer of the nail plates."

"What about Luke and Tom and Russell? They aren't living hand-to-mouth. From what Dad says they have healthy savings accounts."

"They aren't married, either. Who do you think is the one who insisted on their putting money away for those rainy days? Me, that's who. The boys and I have had plenty of heart-to-heart talks like this one. They listen to me."

Cat had to duck her head to keep her mother from seeing her smile. The boys might have listened, but they did as they damn well pleased. Both Tom and Luke had been living with their sweethearts for the past couple of years. Russell had his eye and his sweet tooth on the owner of a small ice cream shop. James was just waiting for the right timing to announce his engagement.

Yeah, they listened...with deaf ears. Her brothers' motto was "What mother doesn't know won't hurt us!"

"If Hank goes into partnership with them, we can help each other over the rough spots."

"We?"

"I'm the one who's trained to make certain the roller coaster only hits a few bad curves."

"No. You're not on the same ride. If I were you I'd keep it that way. If they go off the track, you won't be crashing down with them."

"You don't want me to be a part of McGillis and Collins?"

"No, I don't."

"What about Hank? Is it okay if he's part of it?"

"Only if..." Maude paused. Her eyes scanned from one end of the porch to the other. "What if I could prove to you that he'll put his business before you and any children you'd have?"

"You don't know Hank."

"Don't I?" Again she laughed. "Honey, he and your dad might as well have been cut from the same oak tree. That's why I know what's going to happen if I don't step in and speak my piece." She watched Cat shaking her head. "And, whether you'll admit it or not, you and I are alike. Sometimes I think we're too much alike. Your father says that's why we bicker with each other."

"How can you prove Hank will put business before his family?"

"You aren't going to like what I've done," Maude warned.

"What you've *done*? You did something *before* you talked to me?"

"It was the only way I could protect you, daughter." Maude stared blankly at the boat disappearing around a promontory in the lake. "You may think you'll never forgive me for it, but you will. Once you've gotten over Hank Collins, everything will be back to normal. You'll find a nice steady man."

Over Hank! "Mother, what have you done!" Cat jumped to her feet. The rocking chair teetered precariously back and forth. "Tell me."

"I'll tell you, but only if you give me your word you won't say anything or do anything to stop what's going to happen. You're going to have to act as though I haven't breathed a word of this to you."

Cat felt a cold sweat breaking out beneath the hair hanging down her back. "I can't do that!"

"Then I won't tell you. You'll just have to learn the way I did . . . the hard way." She impaled her daughter with a meaningful glare and folded her arms across her middle. "This will be a painful lesson, but at least I've made damned certain it won't last a lifetime."

"Whatever it is, I'll find out by asking Hank."

"He won't tell you, unless he's not the honorable man of integrity you say he is. He gave his word to your father over the telephone that he wouldn't. But even if he does break his word, one way or another the final outcome will be the same . . . you won't marry Hank Collins."

"Mother, I won't let you manipulate me."

"Then don't," Maude simply replied. She rocked forward. "All this talking has made me thirsty. I think I'll get a cold glass of lemonade. Would you like some?"

"You can't do this to me!"

Maude gave her a haunted smile. "I have to protect you from yourself, just like I did when you were little. You couldn't swim, but you wanted to jump in the lake like your brothers. I must have told you a dozen times to stay off the dock, that I didn't want you to drown. You ignored me. So, to keep you safe, I fenced off the dock. Your brothers could get over it, but you couldn't. Do you remember how furious you were with me? You threw one tantrum after another, but I didn't listen to your screams because I couldn't bear the thought of permanently losing you. I kept that fence up until you finished taking swimming lessons at the YMCA."

"I am not a child. You can't tie a rope around me to keep me safe from Hank."

"No. I wish protecting you was that easy." She arose from her chair. "While you're storming around your condo, giving me the silent treatment, just remember I did what I did because I love you."

Trailing her mother back inside, Cat felt utterly frustrated. "Dad will tell me what you've done."

"Will he? He's the one who brought fencing from the job site to bar off the dock. He wants you to be safe, too. I'll admit, we've fussed at each other over this. He fussed about the fence." Maude poured each of them a glass of lemonade. "But in the long run, when it comes to you kids, he backs me one hundred percent."

"There's one major difference between me and the kid trying to get on the dock. She thought the only way into the water was by jumping off the dock like her brothers. You could build a fence ten feet high now, but I'd get around it by wading into the lake."

"And you'd stop when you saw that you were in over your head?" She handed Cat the glass. "Take a good look at me if you need more visible proof, sweetheart. Admit that I'm right, before you're hurt.''

"Maybe we aren't as much alike as you believe. I look at you and I see good times, not hard times. I remember you taking all of us to the zoo.''

"It's free.''

"I remember fancy little dresses you made for me that were the envy of every little girl at school.''

"Because it's cheaper to make clothes than buy them.''

"I see all of us playing games on the living room floor in front of the fireplace.'' Cat leaned close to her mother. "I see a home that was filled with love.''

"You saw what we wanted you to see. We protected you from the ugliness. We're protecting you from it now.''

Cat sipped her drink; the tart yet sweet flavor matched the flavor of their discussion. Bittersweet. Her mother's viewpoint was bitter; Cat's was sweet.

"You love Dad.''

"Yes. I love him. But it wasn't always an easy kind of love. We had hellacious fights.''

"But looking back, wasn't it all worth it?''

Maude smiled. "I wished I'd marked the day on the calendar when I looked in the mirror and asked, 'Is this all there is?' and answered, 'It's enough. I'm happy.' I didn't. The point I've tried to make is that you never have to ask yourself that question. Find yourself—''

"A steady man, with a monthly paycheck and fringe benefits,'' Cat supplied for her, tired of hearing the same litany. "Well, I've looked for him, Mom. I honestly tried to find your Mr. Perfect, just like I did when I signed up for courses in college that bored me. I don't want to yawn my way through life because it's what you think will make me happy. If sharing my ups and downs with Hank Collins means riding through life on a roller coaster, I'll love every thrilling moment."

Maude shook her head regretfully. "You haven't heard a word I've said, have you?"

"I listened with my heart, Mom." She placed her glass on the counter, then moved her hand over her heart. "I don't know what you've done, but I know Hank Collins cares for me. And I care for him." Her hand moved until it rested on her mother's shoulder. "And I care for you, too."

Maude hugged Cat in her protective arms; Cat returned her hug with loving arms.

"I did what I had to do," Maude said softly.

"I know, Mom. I'm just doing what I have to do, too."

Later, while Cat skirted the lakeshore trying to catch sight of the men, wishing they'd taken her with them, it dawned on her that this was how her mother had chosen to protect her. Hank would ride off with the McGillis men and leave her standing on the front porch. Likewise, Hank would be part of their newly formed company, but she'd be excluded.

Cat plopped down on the shore, picked a blade of grass and thoughtfully chewed the end of it.

The whole family knew she hated being shut out of what they were doing together. Did they think by excluding her from McGillis and Collins that she'd take her anger out on Hank? Was this the wedge that would drive them apart? Had Hank given his word not to include her?

Thinking back, she remembered how reticent he'd been about discussing the partnership. Although he'd said he didn't mind having her as a boss, he only had one vote. The votes would be split, just as they'd always been.

Except that the Mean Musketeers and her sidekick, James, wouldn't have to listen to her carrying on. Hank would. But knowing what she did about Hank and his past, she figured he wouldn't see her persistence as her wanting to be included; he'd view it as her being ambitious.

She bit off the pale stem of the grass and spit it on the ground.

They'd counted on her strength to penetrate Hank's vulnerability. Eventually, with them working on him in the background and her confronting him daily, Hank would make his own conclusion that he didn't want to marry a woman like the one he'd divorced.

Very clever, Mom, she silently congratulated. Maude had made only one mistake. Cat decided she wasn't going to throw an adult version of a childish tantrum, demanding to be part of the new company. They could exclude her all they damn well pleased, but she wasn't going to open her mouth to Hank . . . other than to encourage him.

"Things are off to a good start," Joshua reported. "Would you pass some of that terrific coleslaw, Luke? Here, Hank, you have some, too. I noticed you ate two helpings the last time you were here."

Beneath the table, James nudged his sister's toe. As a peace offering he said, "We're going to alphabetically rotate who's president of the company. Hank has the toughest year, it being our first year in business. The rest of us are vice presidents in charge of our special areas."

Playing her role perfectly as the daughter who wants to be one of the guys, she said, "I could help write job descriptions."

Luke looked at Russell and they both laughed. Tom joined in, too.

"I'll just bet you'd like to make a list of things I should do," Luke said, chuckling. "Clean your truck. Polish your boots."

"Take out the trash," Russell chimed in.

"Mow your yard?" Tom asked, sniggering.

Cat glared at her brothers, hoping they'd choke on their next bite of food. She had to curb her sharp tongue and prove she could take their teasing without blowing her cork. Sweet as sugar she drawled, "You seem to have forgotten that Goldcoast considers me an extremely competent manager." Cat lifted her shoulders. "I just wanted to help. Goldcoast had a consultant write their job descriptions because the officers got into a squabble over who was supposed to do what."

"We're family," Joshua said. Grinning at Hank, he added, "Plus one. You might let him borrow those manuals."

"Can't. Copyright laws. Mother, could I have some more potato salad, please."

Maude passed the bowl to James who passed it down the line until it reached Cat. "You're all going to be too busy building those roof trusses Hank needs to worry about writing anything."

"We're stringing lights outside the storage shed." Joshua paused, savoring the smoked brisket. "None of us can shut down our jobs, so we'll be working nights."

"Cat said I have to be putting them up by Wednesday," Hank said. "We'll have to hustle. I might be able to talk some of my men into giving a helping hand. I'll pay them extra, but it'll have to be after I get a check from Butler."

"What about payroll on Friday?" Tom asked, his mouth half-full of beans.

"Please, son," Maude corrected, dabbing her mouth with a paper napkin.

"Sorry, Mom."

Hank came to Tom's rescue. "I can cover payroll for this week and next. Don't throw those beans away though. They may be all I have to eat."

"You can eat at my house," Cat offered.

"He won't have time for a sit-down dinner," Joshua contended. "None of us will."

"Thanks, Dad. I'm glad you included me."

"I didn't. You've got enough to handle at the Lemontree without working past midnight at the storage shed. Maude, do you remember those jobs I worked on out of town when the kids were little?"

She sure does, Cat thought, not showing that she was the least bit upset by her father restricting her from working with them. She wanted to stay in character by subtly pushing to be included, but they expected her to exert the most pressure on Hank.

"Sixteen hours a day. That's what we worked." He glanced around the table. "That's what you men are going to be doing, too. 'Course when you're out of town, missing your family, all you're thinking about is getting the job done so you can get home with money in your pocket. The older I got, the tougher it got to leave home." He smiled warmly at his wife. "Maude had the toughest job though—twenty-four-hour duty, seven days a week."

Maude returned his smile. Cat guessed at the bittersweet feelings her mother was disguising.

Unfolding his legs from under the table, Luke picked up his plate and headed for the kitchen. "I don't know about the rest of you, partners, but I'm going home to take a nap. Just listening to Dad has tuckered me out."

Russell and Tom exchanged man-to-man grins. "We'll help clear up the dishes, then we'll head home, too."

"What about dessert? Fresh strawberry shortcake," their mother tempted, sorry to see them leave early. "The hammocks are in the attic if you want to laze around here."

"I'm going to soak up the air-conditioning while I can," Russell replied.

Knowing full well her brothers were going back to their girlfriends, Cat grinned at Hank. Make our excuses, her eyes pleaded. He pressed his knee against hers in response.

"Yeah," Hank chimed in, "I hate to eat and run, but I need to make some phone calls to my men." The wistful look he gave Cat's mother was enough to soften the hardest of hearts. "Strawberry shortcake is my favorite dessert, too."

"This isn't a take-out restaurant, but I guess I could fix a bowl for each of you young men to take home. You, too, Cat."

"Great!" James enthused. "By the time I get to town I'll be hungry enough to eat two helpings."

Cat silently groaned. James was so transparent. He constantly dropped little hints, but Maude either didn't catch them or she purposely ignored them. Cat didn't know which.

On the way back to her condo, Cat dunked a strawberry in whipped cream and held it between her fingers in front of Hank's mouth.

"Mmm. Good." He bit the tip off the berry, then sucked the remainder into his mouth along with Cat's fingers. She started to withdraw her hand, but he reached up, snagged her hand and licked off the whipped cream.

"You've been awfully quiet since we left your parents' house. I thought you'd be ecstatic!"

"I'm happy for you." Uh-huh, she thought. My big brothers probably warned you that I'd pester you for details, not that Hank needed warning. She smiled happily at him. "Want another one?"

"It's every man's fantasy to have a beautiful slave girl hand-feed him."

"Grapes."

"Strawberries and whipped cream will do in a pinch." He opened his mouth. "I'm ready."

Her eyes lit with mischief. She raised another to his lips, teasing him by keeping it just out of reach. His tongue flicked out, missing the whipped cream.

"C'mon, little hellcat, don't tempt me or I'll pull over and make wild, passionate love to you."

Her heart skipped a beat. "Don't be impatient. Half the fun is anticipation."

"When you're around, I'm in a constant state of...anticipation."

Laughing, Cat pushed the berry into his mouth. "You're starting to sound like Geraldine."

"I wasn't making fun of her speech problem," Hank swiftly denied.

"Speech problem?" Cat chuckled. "Geraldine's problem doesn't have a thing to do with how she talks. I suspect her dramatic pauses are meant to be sexy."

"Since you mentioned her, how much have you told her about us?"

"Not much. She thinks you're hot stuff. I confirmed her opinion, but didn't go into details." She stressed the last phrase. "Which only goes to prove that men discuss their secrets more openly than women."

Hank glanced at Cat. She looked as innocent and helpless as a newborn kitten. He knew better. His Cat had claws, and she didn't mind using them. Her brothers didn't know she expected to be invited into the partnership; he did.

"We did discuss you."

"You discussed me with Geraldine?"

"Don't be obtuse, Cat. I meant the male portion of the McGillis clan, and you know it."

"Oh?" She rammed a berry between his lips. "I guess with the letter *C* alphabetically coming before *H*, that my name was mentioned then?"

"Your brothers agreed that you do have the most administrative experience, not to mention your education."

"And then you all voted and they skipped the first part of the alphabet?"

"Actually, no." He disliked hurting her feelings, but he had to tell her the truth. "Your Dad spoke up."

Cat recalled her mother's words—*Your father supports my decisions one hundred percent*—and wasn't surprised. Her brothers had been clued in, so they undoubtedly appeared to let their father sway their judgement and supported him. Five against one. Hank didn't stand a chance.

"What'd he say?" *As if I don't know already,* she silently added.

"Not much. Nothing derogatory." To his extreme delight, Joshua hadn't even mentioned the stipulation of breaking up with Cat before they'd consider saving his ass. "Your family admires what you've accomplished."

Very diplomatic, Cat mused. Not explicit, but diplomatic.

"That's nice."

Hank gave her a sidelong glance. Something didn't quite jell. She appeared to be uninterested. He'd expected her to be, at the minimum, mildly displeased. No, he reconsidered, he'd expected her to spit and hiss like a real hellcat!

"You're taking this extremely well."

Huh! Like hell I am. I'm just not going to let Mother manipulate me into making the wrong move with you! You're more important to me than ten McGillis and Collins companies.

"Remind me to cry on your shoulder, later," she dryly replied. "More strawberries?"

"Thanks." Suspicious that her mother had warned her of her father's intent, he asked, "What did you and your mother talk about while we were in the boat?"

"This and that."

"Could you be a little more explicit?"

"Mostly she reminisced about how tough things were when she and my father were first married. And how the two of us were alike."

Inwardly Hank cringed. "Nothing about the two of us kissing in front of her?"

"She suggested we should have made a few more stops on the way down the lane."

"A few more? We didn't make any."

Cat nibbled on his earlobe. She put her arm across his shoulder; her breast brushed against his arm. "We could park on one of the side roads now and make up for lost time. Is necking in your pickup truck one of your fantasies?"

"Not in broad daylight."

"There's a lot of untraveled roads between here and Houston." Her tongue flicked around the shell of his ear. "Don't you want to celebrate?"

His foot pressed down on the gas pedal. They were twenty minutes from her place, but he could make it in fifteen. Maybe less.

Chapter Eleven

"Hey, boss lady!"

"Yes?" Recognizing Bubba Clark's voice, Cat slowly turned around. She'd nicknamed him the Gray Ghost because he had the uncanny ability to disappear into thin air when she was anywhere in his proximity. She caught a glimpse of Hank as she waited for Bubba to catch up with her.

"I completely changed the wirin' on that circuit box. Did you notice?"

She'd paid the full amount of his bill. Did he think she'd done so without checking to make certain he'd carried out her orders?

"It looked fine. The building inspector passed it this morning." Since she'd also noticed his men had finished the next building ahead of schedule, she said, "Looks like your men are on a roll."

"I built a fire under them by promisin' them a bonus. I'm going to be pushin' wire up Hank's—" his teeth snapped together to bite off a crudity "—uh, Hank's rafters by Friday."

"Don't worry, Bubba." Good news must not travel as fast as bad news, she mused, grinning at the electrical subcontractor. "Hank will have those roof trusses on before you get there."

Bubba fell into step beside her, shortening his stride. "Butler Mills shipping them after all?"

"No."

"Found somebody locally, huh?"

She held her tongue. Let him have to ask Hank, she thought. "I don't care where he gets them from. I only care about your men and Flint's twiddling their thumbs while waiting on another subcontractor."

"He's a good man. I hated to see him with his feet held to the fire." He loudly cleared his throat. "You aren't so bad yourself. Me and the boys have been talkin' about what a fine job you've been doin', too."

Praise? From Bubba? Cautiously, she asked, "Are you having supply problems?"

"Hell, no. My supplier dropped the price of wire a couple of cents a foot. That's why I can offer a bonus. That, and I'm connectin' those boxes up myself. Did Geraldine tell you I gave her those insurance papers you asked for last week?"

"Yes. You're in good shape."

Bubba gave a heh-heh-heh chuckle and sucked in his stomach. "It's all the walkin' I been doin' lately. My wife—she's pregnant, you know—says I'm losin' weight and she's findin' it."

Grinning, Cat noticed the bright red suspenders he was wearing to keep his jeans up. Curious, she asked, "How many children do you have?"

"Two back in Oklahoma from my first marriage, and this is the third by my second wife." He pushed his hard hat back off his forehead and wiped his receding hairline. "She's a bit younger than I am."

"Five kids." She wondered if Bubba's divorce was caused by the roller coaster effect on his marriage. "My folks raised five kids. Expensive, huh?"

"Darn tootin'. My oldest boy—he's seventeen—is comin' to visit for the summer. Would you mind if he sort of tags along with me? He wants a car, real bad. His mother says he has to earn it, so I thought, if it's okay with you, I'd let him learn somethin' about his old man's business instead of him slingin' burgers."

"I don't have any objections." How could she? Her brothers had worked in construction to pay for their first cars. "You hire your own men, not Goldcoast."

He flexed his red suspenders with his thumbs. "Well, he's a good kid, but I'll keep a sharp eye on him. He won't be a problem to you. Good talkin' to you, Cat."

"Yeah. Same here."

Surprisingly, it had been good, Cat mused. For once, she hadn't had to chase him down. And for once he'd treated her as though she was a business associate instead of a not very bright female lost on a construction site.

"You aren't so bad yourself," she murmured, her smile growing wider as she quoted Bubba's earlier remark.

She circled the building where she'd seen Hank talking to his men. Yesterday he'd left her place before dawn. She'd had only an occasional glimpse of him since.

"Juan," she called, spotting one of Hank's men. "Have you seen Hank?"

"*Sí*, Señorita McGillis." He pointed his nail gun toward the back unit of the building. "He's talking to Pedro."

She nodded and looked in the direction Juan had pointed. Pedro was supposed to be at home recuperating from his accident. Easily sliding between the erected studs, she made a direct path to where she heard Hank's voice.

Not wanting to interrupt, she slowed her steps when she heard Hank say, "You can't work day and night when you've got a concussion. Why do you think I sent you home yesterday when you showed up at the lumber shed?"

"I'm okay, boss. You need me."

"Damned right I do, but what happens if you're walking the rafters, get dizzy, fall and break your fool neck?"

"No fall. No break neck," Pedro protested. "You need me."

She observed Hank put his arm around the smaller man's shoulders and escort him to the edge of the concrete slab. "I don't want to see your face until the doctor gives you a clean bill of health. *¿Comprendes, amigo?* You're too valuable for me to take a chance on having you get badly hurt."

"But, *patrón* . . ."

"No buts. You go on home, Pedro. Don't worry your aching head about the job or the roof trusses or your paycheck." Hank gave Pedro's shoulder a friendly squeeze. "There'll be plenty of work left to do when you get back."

Watching Pedro reluctantly depart, Cat admired Hank for putting his men's welfare ahead of his own interests.

"I think Pedro would give you his shirt if you asked for it," she commented, stepping out of the timber's shadows. She loved how his eyes lit up with pleasure when he turned around and saw her. "How'd it go yesterday?"

"Slowly. It's been a while since your brothers worked with wood."

It was said as a statement of fact, not a criticism, Cat realized. She nodded. "Too many bosses and not enough carpenters?"

"That, too." He returned her smile, feeling better just seeing her and hearing her voice. "Joshua threatened to put duct tape across their mouths if they didn't stop bickering."

"Wouldn't be the first time they've heard that threat." Knowing her father, she dropped her voice and mimicked, "All I want to hear is the sound of hammers striking nails. One more word out of any of you and I'll tape your mouths shut."

Without either of them being aware of it, they had closed the distance between them until they stood toe to toe.

Hank chuckled as he heard the precise words her father had bellowed, then leveled his eyes on her mouth. "I missed you."

"Good."

She doubted he'd had a spare moment to think of her. What her brothers lacked in speed and skill, Hank had probably made up for by working twice as hard. She had all she could do to keep from wrapping her arms around his waist and laying her head on his shoulder. Only where they were and the possibility of being seen kept her hands in her back pockets.

"Good?"

His eyes lowered to the fabric stretched tautly across her breasts. Remembering the lacy underwear she wore beneath her Goldcoast jumpsuit had his tongue raking against the roof of his mouth.

"You wouldn't want me to make you cocky by saying that I missed you, too, would you?" she teased lightly to cover up the effect his eyes were having on her. Her nipples puckered under his intent stare; she could feel them tighten.

"I don't think there is a cocky bone left in my body. They're too tired."

"You're welcome to use the whirlpool tub at my house." She dared to trace her finger along the edge of his unbuttoned shirt. "I give a mean message, too. Guaranteed to take the kinks right out of your muscles."

His skin quivered at her light touch. "Boss lady, if you don't remove those curious little paws from me, in two seconds flat we'll be on that pile of drywall over there doing something deliriously kinky."

Cat glanced over her shoulder as though she seriously considered his outrageous statement plausible. She rolled her impudent tongue in her cheek.

"Looks more comfortable than a bed of nails," she quipped. Her blue eyes sparkled with mischief. "Of course you'd have to let me be on top, just in case one of the men happened to notice us. I do have my position as boss around here to consider."

"Hilda Catherine McGillis, I think I'm going to borrow a roll of your father's duct tape."

She knew perfectly well what he meant, but chose to misunderstand him. Primly she said, "I think I ought to tell you, I'm not into S and M."

"Oh, but you are, sassy-mouth," he contradicted, reaching around her and giving her behind a swat. His hand lingered, soothing the curve of her derriere. "You'd better get out of here while I can still concentrate on my job or I'll be the one taking a nosedive off the rafters."

"I would, if you'd kindly remove your hand from my posterior." She grinned up at him and gracefully twirled out of his arms, which wasn't an easy accomplishment considering she was wearing boots and her hard hat. She backed away from him until she felt a two-by-eight between her shoulder blades. "Incidentally, to keep the records straight, I missed you, too."

He followed her to the front of the building, his heart gladdened by their short encounter.

Raising her voice in case anyone was listening, she said briskly, "You haven't turned in your bill, Collins. I'll expect it on my desk by noon if you want to be paid on Friday."

"About my bill." He stopped her by touching her elbow. "Any chance you can get Goldcoast to take Butler's name off this check? I don't owe them anything since they haven't delivered a shipment."

"I'll try." She hadn't told him she'd tried once before and Kent had refused to talk to the accounting department. "Don't count on it, though. You need to contact a lawyer, Hank."

"Tom offered to do that for me. I'll get in touch with him at lunch."

"You can use the phone in the office," she quietly offered. It seemed the least she could do to help him.

Hank stuck his hand in his pocket and jingled his coins. "And break one of Goldcoast's rules? Not me, boss lady. I'll use the pay phone."

Nodding, remembering the lecture she'd given him about his hard hat, she gave him a slight wave and strode back to the office trailer without a backward glance.

Much as she wanted to get one last sight of him, she did have to keep up appearances.

It rankled her that her whole family could pitch in and help Hank and she couldn't do a thing for him. She worried her bottom lip. Maybe she should go around Kent, straight to the head of the accounting department. With the news media coverage of the mill shutdown, she might be able to convince them to drop Butler's name off Hank's check.

She had her hand on the doorknob as she muttered, "It's only fair to ask."

"Ask me what?" Geraldine swiveled her chair toward Cat.

There's something different about Geraldine today, Cat noticed, then dismissed the thought. Automatically, she chafed her arms before she realized the room temperature wasn't subzero.

She closed the door behind her and replied, "Not you, the main office. Since Collins isn't getting his materials, I think it only fair to have the payee's name changed on his check."

"Good luck! You know how Goldcoast sticks to the rule book. Unless you can find a loophole, I don't think they're going to be accommodating." She handed Cat the daily bulletin from headquarters. "The decorators are in the display units. You might want to go down there. Oh yes, and the security guard company you called? They're mailing you a brochure of their services."

Cat studied Geraldine thoughtfully. They were wearing identical jumpsuits. It wasn't that. "Have you changed your hairstyle or something?"

"Nope." Her hand flew to her hair. "Should I? Do you think it's too curly?"

"I think it suits you." Cat shrugged. She had too much to do to discuss hairstyles. "I'd better read these. Once the decorator starts moving furniture into the display units I'll need a work order typed to send to the security guard service."

"I think you'd better read the bulletin first."

"Why?" She switched the bulletin to the top of the pile she had been handed and quickly skimmed over it.

"They've changed a couple of procedures. No more express mail. No more overtime for office employees. No more special work orders initiated on the job sites, unless they're approved by your immediate boss."

"Looks like Bubba isn't the only one tightening his belt," she mused aloud. A smile flitted across her lips as she read the directive concerning the thermostats in the general offices. "I don't think they meant the window air-conditioning units in the job site trailers, Geraldine. We don't have thermostats to turn down."

"No problem. I'm fine. If you're hot and bothered, you can turn it down."

Cat gave Geraldine a wary look. Was that a cardigan sweater hanging on the back of her chair? At lunch she'd definitely have to find out what had happened to Geraldine over the weekend. Right now, she had to call Kent about the security guard before she checked on the decorators.

"Give me five minutes to read through this bulletin, and then get Kent on the phone, would you?"

"You got it. Five minutes."

Geraldine had summed up the high points of the communication, but she'd overlooked an item on the back of the page. Goldcoast had hired a team of consultants who'd be starting at the top of the organizational chain and working their way down to individual job sites.

"Great," Cat muttered with sarcasm. That's what the subcontractors didn't need, more eyeballs going over their work. She'd have a few things to tell the consultants before they set foot in one of the Lemontree's buildings.

"Line two!" Geraldine bellowed. "Kent is in a meeting, but I think you'd better talk to his secretary."

"Cat McGillis speaking. I have decorators here. I need an okay on a special work order to hire a security guard."

"This isn't a good time to interrupt the meeting." Kent's secretary's voice trembled and dropped to a mere whisper. "All hell is breaking loose around here. People are getting fired left and right. I'm not going into the boardroom."

Rocking back in her chair, Cat asked, "The consultant group?"

"Yes," she hissed.

"How long do you expect the meeting to last?"

"Forever."

"Seriously."

"Forever," the secretary repeated, her voice remaining hushed. "The accountants are in there, too."

"You'd better take a message and leave it on his desk. Tell him I couldn't get in touch with him, so I took it upon myself to go ahead and hire a guard. I'm following standard operating procedure."

"Forget the procedures manual. They've been collected here in the office...and shredded!"

"If there's a problem, have him call me, immediately," Cat concluded. Feeling compassion for Kent's secretary, she added, "Hang in there. They can't get rid of everybody."

"Thanks. I'll put your message on top of the others."

Cat hung up the phone. The consultants started at the right place, she thought. The offices were impressive;

people strutted around looking dedicated, but anyone with a lick of sense knew the money earners were on the job sites. She could think of two or three people that qualified as deadheads who soaked up the profits and gummed up the works.

Goldcoast was one of the biggest multifamily builders in the entire country, with work sites in various stages from Miami to Seattle, from San Diego to New York City. She wasn't worried about her job, unless the consultants stopped firing the deadheads and started demoting them. That didn't particularly bother her, either. The ones she'd met hadn't worn a hard hat in decades. They'd quit the instant a drop of perspiration beaded their foreheads.

Getting back to her immediate tasks, she discarded the idea of discussing Hank's check with the payroll department. Asking for a favor from the accountants today would be like praying for rain in the Texas panhandle.

She was dialing the number of the company that supplied guards just as Geraldine brought in lunch. Glancing at her watch, she decided she'd call them later, instead, and put down the phone. Maybe Kent would call with an okay on the special order.

"Next week it's your turn to bring lunch," Geraldine reminded her. "I'm getting sick of rabbit food. Any chance you'll make some of your delicious chicken salad?"

"Sure." She could fix a couple of sandwiches for Hank, too, she thought, then remembered he hated chicken salad. "So how was your weekend?"

"Peaceful."

Cat took the packet of French salad dressing from Geraldine. "What happened to Mr. Hot, Hotter, Hottest?"

"I dropped him. I've met the man of my dreams."

"Anybody I know?"

Geraldine shook her head. "I doubt it."

"Where'd you meet him?"

"At church."

The bite of lettuce Cat had lifted toward her mouth stopped in midair. She tried to imagine Geraldine singing from a hymnal, but the picture was fuzzy.

"Well, not exactly at church. Mother had bridge at her house and insisted that I be a fourth."

"Fourth what?" Cat asked, forking the lettuce into her mouth. She felt at ease now that Geraldine was back to normal—not making sense. The fact that Geraldine's mother had built a bridge in her house didn't faze Cat. She'd been to her secretary's apartment.

"Bridge, as in card game played with four people at the table. Somebody got sick at the last minute so I filled in for them. Didn't they play bridge at the college you attended?"

"I didn't have time for card games."

Geraldine shrugged. "I didn't go to college. I just thought bridge and college went together like...Hank and Catherine?"

"Stop fishing for information and tell me about the man you've met."

"I didn't just meet him. I've known him since we were kids." Her brown eyes took on a dreamy glaze. "We were in the same Sunday school class. He kissed me in the back pew. I should have known then that our love was ordained from up above. He's a minister."

"You're dating a minister?"

"Why not?" Geraldine demanded, put on the defensive.

"I don't know. I just have trouble picturing you with a man of the cloth."

"Men are men. They come in different sizes and shapes, but basically they're men."

"Very profound, Geraldine. I had a philosophy teacher who made comments like that. Everyone thought he was brilliant."

"I'm smarter than I used to pretend. Mistakenly, I thought men preferred women who had great bodies and no brains." She gave Cat a sly smile. "I'm an excellent bridge player."

"You're an excellent secretary. I've yet to find a mistake you've made."

"I know. I'm exceptionally efficient."

Cat leaned across her desk and patted Geraldine on the back.

"Why'd you do that?"

"I didn't want you to break your arm doing it yourself," Cat teased. "My 'exceptionally efficient' secretary needs both hands to continue being 'exceptionally efficient.' "

"I had you . . . fooled." She fanned her eyelashes and gave Cat a blank look. "You believed every erotic tale I spouted, didn't you?"

"That's it!" Cat said, realizing what was different about Geraldine. It wasn't how she looked; it was her speech pattern. "You aren't pausing before the last word of every sentence."

"Pauses, followed by double entendres are very, very . . ."

"Ditzy?"

"Sexy," Geraldine corrected. She raised both hands palms upward. "Maybe a little ditzy, too."

"I like the real Geraldine," Cat said sincerely.

"So does my beau. I think this is I-T for me."

"Wedding bells? Long white dress? Flower girls?"

Geraldine nodded to each question. "I love him."

"Does he feel the same?"

The phone buzzing stopped Geraldine. She swallowed, then picked up the receiver. "Goldcoast. Can I help you?" She held the phone away from her ear.

"Put Cat McGillis on the line. Now!"

Geraldine banged the mouthpiece on Cat's desk, twice, then handed it to her. "Nobody yells at me!" she mouthed.

Holding the receiver at arm's length, Cat grinned as both of them listened to a long string of vicious expletives.

"Good afternoon to you, too, Kent," Cat purred.

"Sorry. I'm having one hell of a Monday! Those goddamned son of a bitch consultants have been picking my brain until it's mush. My secretary just threw my messages in my face and ran out the front door in tears." Kent took a deep breath. "There's no such thing as a special order around here anymore!"

"How do I go about making arrangements for security guard services?"

"You don't. If those prissy-assed decorators want somebody to look after their furniture all night, let *them* hire a guard!"

"And if they refuse?"

"Lock the doors!"

"This place is deserted at night. The thieves will have to start a lottery to decide which one of them gets the furnishings!"

"That's why we have insurance. The cost analyst says rent-a-cops are a waste of money."

"That's asking for trouble."

"They're the experts. If you don't believe me, ask them. And after you do, they'll fire you for asking dumb questions."

"I don't want trouble at the Lemontree."

"Listen to me, Cat, you'd better follow my example and sit tight, with your mouth shut. Don't ask questions. Don't volunteer information. That's the only way to survive."

She heard him mutter an obscenity under his breath, then the line went dead.

"Trouble in Austin?" Geraldine asked.

"Trouble at the Lemontree. How much money is in the discretionary fund?"

"Petty cash account? I'd have to look, but the only thing I've paid out of it is those small bills the subcontractors turned in to fix the fire damage."

"That's another good reason to hire a guard." Cat had lost her appetite; she pushed her salad to the center of the table. "We may not be able to afford the guys with the fancy brochure, but I'll find somebody to keep an eye on things."

"I don't think you should," Geraldine advised. "Kent sounded...emphatic. I could hear every foul word he screamed."

"What you heard won't compare with what he'll say if something goes wrong on this job. He won't need the telephone. You'll be able to hear him scream all the way from Austin."

"Cat, there never was much money in that account. I know I only have to make a quarterly report on it, but you're taking a big chance countermanding Kent's direct order."

"He may not be working there in three months. From the turmoil going on, I may not be here in three months, but by damn, the Lemontree will be here. I'll make certain of that!"

Chapter Twelve

You could at least call me after you finish at the lumber shed, Cat wanted to scream at Hank. She forced a smile. "What time did you quit last night?"

"Your brothers went home around midnight."

Hank's hand moved to his hard hat, but, too fatigued to complete the effort, he dropped it limply to his side. He felt drained. For two weeks he'd lived on fast food and no sleep. Roof trusses and his men's payroll; those were the only thoughts keeping his adrenaline pumping. And Cat, always Cat. He couldn't let her down.

"What time did you go home?"

"Who knows? One. One-thirty. Your dad and I stayed and put the electrical tools away."

Tired, unable to concentrate, his mind wandered. While they were putting the tools away, Joshua had answered several of the questions that had bothered Hank.

Why, Hank had asked, did you want me to agree to stop seeing Cat before you offered to help me? Joshua had replied with his own question. Why did you refuse?

Hank's answer had been simple. Cat meant more to him than a stack of wood. Joshua's reply had been complex. He'd done it out of respect for Maude's ambitions for her only daughter. Between the Wednesday when he'd spoken to Hank on the telephone and made the first offer, and the Saturday when he'd removed the stipulation that Hank break up with Cat, he and Maude had had a royal battle. Maude wanted what she thought was best for Cat; he'd wanted Cat to make her own decisions. He seldom countermanded Maude's decisions—after all, he'd been gone for weeks on end while his kids were growing up, but Joshua felt Hank and Cat complemented each other. Just as he and Maude were two halves of a whole; so were his daughter and Hank.

Hank felt Cat shaking his arm. He dug the heels of his hands into his sunken eye sockets.

"I'm awake. I was checking out my eyelids for nail holes. Something has to account for this burning sensation." He focused his eyes on Cat, gathering his thoughts as he asked, "Did you ever get hold of the accounting department at Goldcoast?"

"It's still in an uproar there. New policies are being sent out daily. Then the next day, the new policies are rewritten and shipped out again. I don't think they know their left hand from their right. It's a mess. Did you talk to Tom's lawyer? It's more than time."

Hank felt his head reel. He propped his shoulders against a concrete block fire wall. "Time. Hell, it's been two weeks. I don't know how the hell I'm going to make payroll next Friday. My bank account is tapped dry. I can't believe Goldcoast keeps shipping my checks to Butler Mills!''

"Hank!" She had to shake his arm again to get his mind back on her question. "Tom's lawyer. What did he say?"

"He contacted Butler's lawyers. Butler's people say this will be over in a couple more weeks or they'll close down the mill permanently. Since they've broken the agreement and I'm providing the lumber and building the trusses, they're willing to issue a check."

"Thank goodness. Did you tell them to express-mail it to you?"

"They're computerized." Hank sighed. "The computer operator changed the password to access the files just before she went on strike. Without the password the new accounts manager can't get into the computer's bank file."

"They'll get it to you by next Friday, won't they?"

"Hell. Who knows?" Hank yawned. "God, I need a good night's sleep. I drop into bed like a ton of bricks and my mind keeps spinning. The alarm seems to ring before I doze off."

Her heart went out to him. He looked exhausted. Red-rimmed eyes, sagging shoulders.

Along with her heartache, her temper simmered, rapidly approaching the boiling point. Her family had to see what they were doing to him. Her brothers should have stayed to help store the electrical tools. They were shirking part of the work, taking advantage of Hank.

Cat sighed in frustration. Only the realization that her brothers probably looked in just as bad shape stifled her impulse to call them and ream them out! She couldn't fault them for helping the man she loved.

She wanted to volunteer to take Hank's place on the night shift. But she knew he'd refuse her offer. It must be part of the bargain he'd made with her family. The only satisfaction she had was knowing her mother's little plot to manipulate her future was failing.

"Tomorrow, as promised," Hank mumbled, "the next flatbed truck will deliver enough trusses for the next building."

Through bleary eyes he watched Cat worry her lip. Her bad habit, the one that always made him want to kiss away her problems, should have caused a flicker of desire to hammer through him.

But why would it? he mused. He felt dead from the neck downward.

His eyes closed. He'd rest for a minute, let Cat's voice wash over him, revive him. Just for a couple of minutes, then he'd have the vitality to get back to work.

"Hank?" Cat softly called. They'd been together less than five minutes and he'd fallen asleep? Standing up? That does it, Cat thought. Hank could scream and yell, stomp his feet and pull out his hair, but she was taking him to her place.

Quietly she moved to the far side of the building where his men were working. The nail guns jetting out sixpenny nails made a cracking noise that should have woken a dead man. She glanced over her shoulder. Hank remained slumped against the wall.

She motioned to Pedro to join her.

"I'm taking Mr. Collins home. Can you take care of everything here for him?"

"*Sí!*"

"Are you going to the work shed tonight?"

"Boss won't let me, but my cousins will be there."

She was about to arrange for one of Pedro's cousins to tell her brothers that Hank was asleep on his feet and she'd be covering his share of the work, but decided against it. No, she would do her dirty work personally. She could wield a hammer better than most men. If they didn't like it, they could get in line behind Bubba, Kent and Maude to file their complaints.

"Tell them I'll see them there."

She bit into her lip as she suddenly realized she couldn't go to the shed; she'd promised the new night watchman she'd hired that she'd walk him around the job site. She couldn't be two places at once.

"Is there something else I can do?" Pedro asked. "Everybody works. I go home an rest. Makes me feel bad, like I'm not doing my share to help Mr. Hank. He's been so good to me and my family. I wish I could do something, anything, to help him."

"Me, too." A bright idea came out of nowhere. The man Hank trusted the most could help. "While I take Hank's place building the trusses, would you do something for me?"

Pedro's face brightened. *"Sí!"*

"The man I hired to patrol the Lemontree at night quit. A new man is being sent out to take his place. Would you mind staying around here until he arrives?" *If* he arrives, Cat thought, her lips compressing into a tight line.

"No, Señorita McGillis. I'll stay."

The temporary agency hadn't been certain they could replace the watchman who'd quit on such short notice. Cat removed her key ring from the front of her jumpsuit. Flipping through the keys she found the one to unlock the building with the display units.

"Here's the key to Building 1. It's furnished. If the new watchman doesn't arrive, would you mind spending the night there?"

Pedro shook his head; Cat felt her heart sink when he refused to take the key.

"New furniture?" His hands gestured from his sweat-stained work clothes to the sawdust on his boots. "No, I'll have my wife bring me a sleeping bag." He grinned. "I sleep under the stars, like in Mexico when I was a boy."

Relieved, Cat extended the key toward him. Pedro backed away. "You're sure?" she asked.

"*Sí*, I watch Lemontree. You help Mr. Hank. It's . . . what you say, good deal?"

Cat grinned at Pedro's mastery of American slang. "Yeah, it's a good deal, Pedro. Take the key, though. There's no furniture in the upstairs apartments. It won't bother you to go in one of them to wash up, will it?"

Reluctantly, Pedro held out his hand. "I be careful not to make a big mess."

"Use the phone in the back display unit if you need to call your wife, Pedro. And thanks, I really appreciate your help."

"No thanks needed. You help me to help Mr. Hank. Make me feel better." His dark skin accentuated the whiteness of his teeth when he gave her a big smile.

"I'd better get your boss into my truck. I'm leaving his truck here, so keep an eye on it, would you?"

"No problem. Do you need help with him?"

They both turned to the place where Hank had dropped to his haunches, folded his arms around his legs and used his knees as his pillow.

"I'll take care of him."

Like Pedro, Cat began to feel better, too. If she had to carry Hank piggyback the two blocks to her condo, her determination to help him would give her the strength to do it.

"Can't go to bed," Hank mumbled, sleepwalking to her bed. "Got to get over to the timber shed."

Brute dodged around his feet, happy to see him.

"It's taken care of, Hank."

She put her finger to her lips and patted the pillow, motioning for Brute to keep quiet and to get up on the bed, which was a special treat for the poodle.

Tail wagging, hind end shaking with delight, Brute scrambled onto the bed. He rested his head on his forepaws. Eyes round, he blinked at his second most favorite person as though he didn't understand what was going on.

"Payroll Friday. Need time." The back of Hank's knees touched the edge of the bed; he crashed into the softness of her bed like a mighty oak falling into a pile of oak leaves. "No time. Broke."

Cat unlaced his boots, gently tugged them off his feet and placed them at the end of her bed. Quietly moving to the closet, she pulled a spare blanket from the cedar chest to cover him. She could hear his breathing, slow and deep and regular.

As she tucked the covers around him, she watched his face. To her, he was beautiful, puffy eyes, wrinkled brow and all. Lightly she brushed his forelock off his face, touched the stubble of dark whiskers on his cheeks. Reflexively, his head turned toward the soothing coolness of her hand.

She more than cared for Hank. She loved him. In sickness and in health, for richer or poorer. She wanted to cherish and protect him. She would love him until death parted them, and beyond that point. Slowly, she straightened, realizing the source of the familiar phrases.

"I do love you," she whispered, backing away from the bed.

The impulse to curl up beside him, to magically let her strength pour into him, pulsed through her. She stifled the urge.

She knew that when he wakened he would instantly resent her for kidnapping him and putting him in her bed. His strong work ethic and sense of fairness would make him feel guilty about not carrying his share of the load. Once she told him that she'd substituted for him, at least part of the guilt he felt would be vanquished.

She'd taken care of Hank and her responsibilities at the Lemontree. Now she had to get over to the lumber shed.

"You watch over him, Brute," she mouthed. "Stay here."

Turning, she tiptoed from her bedroom, silently closing the door. Her mind instantly flashed to what was ahead of her. If, as she surmised, her family had plotted to exclude her from working with them, it logically followed that they wouldn't welcome her help with open arms.

As she drove to the work area, she mentally fought the imaginary dragons she'd have to face—all five of them, her brothers and her father.

Since her dad was following her mother's plans to split her and Hank apart, he'd be honor bound to dissuade her from helping Hank. Talk wouldn't stop her. She could turn a deaf ear to him while she worked.

Her brothers were an entirely different matter. Tom and Luke would have no qualms about physically ejecting her from the property. They'd certainly had no problems with physically removing her from their rooms when they were kids.

"Well, boys, we aren't kids," she muttered with determination.

Her jaw clenched; her hands held the steering wheel so tightly her knuckles turned white. For Hank's welfare, she'd kick, fight and scream bloody murder if they tried to pick her up bodily and remove her.

Her eyes dropped to the handle of the small "shark-killer bat" James had given her as a joke the day she'd first started working on a construction site. "A friendly persuader," he'd teased as he'd shoved it under the seat. "With your sharp tongue, though, you'll probably never need it."

She smiled grimly. James would pass out if she pulled it out and threatened to use it on him and her other brothers!

Steering her truck to the right, she followed the dirt road leading to the lumber shed. As she drove closer, she could hear the buzz of the power saws slicing through slabs of wood. She sniffed the clean fragrance of cut pine through the open windows.

A band of scrub brush circled the cyclone-fenced area, obstructing her view of the workers. She parked between Russell's and Tom's trucks, thinking, "They're all here." Had only James and her father been here, her job of convincing them to let her help would have been a whole lot easier.

She shoved her Goldcoast hard hat on her neatly bound hair, grabbed the carpenter's belt off the back of her truck and strode purposefully to the double gate as she buckled the belt at her waist. They must have spotted my truck, she thought, hearing the whir of saw biting into wood gradually grind to a stop.

"What the heck are you doing here?" Tom bellowed, glancing at Joshua, who'd dropped his hammer and was rapidly walking toward her. "We sure don't need you around telling us what to do."

Cat yanked the hammer from her belt loop, sidestepped around her father and kept right on marching toward the pile of mitered wood stacked where her father and James had been working. Her eyes flashed blue bolts of lightning, daring any and all to try to stop her from helping Hank.

"Welcome aboard the train leading to Exhaustionville," James muttered, moving to one side to make room for her. "Hank's collapsed, right?"

She nodded. Good ol' James, she mused. We're still sticking together. From behind her she heard her father's footsteps.

"What took you so long to get here?" Joshua asked. "I expected you to show up last weekend."

Cat filled one pouch with nails from a cardboard container as she replied, "No one asked me to join this partnership. I figured my being excluded was part of Mother's plan to split up Hank and me."

She saw her father glance at James, who became extremely anxious to get back to work. Though not a word was spoken, she could almost hear her father demand, *Did you blab?*

Selecting a nail, she joined two timbers together with one sure stroke. Shooting straight from the lip, she said stubbornly, "That ain't gonna happen! Hank has worked until he's dropped—in my bed. I'm here to help him and nobody, I repeat, nobody is going to stop me."

Other than the *k-whack* of her hammer driving another nail, there was no sound. For several long seconds, Cat was certain she could have heard a pin drop into the sawdust.

Then she heard her father shout, "What's going on here? Just because your sister's arrived, it doesn't mean this has turned into a social gathering. Let's stop lolly-gagging around and get busy!"

During the next two hours each nail she drove, she drove for Hank, swiftly and surely. Each piece of lumber she balanced on her shoulder, toted and put into place was one piece less weighing down on his back. Each fabricated roof truss she watched being loaded on the flatbed truck gave her the same sense of accomplishment that Hank would have felt.

She grew increasingly hot, sweaty and dirty, but she didn't notice the grime. Tomorrow she'd feel it in her knees and across the muscles of her shoulders, but tonight she performed like a well-oiled machine. All for Hank.

"Hey, sis, take a break, would you?" James said, unable to keep up with her production rate. "We can't get all of them finished in one night!"

The note of admiration she heard in his weary voice broke through her focused concentration. Hunkering down, she let her bottom drop to the ground. Her arms supported her aching back by wrapping around her legs.

"I don't know about you, but my mouth tastes like I've planted a box of toothpicks in my stomach." He pulled a handkerchief from his back pocket and blew his nose to rid himself of the minuscule pieces of sawdust he'd breathed in. "I need to water them to get them growing. Want a cup?"

"Yeah. That'd be great," she answered, smiling. His reference to the toothpicks growing had sparked a memory of the watermelon-eating contests her brothers had had when they'd been teenagers.

James always won because he never took time to spit out the seeds. The whole family had teased him. Maude would pat his swollen belly, warning him that he'd have watermelon vines sprouting from his ears if he didn't quit swallowing the seeds.

Cat wondered how her mother remembered that incident. Swiping a damp strand of hair off her neck, she had difficulty understanding how she only remembered the good times and Maude saw them as hard times.

Was the difference in how they perceived this kind of incident due to the age difference, Cat wondered, or to her own self-confidence and spirit of optimism? She had to admit, she and her mother did share many personality traits. Was her mother's lack of education and of time to dream the barrier that made it impossible for them to communicate?

Her memory flew to her college years. In her endeavor to find an "acceptable" vocation, she'd taken a few psychology courses. She recalled something that Zany Zinfield, her psych professor, had said in class. A woman marries a man like her father, and if she takes a lover, he will have the same personality traits as her mother. Back then, along with her unbelieving classmates, she'd laughed.

Her gaze moved to where her father sawed lumber. Maybe her teacher had been closer to the truth than she'd realized, she mused. Hank was like Joshua—hardworking, honest, capable. They both had tough exteriors that shielded a vulnerable heart. And they'd both been through rough times.

Cat loved her father devotedly. She knew without a doubt there would be no lovers in her life. She loved Maude, but there were times when she did not like her.

Since there were similarities among the four of them, she speculated on her future with Hank. Thirty years from now, if they married, would she be manipulating her daughter? Would she be the one determined to prevent her daughter from following the path in life that she'd chosen?

Cat didn't have the answers to her own questions. Forecasting future behavior was Zany Zinfield's specialty.

"We're so similar, and so damned different," she mumbled.

"Only crazy people talk to themselves," James tormented good-naturedly, handing her a large paper cup. "Since I know you're sharper than a carpet tack, talk to me."

She drank thirstily from the cup. The water wet her throat; the taste of fresh lemon quenched her thirst.

Cat chuckled. "If I tell you what I was thinking about, you'll book reservations for me in a padded cell."

"Crazy in love?" he prompted. "That eventually happens to all of us . . . if we're lucky."

"When are you going to tell Mother about Grace?" she asked, diverting her thoughts from her own problems to James's problem.

James knew his sister too well to fall for that tactic. He scooted closer to her to keep from being overheard. "Let's talk about you and Hank Collins."

"I love him. I want to marry him, if he'll have me . . . and if I can keep Mother's little strategy to split us up from working."

"Bam!" James said, pounding his fist against his palm. "You always hit the nail right on the head, don't you?"

"No. Sometimes I miss." She glanced at the stacks of lumber in the shed. "Mother told me she had some trick hidden up her sleeve, but I wouldn't let her maneuver me into promising not to divulge her 'secret plan' to Hank. I should have come here sooner, like Dad said, but I've been too busy second-guessing Mother.''

She leveled her eyes on a pair of eyes as blue as her own. "Maude thinks I'll nag at Hank to be part of McGillis and Collins until he walks out on me, doesn't she?''

James slammed his fist into his hand again, but compressed his lips together.

"I won't bedevil Hank, dear brother, but I don't mind harassing you.''

His eyes dropped, then slowly made a circuit around where their brothers and father worked.

"We've always stuck together, James. You tell me what's going on.''

"You won't like it." He downed the remains of his water, wishing it was something stronger. "You won't like it one damned bit.''

"You're probably right. But if you don't help me, I have this gut fear that I'll lose Hank.''

James nodded. His mouth twisted in distaste for the unpleasant truths about to pass through his lips. "You're wrong about the 'secret plan' Mother instigated. At least, excluding you so you'd henpeck Hank to death wasn't discussed before Dad called your place and talked to Hank.''

Cat leaned closer to James, until their shoulders touched. When her brother hesitated and glanced furtively around the area, she prodded, "Yes? Go on.''

"Dammit, Cat, they'll have my hide if they find out I told you what's going on.''

She ran her finger over her lips, then crossed her heart—the same gesture of sworn silence they'd made as children.

James took a deep breath, then blurted, "Joshua offered our help to Hank, but only if he broke up with you. You know how Mom feels about you dating someone in the trades. Dad is just going along with her... as usual."

Appalled that her family had dared to make such a despicable offer, flabbergasted that Hank must have accepted it, Cat dropped back on her elbows as though she'd been struck a deadly blow. Her mouth opened and closed, opened and closed before she could think straight.

"Let me finish, for crying out loud, before you go off half-cocked. On the phone, Hank turned the offer down, without a second thought."

Cat sat up again, and her hand grabbed James's shoulder for support. "He did?"

"Absolutely."

"Then what happened?"

James hung his head. "The whole thing made me sick to my stomach. After Dad told us Hank's answer and hung up the phone, everybody starting shouting at once. I left."

"You left? You mean you don't know if they badgered Hank into changing his mind?"

James nodded. "I guess I should have stayed, but I didn't want to be a part of their scheme. Hank hasn't been acting differently toward you, has he?"

Her mind raced back over the past couple of weeks. She tried to recall specifics of how Hank *had* treated her. He hadn't spent a night with her; he'd been working. They'd spoken to each other on the job, but hell, she was his boss! He had to talk to her.

Had he hugged her? Kissed her? Made any show of affection?

No. No. No!

He'd yawned in her face! And she'd felt sorry for him!

Her hands knocked the hat off her head as her fingers scissored through her hair. She blinked her eyes, to keep tears from spilling down her cheeks. She couldn't recall one single instance when Hank had reached out to her!

She'd only clung to him!

She had to accept the harsh truths: The roof trusses had been delivered to the Lemontree. Hank had sold out to her family. His ambition to succeed had superseded his love for her!

And last of all, she realized her mother had won the test of wills.

She clambered to her feet; her knees trembled as she fought for balance. Her face lost all vestige of color.

Hurt by her family's betrayal, Hank's betrayal, she had to mentally give herself a shaking. Her pain-filled eyes glanced from the hammer Joshua had given her as a gift to the men who'd not only molded her past and present life, but ruined her future.

"Cat? Are you okay?" James asked when she didn't answer his question.

Zombielike, she turned to stare at James, her eyes devoid of emotion. "I'm going home."

"Now? I thought..."

"Thought I'd stay? After you made me aware that the only people in the world I love have betrayed me?" The tears she could no longer contain streamed down her face. Angry with herself for losing her composure, she scrubbed the droplets away with the back of her hand. "I think not."

"I'll take you home. You're too upset to drive," James offered, walking beside her.

"I can make it on my own."

I can make it on my own? That has to be the biggest fib I've ever told...and to no one's benefit, which makes it a damned lie! I'm dying on the inside. My body just hasn't been notified yet!

"You're in an emotional turmoil. I don't think it's wise to drive," James said.

Her head jerked toward him. The concern she witnessed on his face did not register in her brain.

"Wise?" A hurt-filled laugh clawed its way up her throat. One hand lifted, fingers curled and uncurled, as though she could hold on to the air around her for support. "I'm not wise, James. I'm the biggest goddamned fool in Texas. But I'm driving home...alone."

She blocked him when he opened the driver's door and started to get in. Pushing against his chest with the strength of her building anger, she warned, "One well-placed knee and you won't have to worry about your love life, either, James Joshua McGillis. Step aside. I mean it. And don't even consider following me. Got it?"

It could have been the threat or it could have been the look in her eyes that caused James to step away from her truck.

"Dad'll come after you when I tell him—"

"Not one word, James. I have something to take care of before I speak to any of them."

The "thing" she planned on taking care of was getting Hank Collins out of her bed...and forever out of her life.

Chapter Thirteen

Neither Brute nor the brute she loved stirred when Cat entered her bedroom. She stared down at Hank, who was sleeping peacefully snuggled up to her pillow. Devastated by hurt and anger, she hadn't been able to think clearly enough to decide on what course of action she'd take once she arrived home, although she'd considered several during the drive.

You could be a lady, she thought. Wake him up and docilely ask him to leave. When he asks questions, refuse to answer them. That was how a lady born and raised in the South with genteel manners would react.

To a man who'd dumped her for financial gain?

Not this lady, Hilda Catherine McGillis decided.

Nor was she capable of extreme physical violence. She was fighting mad, but she recoiled against the thought of deliberately injuring someone she loved. Too much blood, too much mess, too many years in prison paying for the crime, she rationalized.

And yet, it infuriated her to be in such a wild emotional upheaval while she watched him lie in her bed peacefully sleeping. She wanted him wide-awake. Instantly!

Utterly frustrated with herself for doing nothing to vent her anger, she reached down and pinched his nose. Hard.

Hank's eyes flew open. His heels sprang straight upward; his legs bounced as they rebounded on the mattress. Astonished, momentarily disoriented by the sharp pain, he thought he'd been stung by a bumblebee. Expletives peppered the air as Brute yapped in his ears and jumped back and forth on his shoulders.

He saw Cat. Or he thought he saw Cat. She looked more like an avenging angel. Why was she pushing him, rolling him off the bed?

"Stop it!" His shout was muffled when his face pitched into the pillow. The coverlet wrapped around him. Arms at his sides, he felt like a damned mummy. The next thing he knew, he was facedown on the carpet. "Stop it!"

"Get out! Get out of my house and don't you ever, ever, ever come back! Me ambitious? That's like J.R. on *Dallas* accusing his brother of being ambitious. Out! Out! Get him, Brute! Sic 'im!"

The jarring ring of the phone had Cat crawling backward across the width of the bed. If this is a member of my family, she thought viciously, they're gonna get it, too! She swiped loose strands of hair back from her face.

"Hello!" she shouted. Her heart pumping, chest heaving, ragged breaths blowing into the mouthpiece, she could hardly hear the voice of the person speaking to her. "Hello!"

"Boss lady?"

"Yes!"

"Come quick. Bring Mr. Hank. Somebody is sneaking around here."

"Pedro? Are you at the Lemontree? Didn't the night watchman arrive?" The line clicked. "Pedro?"

The project was less than a mile away, she thought, grabbing her truck keys, racing through the bedroom. She glanced briefly at the tangle of arms and legs sprouting from under her bedding. He'd slow her down by wanting explanations, she hastily decided, hurrying through her condominium and out the front door.

Bitterly, she blamed Hank Collins for whatever problem there was at the job site. Knowing how deceitful he'd turned out to be, he'd probably been the one who'd instigated it!

Hopping into her truck, she started the engine, slammed the gears into reverse and burned rubber backing down the driveway. She hunched over the steering column and threw the truck into forward.

Her thoughts traveled faster than the truck she whipped around corners at fifty miles an hour. Pedro! Hank's lead man! Hank was the one who had "discovered" the small fire! Fire! Hank's money problems! Insurance! Oh Lord, had she assigned the fox to guard the chicken house? No, if she had, Pedro wouldn't have called her.

She fought the wheel as she turned onto the main street that led to the Lemontree. She cut the corner too closely. The rear wheels bouncing over the curb caused the truck to buck like a renegade bronco. Overcompensating, she swerved into the oncoming lane. Twin beams of light blinded her. Reflexively her foot moved from the gas pedal to the brake. Yanking the steering wheel in the opposite direction, she swerved back into her lane.

Air whooshed from her lungs as she realized how close she'd come to having a head-on accident. Calm down, she ordered. A dead woman isn't going to stop vandals on the job site.

"No, Hank's innocent, he's not involved," she muttered between her teeth. She couldn't believe that of him. He'd dumped her because this job was important to him. He took too much pride in his work to destroy it. No, whatever he might have done to her, he was innocent of this.

Then who? Who could be sneaking around the apartments? An electrician? Plumber? Drywaller? Roofer? A disgruntled laborer? Kids out having fun? It could be any one or all of them!

She realized she was pointing her finger at all the subcontractors as though she were playing Russian roulette. She had to know for certain this time. She not only had to stop them, she had to catch them. Had to be able to identify them.

As she came close to the entrance, she slowed down and turned off her headlights. Her eyes blinked to adjust to the darkness. Moonbeams lit the road, distorted by the limbs of the giant overhanging oaks.

Eerie, she thought. A rash of goose bumps shivered down her spine. Stop being a ninny, she chided sternly. You know this apartment project like the back of your own hand.

Her eyes swept from right to left, searching for anything unusual. Two trucks parked on the unpaved lot, she observed. She couldn't tell what color they were, but she felt certain one was Hank's and the other Pedro's. Mentally, she struck teenagers out having fun off her list of vandals. The trucks would have deterred a bunch of kids.

Unless they used the back road into the project, she amended, and didn't see the trucks.

She drove as close to the building housing the display units as possible, hoping no one had detected her presence. Shutting off her engine, she located her flashlight, pulled the shark-bat from under the seat and as quietly as possible got out of her truck.

Crickets chirped, a mockingbird called, a light breeze whispered through the timbers Hank's men had built. Her heart thudded in her chest; to her, it sounded louder than the night's noises.

Should she turn on the flashlight? Would anyone skulking around spot the strong beam of light? She decided not to turn it on, not yet. Her eyes strained to see into the blackness.

Cautiously, she crept from tree to tree, steadily moving toward the building, staying off the ribbon of concrete sidewalk. Through the soles of her boots she could feel the squares of newly planted sod.

The landscapers must have finished leveling and grading after I left. Where's Pedro? The thoughts had barely flickered across her mind when she stumbled over a mound. She heard a groan. Retrieving her balance, she turned and cupped her hands around the flashlight to see what she'd tripped over.

Fear ricocheted through her. She hadn't stumbled over a pile of dirt. Pedro lay sprawled facedown in the grass. A trickle of blood oozed from a scalp wound. She dropped to her knees beside him.

"Pedro?" Her voice sounded thin, harsh in her ears.

As gently as possible she grabbed Pedro by his shoulders and rolled him over. She hunched over him protectively, after glancing over her shoulder, expecting at any moment to feel a blunt object crashing against her skull.

He's breathing, unconscious, but breathing. She had to get help.

Get to the phone, call an ambulance, she thought. Automatically her hand reached to her belt. She touched the loop where she normally kept her keys. Nothing! In her mindless rush to find out what was happening, she must have left them back in the truck.

"Pedro?" She'd given him the key to the display apartment in the building behind her. "Where's the key? I've got to call an ambulance."

A crashing noise coming from inside the building distracted her from searching Pedro's pockets. Killing the beam of light, she picked up the bat, stooped low and moved closer.

Her frown deepened. The double door stood wide open. Had Pedro left the door open when he heard the prowler, or had the prowler banged Pedro over the head and taken the key?

Whatever he did, he must think he's safe, she silently speculated. She made a dash for the side of the building near the open door. To her own ears, her boots pounding on the packed earth made enough noise to be heard from the Lemontree to China.

While she tilted her head to one side, she unlaced her boots and removed them. She heard something that sounded like splashing liquid . . . and someone whistling through his teeth.

The empty corridor must be acting like an echo tunnel, she mused, amazed by how clearly she could hear.

She crept into the entry, flattening her body against the wall. Three doors on each side of the hall. The intruder could be in any one of them. The textured drywall caught at the fabric on the back of her uniform as she inched toward the back apartment on the first floor.

What's that smell? she wondered. Why did her shirt feel wet where it had touched the wallpaper? She ran one finger down the drywall and sniffed it.

Instantly she placed the odor. Kerosene!

The whistling stopped; she stopped.

Had he seen her? Her heart hammered like a wild thing in her chest.

She ducked into a doorway, almost tripping backward when she no longer felt anything against her back. Were all the doors open? She couldn't tell.

Her grip tightened on the weapon in her hand. She wondered what the prowler had used on Pedro. She hoped to God it wasn't a gun. Her throat constricted as she remembered the joke about the dead man who'd brought a knife to a gunfight.

Fleetingly, she regretted not bringing Hank along, not calling the police before she'd left her condominium. By now, they'd have been here!

I'm the only one here, she thought, scared, chewing her lip. She glanced back at the front door. The possibility of being trapped in a burning building horrified her.

Her eyes began to tear from the concentration of fuel fumes. One small spark and she'd be engulfed in flames!

What the hell am I doing here? I'm no damned hero! Whatever damage is done, it's covered by insurance. Why should I risk my life? Goldcoast probably can't even afford to pay for my funeral!

Her self-preservation instincts warred with her compelling desire to know which subcontractor was responsible for lighting the match. They'd point the finger at Hank first, because everyone knew he'd had a hell of a time getting those roof trusses. She doubted his personal integrity because of the deal he'd made with her family, but his professional integrity was pristine. Deep in her twisting gut, she knew for certain Hank was not involved. But he'd take the blame, unless...

Cat shook her head, clearing her cowardly thoughts from her brain.

You can be a fraidy-cat and make a run for it. But if you do, this building is going to be torched and the arsonist will probably get away before you can get to a phone. You'll never know for certain who started the fire.

The hollow sound of a near-empty container banged against a wall sliced through her thoughts. She turned her head from one side to the other, trying to locate which apartment the sound came from, but the vaulted ceiling distorted the acoustics. The arsonist could be in any of the apartments.

One more door, she coached herself. Just move your feet down the hall one more door and you're home free. Call the police and the fire department. Get out of the building. And maybe... maybe once I'm safe, I'll try to whack the guy over the head as he tries to escape.

Her courage bolstered by having a definite plan of action, she edged silently down the corridor. Finally reaching the back apartment, she ducked through the open door.

Her eyes grew round in astonishment as she recognized the man holding a gasoline container.

"Brute! Get off me! Cat, help for heaven's sake." Through the coverlet Hank could feel the dog's needle-like paws. He touched his nose, dead certain it had to be bleeding profusely. It hurt like hell. "This isn't a damned game!"

Kicking his feet free, he used one arm to unwind the bedspread from his torso. He opened the hand that had held his nose. No blood. What'd she do to him? he wondered.

"Cat?" He levered himself upward, twisting his shoulders until his eyes completely scanned the bedroom. He heard the front door slam. "Cat! Wait!"

He made it through the door in time to see the taillights of her pickup truck swerving down the road. His head jerked toward the driveway. Where was his truck?

Vaguely he remembered his arm across Cat's shoulders as they had left the Lemontree. He glanced back at the door, then down at his watch. It was after eleven. She must have brought me here and left my truck at the job site.

The phone jangling halted his mental reconstruction of what had taken place in the past six hours. His eyes widened as he retraced his steps back into the condo. The phone had rung just as he'd hit the floor, too. His groggy mind had only caught two words: Pedro and Lemontree.

He picked up the phone.

"McGillis residence."

"Hank? This is James. Is Cat there?"

"No." He kept his reply curt. How could he explain what had happened in the past five minutes? He didn't understand what had happened! "She isn't here."

"Was she there?"

"Briefly."

"Mad as a hornet?"

"An apt description." He gingerly touched the bridge of his nose. What the hell, he decided. Cat was James's sister. He'd find out sooner or later. "I think she punched me in the nose while I was sleeping!"

"Oh, damn! She was in a tizzy when she left the lumber shed. I knew I should have driven her home."

"She rolled me up in the coverlet and dumped me on the floor while screaming for me to get out of her bed." Hank's fuzzy sleep-laden mind finally cleared. He jumped to full alert as he said, "Somebody called. She mentioned Pedro and the Lemontree." A shaft of fear bolted up his spine. He let loose with an expletive. "I gotta hang up. Something must have happened at the Lemontree. Cat is on her way over there."

Without waiting for a response, he banged down the receiver. No truck. How am I going to get there? There was only one way...on foot. In a flash, he was out the door, running as hard and fast as he could. He'd barely noticed his feet were bare, until a sharp object pierced his heel.

He kept running. A mile, he thought. How long? Eight, maybe nine or ten minutes. Knowing Cat would fearlessly jump feetfirst into any situation, he only hoped he could get there before something happened to her.

His arms pumped harder; he ran faster.

He couldn't let anything happen to her; if it did, he knew his life wasn't worth living.

Her watering eyes had to be tricking her. Cat shifted the bat until it was behind her. "Kent? What are you doing?"

Only for a second did he stop splashing the contents of the five-gallon fuel can on the walls. "Saving Goldcoast. Want to help?"

"Are you crazy?" Cat gasped. His calm determination unsettled her. She didn't see a weapon, but Kent had to have one. He'd hit Pedro with some sort of blunt instrument.

"Perfectly sane."

"Why, Kent?" Her voice shook. "How can setting fire to this building save Goldcoast?"

"Insurance money. It's done all the time, Cat. The general contractor gets paid twice for building the same building. Once by the owner and once by the insurance company."

"That's insurance fraud. You could go to jail!"

Her eyes snapped downward as Kent swung back his arm and spilled kerosene near her bare foot. She curled her toes toward her heels to avoid standing on a carpet soaked with fuel oil.

"Not if I don't get caught. Who's going to tell? You?"

Her fingers tightened on the bat. He'd made his intentions perfectly clear. She could be his accomplice, or... what? He'd kill her? She shuddered at the second possibility.

"This wouldn't be necessary, Cat, if you'd fouled up like everybody thought you would. When Goldcoast bid this job, they stripped the profit out of it because they counted on half the subcontractors pulling off the job site after the first month. You're a bright lady, Cat. You figure it out. Add ten or fifteen percent of the subcontractors' money to our cash flow. I wouldn't be here tonight if you hadn't made those men knuckle under."

Insulted, Cat thrust her chin forward. "You miscalculated again if you think I'm going to be part of this scheme to defraud the insurance company."

She had to reason with him, change his mind, convince him there was some other way for Goldcoast to solve their financial trouble. Scared spitless, all her mind could do was shriek Hank's name!

Kent flicked open the lid of his lighter. "I did tell you not to hire a watchman. Lucky for him he didn't see me. You aren't going to be that lucky."

Cat flinched, hanging on to her weapon for dear life. Why hadn't she told Hank about the call? Why hadn't she waited for him to come with her? Her stubborn independence could cost her her life! All Kent Shane had to do was splash fuel on her, toss the lighter, and she'd be a human torch.

The fingers on her free hand balled into a tight fist. She wasn't going to die! Think, goddamn it! Stall him! Keep him talking. Oh, Lord, how long could she prevent him from burning her alive?

"I always thought of you as my mentor, Kent." Her throat constricted so tightly in fear that she could barely speak.

"I am." He held up the lighter. "Right now I'm giving your last lesson . . . in profit and loss."

"Just a minute, Kent. Think about what you're about to do. Arson is one thing. You might get away with it. But murder? Would you kill for Goldcoast?"

He slowly began to circle to her side, getting closer and closer to the door as Cat pivoted around to keep him facing her.

"It's a matter of survival."

"But you've never killed anyone. Have you?"

"No, not yet." His hand with the lighter in it moved toward her. "You're the one who needs to reconsider. You start the fire and I'll keep my mouth shut. We'll both walk out of here with no one being the wiser."

"I can't," Cat blurted. She knew by the muscle tightening along his jaw that she'd given him the wrong answer. She should have lied, promised him anything he wanted to hear.

He paused for a second, then continued his slow-motion journey that would lead to his escape.

"You can't kill me, Kent. You know you can't. Just let me walk out of here."

"And have you call the cops? And then testify against me in court? I'm no fool, Cat."

As she watched Kent skirting around her, she realized he was completely ruthless. He had every intention of killing her.

"Let me go. I promise," she lied, "I won't report you. Just let me walk out of here. It'll be our secret."

Kent chuckled with ominous softness; it sent chills up Cat's spine.

"Only one person can be trusted to keep a secret. Why do you think I didn't hire someone else to do Goldcoast's dirty work?"

Remembering the small fire that had been started in the apartment upstairs, Cat said, "But you did trust someone else, didn't you? You hired someone to try and burn this building down a couple of weeks ago."

"Yeah," he admitted. "Loyalty and competence don't always go hand in hand. That man will be on the Goldcoast payroll forever. But thanks to you, that fire wasn't reported. There's no paperwork that connects Goldcoast and the first fire." He rocked back on his heels, then to the balls of his feet. "What about your loyalty, Cat? You can start the fire, or you can be a hero and die trying to save Goldcoast's building. An ironical choice, huh? Either way, Goldcoast wins."

Her eyes never left Kent's face. Instinctively, she knew his eyes would warn her of when he was about to strike the flint. If he'd only get a little bit closer, a foot or two, she could swing the bat and hit him. But he wasn't going to risk getting too close. She had to close the gap. She didn't realize how fear could paralyze a person until she found she couldn't move a muscle other than her mouth.

"Kent, I've always looked up to you. Don't do this!" Soon. At any second, he'd toss the lighter into the kerosene.

Her throat clogged with the fear of dying. She didn't want to die. She wanted to live, with Hank! Her mind echoed his name; her lips moved without making a sound.

Kent dropped the container; his foot kicked it on its side, spilling the remainder of its contents. He held the open lighter out to her, his finger poised over the wheel. "This is your last chance, Cat."

For a fraction of a second he glanced toward the darkened hallway. Cat saw her chance and took it. She swung the club with all her strength . . . and missed.

Hank swiftly, silently ran up the steps of the apartment building. He'd heard voices from outside: a man's voice, deadly and cold, and a woman's voice, steady and clear. He recognized the stench of kerosene the second he dodged inside the front door.

The same building, he thought, sucking air through his nostrils, probably the same man trying to finish what he started. Just keep him talking, sweetheart! Lead me to you! I won't let him hurt you!

He felt his way down the ebony-dark hall, his ears guiding him more than his hands. A flicker of light from the back apartment lit the open doorway. The light pierced the corridor as the man stepped back. For only an instant, Hank caught a glimpse of the man's face as it twisted into a grotesque mask of indecision.

"See you in hell, Cat!" the man said.

"No!" Hank bellowed in a last-ditch effort to draw the arsonist's attention toward him and away from Cat.

"Hank!" Instinctively, Cat rushed toward the door, fearing Kent would touch the lighter's flame against the wallpaper in the hall. "No! Get back!"

To save himself from getting caught, Kent lobbed the lighter into the apartment and darted backward across the width of the hall.

A sunburst of orange flames blinded Hank as he propelled his body forward into a flying tackle. Sightless, he wrapped his arms around the man's thick waist. He felt a blast of heat coming from the apartment. The man under him took the brunt of Hank's weight as they fell in a snarl of arms and legs.

Cat! he silently screamed. My God, he's killed her!

A murderous rage consumed Hank. He raised his fist to punch the arsonist out cold, opened his eyes to take aim and saw Cat with her arms clenched to the man's thighs.

The arsonist didn't stand a chance with both of them tangled around him.

"Get out, Cat!" he shouted. Miraculously she'd saved herself. He wasn't going to allow her to take another risk. Fire engulfed the apartment; tongues of flame licked toward the soaked wallpaper in the hall. "This whole building's going to go, fast! Get the hell out of here!"

"Not...without...this...sucker!" she gasped, winded. When she had grabbed him, Kent had repeatedly rammed his bent knees into her ribs. Simply breathing sent waves of pain crashing against her lungs. She held her ribs with one arm, yanked his feet together and struggled to haul him toward the exit. "Help me ... get Kent ... out!"

"Screw him!"

Hank bounced to his lacerated feet and swung Cat over his shoulder. She screamed in agony as her ribs jarred against his shoulder. Hank charged from the building, outracing the flames that ignited behind him.

"Get . . . him!" Those were the last words Cat spoke before a swirling mist of blackness relieved her from excruciating pain by robbing her of consciousness.

Lowering his precious burden to the grass, Hank's arm looped around her shoulders, holding her limp form tightly against his chest. He heard sirens, shouts, footsteps, but he refused to relinquish his hold on her.

"Building empty?" a man in a yellow fireman's slicker shouted.

Much as he hated the son of a bitch who'd nearly killed both of them, he shook his head. "No," he rasped. His throat was parched; his nostrils were clogged from the black smoke he'd inhaled. "First floor. Hallway. Back of the building. Walls soaked with kerosene."

"Get those hoses in position! I'm goin' in," the fireman shouted. "Get a stretcher over here!"

"You'll be all right, Cat," Hank murmured. Hot tears coursed down his cheeks. "You'll be all right. You've got to be all right. Dammit! Don't you give up, Cat McGillis."

The next thing Hank knew, James and Joshua were straining to pull Cat from his arms.

"Leave us alone," Hank said. Cat groaned. "Get away. I'll take care of her."

"You've got to let go of her." Joshua pried Hank's fingers loose from his daughter's shoulders. "Let me have her."

"Never!" Hank snarled, tears trekking down his smoke-stained cheeks. "I can take care of her."

"Jeez, Dad, no wonder he's out of his head. Look at his feet!" James exclaimed. Uncertain he and his father had the strength to break Hank's grasp on his sister, he called, "Get some help over here. We need two stretchers!"

Chapter Fourteen

Groaning, Cat slowly opened her eyelids. Where am I? she wondered, bewildered by the high ceiling and pale green walls of the hospital room. She had to get somewhere, urgently, but she couldn't remember where. Her heart skipped a beat in anticipation as her memory returned.

Fire! Kent Shane! Her eyes blinked as she began to remember what had happened. Goldcoast had started the fire! And she'd thought it had to be one of the subcontractors!

Hank! She had to help him!

Cat made an effort to lift her right hand, to roll to her feet. Her ribs protested the swift action by painfully throbbing. She couldn't lift her hand; it was weighted to the bed.

She turned her head to the side. When she saw Hank's dark hair, and his wide-set shoulders clothed in a torn shirt streaked with soot, her fear abated. He was asleep in the chair beside her bed. They were safe, both of them.

"Hank?" She tried to raise her shoulders to allow her other hand to touch his hair; the gauze bandages under the hospital gown restricted her. Questions popped in her head faster than a framer's nail gun spitting nails. "Hank?"

In his hellish nightmare, Hank heard her calling his name. He ran and ran and ran down a dark tunnel filled with fluorescent-colored flames painted on the walls, but he couldn't get to her. His arms reached out. She was going to die; he was powerless to stop it.

"No," he mumbled hoarsely, the sound louder than thunder, reverberating against the walls of the endless tunnel. Panicked, he threw himself toward her, flying through the air with his arms outstretched.

He could hear her shouting at him. "Go away. Get out. Out. Out!"

Cat watched his shoulder muscles bunch, felt him clench her fingertips and knew he was having a bad dream.

"Wake up, Hank." Her heels dug into the starched sheet. She scooted her bottom down until she could gently stroke the crown of his head. "It's okay, love."

And then her memory slid back to the last moments in her condo. She'd yelled at Hank for betraying her. He'd used her to get his roof trusses, to save his business. He didn't care a damned thing about her.

Lethargically, Hank awoke. He raised his head from the back of her hand. The nightmare receded as he got his first sight of Cat's face.

"Are you okay?" he asked. "You broke a couple of ribs."

"I'm sore, but I'll survive. And you?"

"The same. Pedro is down the hall, but he'll be fine."

"Did you get Kent out of the building?"

Hank shuddered, remembering how he'd wanted to kill Goldcoast's regional manager with his bare hands for putting Cat in danger. "The firemen rescued him. He suffered a few bruises. The policemen took him down and booked him. He spilled his guts about Goldcoast being behind the arson scheme. They planned on using the insurance money to make up for their loss on the Dallas job."

"I blame myself." Cat's sides ached as she sighed heavily. "I must have been blinded by loyalty to Goldcoast. Kent was adamant on the phone about not hiring a night watchman."

"Don't blame yourself. It's only right that you should be loyal to the company you work for."

"Misplaced loyalty!" she derided. "Kent tried to convince me to start the fire, to prove my loyalty to Goldcoast! I still can't believe he did it. I thought one of the subcontractors must have started it because they had a grudge against me, even though the weekly meetings did seem to be going better."

"Vandalism, not arson, is usually a subcontractor's means of retaliation."

"I feel so damned stupid. I'd heard about Goldcoast's financial problems. I knew they were cutting corners. Why didn't it occur to me that they might be the guilty party?"

Hank reached over the bed rail and touched Cat's face. "Maybe because you trusted them, the same way that I trust you."

A sharp twinge of guilt made Cat blush. She must have been crazy to have thought even for a second that Hank's money problems could turn him into an arsonist.

"Did you have the same faith in me?"

She stopped caressing his hair. Professionally? Yes. But in their personal relationship? No. Goldcoast had betrayed her loyalty; Hank had betrayed her trust. Her hand slid across the pristine white top sheet to her ribs.

Hank's nose still throbbed from the twist she'd given it. Reality hadn't brought an end to his nightmare. His gut twisted as he realized the pained expression on her face had nothing to do with her broken ribs or Goldcoast starting the fire.

"Why, Cat?" he asked softly. "Why'd you kick me out of your bed? What did I do?"

"I trusted you. You sold out to my family."

She watched his soot-streaked face blanch to near-white. Guilty as accused, she thought, making a second effort to roll on her side away from him. She couldn't move. It was pure torture lying there, looking up at the ceiling to avoid facing Hank. She could taste the salt of her tears washing down the back of her throat.

"James told you about the offer your father made?"

She nodded curtly. With her ribs bound, she had to fight to take a breath. She stiffened her jaw to keep her chin from wobbling.

"Did he tell you I turned it down?"

She nodded.

"Then why are you saying I sold out to your family?"

"You must have. The roof trusses are on the job site." Her throat worked, hard. "Don't tell me I've impetuously jumped to the wrong conclusion. Since the night we went to my place, after you made the deal, you haven't..." She'd humiliate herself if she revealed how his lack of affection had distressed her during the past two weeks. She'd be a lady and save her pride, if it killed her. "I'd like for you to leave."

"Haven't what, Cat? Slept with you?"

She turned her head toward the window. Strict silence, she thought, would compel him to leave. She felt the tug on her hand, but ignored it. She wouldn't say one word, not one damned word. She clamped her teeth together to make certain she couldn't.

"You listen to me, Hilda Catherine McGillis. I love you. When I saw Kent Shane toss his lighter into the apartment, I felt as though half my body had been torn off me. I wanted to die in the fire with you."

He paused, watching her worry her bottom lip with her front teeth. Although she pretended to have turned a deaf ear to him, he knew she was listening, contemplating what he'd said.

She'd stung his pride with her accusation. The foundation of love was trust. How could she believe he'd sell out?

The longer he paused, the more his irritation increased. "Do you think a man who'd die for you would exchange you for a pile of timber nailed together? Do you think money or the Lemontree is that important to me? You're the one who's gung ho to be a success!"

That swiveled her head toward him. She had to bite the tip of her tongue to remain quiet. Her eyes drilled into him. You are the one who sold out! they silently sandblasted. You are the partner in McGillis and Collins!

On the receiving end of her hot glare, Hank realized he was not getting through to her. His hotheaded little hellcat had made up her mind and she wasn't about to let logic confuse her!

He placed his hands flat on her bed, stiffened his arms and levered himself slowly to his injured feet. He could talk until he ran out of breath, but until she was ready to listen with her heart, he was wasting his breath.

Leaning over her, he firmly grasped her shoulders. His eyes continued to battle with hers, brown against blue. "You're a strong, courageous, *stubborn* woman, Cat McGillis. I wonder if you'll have the strength to come to me when you realize how wrong you are."

And with that declaration, he kissed her, as hard as she'd pinched his nose. He raised his head, nodded as though he knew he'd done the right thing, then turned on his heel and hobbled to the door.

His unexpected kiss made her heart pound with hope. It flopped over when she saw that his jeans had been cut off at mid calf, and both his feet were swathed in bandages. He was out the door before she realized he must have run barefoot across the pebbles and broken glass in the street to get to her at the Lemontree.

More than anything he'd said or done, that was a testimony of his love for her.

She grabbed the side railing of the hospital bed and jiggled it. The slightest movement made her ribs cry out painfully in protest. She didn't notice. The rail remained rigid, locked in place.

"Hank! Come back!" she shouted. "We need to talk!"

The door swung open. When she saw Maude and Joshua enter the room she rattled the railing harder. She couldn't let him leave the building without talking to her!

"What the hell are you trying to do, child?" Joshua demanded as he watched her starting to climb over the bed rail. He rushed to her bedside, blocking her. "You stay right there in that bed!"

Cat lay back down. "Did you see Hank?"

"Yeah. He's going home to take a shower and shave."

"Is he coming back?"

"I imagine."

"Did you ask?"

"No. But he raised enough of a stink around here to make the nurses let him sleep in a chair beside your bed all night. He's also on his way to your place to pick up Brute and take care of him. Why wouldn't he come back?"

Cat covered her face with her hands. Tears spurted from her eyes. Wasn't that just like Hank to battle toe to toe with her and then go care for her dog! Why had she doubted his love?

"He didn't make a deal with you, did he?"

"Of course he did," Joshua replied, too flustered by seeing his daughter cry to deny it. "Do you think I'm Santa Claus? Do you think I've been slaving sixteen hours a day at the lumber shed without making an agreement with him in writing?"

Maude stepped forward. "I don't think the partnership with the boys is what she means."

"Oh!" Joshua had the grace to duck his head, embarrassed. "She means *that* deal."

"The one I instigated," Maude confessed. "Don't blame your father. I badgered him into making the offer to help Hank only if he stopped seeing you." She circled to the far side of Cat's hospital bed. "Hank turned it down flatter than a pancake, sweetheart."

"Why didn't you tell me, Mother? Why did you make me believe there was a secret pact?"

Maude was unable to meet her daughter's look straight in the eye. "I knew the sort of long hours they'd be working. I figured he wouldn't have the time or energy to be very attentive. I thought you'd break off the relationship without giving him a chance to explain if you believed he'd sold you out." Maude sandwiched her daughter's hand between her own. "I'm as stubborn as you are. That's why I didn't tell you. I'm sorry."

"Sorry doesn't right things between Hank and me." Cat turned her head to the opposite side of the bed. "How long will it take you to get me out of here?"

"The doctor thinks—"

"I don't give two hoots what the doctor thinks. Unlatch the bed railing."

Her father stepped back, disobeying her wishes.

"Listen to me, both of you. I love Hank Collins. And I think he still loves me. He ran barefoot over God knows what to get to me. I can and will get out of this bed and over to my place. You can help me or you can try to stop me, but I will get there."

Joshua looked from Cat to his wife.

Maude reached down and pulled the lever to release the railing. "I'll help you. It's the least I can do to make up for the mistakes I've made." She held her arms open in a gesture that pleaded for forgiveness.

"I love you, Mom." She leaned into her mother's arms and hugged her waist. "Be happy that I love Hank... please. I wouldn't have made it out of that burning building if he hadn't carried me out."

Maude cradled her daughter's head against her breasts. "I know." She placed a kiss on the top of Cat's head, then looked up at her husband. She stretched her hand out to him; her eyes expressed her love. "The good times will by far outmeasure the hard times if you truly love each other."

Joshua nodded, his eyes blurred with tears as he squeezed his wife's fingertips.

Her brothers boisterously entering the room had Joshua wiping his eyes and clearing his throat, and Maude issuing orders like a construction superintendent before the boys could say hello.

"Joshua, you take care of the release forms. I'll help Cat get dressed. James, you rustle up a wheelchair. Tom, you and Luke go get the cars and drive them to the back entrance. Russell, you take your car and go to Cat's place. Whatever you do, don't let Hank leave." Maude was in her element. A small smile curved her lips. "Let's get crackin'!"

Joshua helped Cat down from the cab of his truck. Now that Goldcoast was in bad trouble, he'd offered her a position in the McGillis-Collins company. Cat hadn't accepted or rejected his offer. She had more pressing matters on her mind.

"You're sure you don't want me to go in and straighten him out?" Joshua offered.

"No. That would be cowardly." Cat gave her mother a steady unwavering look. "This is between Hank and me."

Maude nodded and placed her hand on her heart. "I hear you, daughter. Here, where it counts the most." Then she opened her arms to her daughter and her husband. "Happy family?"

When she was a child, Cat remembered her dad would be getting ready to work out of town again and the whole family would put their arms around one another and say those exact words. She smiled and returned her parents' hugs.

James came running out of her condominium. He must have remembered, too, because he joined in the tightly knit circle.

"Did you say anything?" Cat asked, knowing her brother truly liked Hank.

"He wouldn't open up to me." James stepped back and glanced toward the door. "He's acting very strange, though. When I arrived, he was talking to Brute and rattling through your pots and pans. Why do you think he's in there boiling chickens?''

Cat shrugged, equally puzzled. "Does he look angry?''

"No, but he should be. You pinched his nose while he was sleeping, didn't you?''

Joshua chuckled. "I remember the time she did that to Tom when they were kids.''

"And Luke, and Russell," Maude added, joining in the laughter. "You were gone when Cat gave them their nose adjustments. Nobody in this family dares to fall asleep around my daughter after they've turned their noses up at her!''

Cat turned toward her front door. She could procrastinate forever by standing outside, swapping stories with her family about the good times, but that wouldn't alter the bad time in her immediate future.

"I've got to talk to Hank," she said, excusing herself.

"You'll bring him out to the house next Saturday," James said, admiring his sister's courage. Matching it, he turned to his mother and said, "I'm bringing my fiancée.''

Cat had her hand on the doorknob as she heard Maude's gasp and her father's chuckle. As she twisted it, she heard her mother say, "Fiancée? I haven't even met the girl! You've been holding out on me.''

Mother hasn't changed, Cat realized. That thought and Brute rushing to greet her made Cat smile.

Hearing Brute's yap, Hank poked his head out of the kitchen. "What are you doing here?''

"It's my home," Cat replied, her voice lilting upward. "What are you doing here?''

Hank ignored her question. "You aren't supposed to be out of that hospital bed with those injured ribs!''

"I had something important to do that wouldn't wait."

"Dammit! Nothing is more important than you getting well!" he bellowed.

Brute growled at Hank.

"Would you mind lowering your voice? Brute is going into his attack-dog routine." Her eyes dropped to Hank's bandaged feet. "I wouldn't want him to hurt you worse than I have."

Hank shook his head. He didn't want her pity. He wanted her trust, her love. It took every ounce of self-control he possessed not to pick her up in his arms and carry her straight to bed, where she belonged. But that would be one mistake he wouldn't allow himself to make. He wanted her more than he wanted to see the morning sunrise.

"My feet are fine." He did lower his voice to placate Brute, though. "Just a couple of little cuts. You're the one who belongs in the hospital, not me. What's so important around here that you checked out of the hospital?"

"You," she replied succinctly.

He watched her visibly gather what little of her strength was left from the ordeal the previous night in order to confront him.

He took one step backward; she took one step forward.

"You need more time to think about what you're going to say, Cat. You said yourself that your impetuosity gets you into trouble."

"It does. But what I have to say to you is something I've known for days."

She stepped forward; he stood still.

"Don't say anything if it's under false pretenses. I don't want you to say what you think I want to hear just because you feel sorry for me."

"Sorry for you," she repeated, desperately wanting him to enfold her in his arms to make her confession easier. "Why would I feel sorry for you?"

"Because, by now you've realized I'm in twice as big a mess as I was before Goldcoast torched the building. Now I have roof trusses for buildings that may never be built!"

"And I may be out of a job." Cat started to shrug, but remembered how lifting her shoulders made her ribs hurt. Instead she extended her hand toward Hank. She didn't want him to feel sorry for her, either. She scoffed. "Big deal."

"I'm broke, Cat. I'm worse off than when Sharon walked out on me. Back then I wasn't in debt up to my ears."

"I'm not like Sharon. And I'm not like my mother in that respect. I'm me, Hank, and I love you." She smiled softly. "I need to be needed. I need for you to need me as badly as I need you."

Hank clasped his fingers around her wrist and drew the palm of her hand to his lips. "Through thick and thin?"

"I'll always be here for you. I would never have doubted you if you'd been honest with me."

"What about when I'm exhausted, too tired to do much more than grumble at you?"

"I just want you here to love."

"You thought I'd abandoned you for a pile of wood." He nibbled the fleshy pad beneath the joint of her thumb. "And I thought I wouldn't be good enough until I proved I could give you the things you'd have if you married the type of man who wears a white collar and has a retirement plan."

"I only want you, Hank."

Gently he put his arms around her, mindful of her injury. "You'd trust me to take care of you?"

"I trust us to take care of each other. I love you, Hank."

"Enough to marry me?"

"Yes."

She stood on tiptoe to kiss him. Her nose twitched. "Is something burning?" she whispered.

"The chicken!" Hank jerked backward and spun around as he saw a tendril of smoke drift by her head. He completely forgot about his injured feet and rushed to the stove. "It's burned to a crisp."

Cat chuckled. "That isn't exactly a catastrophe, Hank. We can order fried chicken from a carryout place."

"Carryout places don't fix that stuff." He grinned down at her. "Chicken salad. I was going to make it and bring some to the hospital for your dinner. As a peace offering."

She touched his nose. "Were you going to eat some of it?"

"I figured that would be the supreme sacrifice I'd make for you. That's true love." The smile she radiated up to him made him feel as tall and brawny as the giant carrying the picket sign at Butler Mills. "I've heard of a great place to get chicken salad."

"Where?"

"At wedding receptions. I'm getting a real craving for chicken salad." The teasing quality of his voice changed to sincerity as he said, "I'm not the man your family would pick for you..."

She put her finger on his lips. "I'll do my own picking."

"But will you marry me anyway?" he finished, his lips moving beneath her finger like tiny kisses.

"I'll marry you anyway, anyhow, anytime," she promised, her heart brimming with joy.

Brute pawed at her leg and whined.

"Looks like you get the forfeit you wanted after all. Something soft and silky that will cuddle up to you," she said, reminding Hank of the bet she'd lost. "I think Brute might run away from home if I don't marry you immediately."

Hank picked Brute off the floor, then nuzzled Cat's neck. "Smart dog."

Choosing to follow a family tradition her mother had begun, Cat hugged Hank and Brute and said, "We're going to be one happy family."

*   *   *   *   *

Silhouette Special Edition

This April,
Silhouette *Special Edition* is pleased to present

ONCE IN A LIFETIME
by Ginna Gray

the long-awaited companion volume to her bestselling duo

Fools Rush In (#416)
Where Angels Fear (#468)

Ever since spitfire Erin Blaine and her angelic twin sister Elise stirred up double trouble and entangled their long-suffering brother David in some sticky hide-and-seek scenarios, readers clamored to hear more about dashing, debonair David himself.

Now that time has come, as straitlaced Abigail Stewart manages to invade the secrecy shrouding sardonic David Blaine's bachelor boat—and creates the kind of salty, saucy, swashbuckling romantic adventure that comes along only once in a lifetime!

**Even if you missed the earlier novels,
you won't want to miss**
ONCE IN A LIFETIME #661

Available this April, only in Silhouette *Special Edition*. OL-1

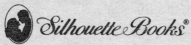

SILHOUETTE'S "BIG WIN"
SWEEPSTAKES RULES & REGULATIONS

NO PURCHASE NECESSARY TO ENTER OR RECEIVE A PRIZE

1 To enter the Sweepstakes and join the Reader Service, scratch off the metallic strips on all your BIG WIN tickets #1-#6. This will reveal the potential values for each Sweepstakes entry number, the number of free book(s) you will receive and your free bonus gift as part of our Reader Service. If you do not wish to take advantage of our Reader Service but wish to enter the Sweepstakes only, scratch off the metallic strips on your BIG WIN tickets #1-#4. Return your entire sheet of tickets intact. Incomplete and/or inaccurate entries are ineligible for that section or sections of prizes. Torstar Corp. and its affiliates are not responsible for mutilated or unreadable entries or inadvertent printing errors. Mechanically reproduced entries are null and void.

2 Whether you take advantage of this offer or not, on or about April 30, 1992, at the offices of Marden-Kane Inc., Lake Success, NY, your Sweepstakes numbers will be compared against the list of winning numbers generated at random by the computer. However, prizes will only be awarded to individuals who have entered the Sweepstakes. In the event that all prizes are not claimed, a random drawing will be held from all qualified entries received from March 30, 1990 to March 31, 1992, to award all unclaimed prizes. All cash prizes (Grand to Sixth), will be mailed to the winners and are payable by check in U.S. funds. Seventh prize will be shipped to winners via third-class mail. These prizes are in addition to any free, surprise or mystery gifts that might be offered. Versions of this Sweepstakes with different prizes of approximate equal value may appear at retail outlets or in other mailings by Torstar Corp. and its affiliates.

3 The following prizes are awarded in this sweepstakes: ★ Grand Prize (1) $1,000,000; First Prize (1) $25,000; Second Prize (1) $10,000; Third Prize (5) $5,000; Fourth Prize (10) $1,000; Fifth Prize (100) $250; Sixth Prize (2,500) $10; ★ ★ Seventh Prize (6,000) $12.95 ARV.

   ★ This presentation offers a Grand Prize of a $1,000,000 annuity. Winner will receive $33,333.33 a year for 30 years without interest totalling $1,000,000.

   ★ ★ Seventh Prize: A fully illustrated hardcover book published by Torstar Corp. Approximate Retail Value of the book is $12.95.

   Entrants may cancel the Reader Service at anytime without cost or obligation to buy (see details in center insert card).

4 This Sweepstakes is being conducted under the supervision of an independent judging organization. By entering this Sweepstakes, an entrant accepts and agrees to be bound by these rules and the decisions of the judges, which shall be final and binding. Odds of winning in the random drawing are dependent upon the total number of entries received. Taxes, if any, are the sole responsibility of the winners. Prizes are nontransferable. All entries must be received at the address printed on the reply card and must be postmarked no later than 12:00 MIDNIGHT on March 31, 1992. The drawing for all unclaimed Sweepstakes prizes will take place on May 30, 1992, at 12:00 NOON, at the offices of Marden-Kane, Inc., Lake Success, New York.

5 This offer is open to residents of the U.S., the United Kingdom, France and Canada, 18 years or older, except employees and their immediate family members of Torstar Corp., its affiliates, subsidiaries, and all the other agencies, entities and persons connected with the use, marketing or conduct of this Sweepstakes. All Federal, State, Provincial and local laws apply. Void wherever prohibited or restricted by law. Any litigation within the Province of Quebec respecting the conduct and awarding of a prize in this publicity contest must be submitted to the Régie des Loteries et Courses du Québec.

6 Winners will be notified by mail and may be required to execute an affidavit of eligibility and release, which must be returned within 14 days after notification or an alternate winner will be selected. Canadian winners will be required to correctly answer an arithmetical skill-testing question administered by mail, which must be returned within a limited time. Winners consent to the use of their names, photographs and/or likenesses for advertising and publicity in conjunction with this and similar promotions without additional compensation. For a list of our major prize winners, send a stamped, self-addressed ENVELOPE to: WINNERS LIST, c/o Marden-Kane Inc., P.O. Box 701, SAYREVILLE, NJ 08871. Requests for Winners Lists will be fulfilled after the May 30, 1992 drawing date.

If Sweepstakes entry form is missing, please print your name and address on a 3" ×5" piece of plain paper and send to:

In the U.S.
Silhouette's "BIG WIN" Sweepstakes
3010 Walden Ave.
P.O. Box 1867
Buffalo, NY 14269-1867

In Canada
Silhouette's "BIG WIN" Sweepstakes
P.O. Box 609
Fort Erie, Ontario
L2A 5X3

Offer limited to one per household.

1991 Harlequin Enterprises Limited   Printed in the U.S.A.

LTY-S391D

Silhouette Romance®

LONG, TALL TEXANS

HARDEN
Diana Palmer

In her bestselling LONG, TALL TEXANS series, Diana
Palmer brought you to Jacobsville and introduced you to
the rough and rugged ranchers who call the town home.
Now, hot and dusty Jacobsville promises to get even
hotter when hard-hearted, woman-hating rancher
Harden Tremayne has to reckon with the lovely Miranda
Warren.

The LONG, TALL TEXANS series continues! Don't
miss HARDEN by Diana Palmer in March . . . only from
Silhouette Romance.

LTT-1